Wrong Sort o

Helen Bridgett

Book 2 – Professor Maxie Reddick Files

Ruby
FICTION

Published 2021 by Ruby Fiction
Penrose House, Crawley Drive, Camberley, Surrey GU15 2AB, UK
www.rubyfiction.com

A CIP catalogue record for this book is available from the British Library.

EPUB ISBN: 978-1-912550-61-6
PRINT ISBN: 978-1-912550-64-7

For my fabulous family and friends - I'm so lucky to have you all in my life.

Acknowledgements

My thanks, first and foremost go to everyone at Choc Lit and Ruby Fiction for giving me the chance to share another Maxie Reddick story with you. In particular the Tasting Panel who passed the original manuscript and made publication possible. A special thanks to: Hilary Brown, Nicola Whittaker, Bee Master, Kirsty White, Donna Morgan, Lorna Baker, Carol Dutton, Yvonne Greene, Julie Lilly, Margaret Marshall, Deborah Warren, Jo Osborne, Sharon Walsh and Alan Roberton.

I'd also like to give a particular mention to my editor for helping me get the story into shape and my designer for the gorgeous cover.
Family and friends are incredibly important to me, and I'm so lucky to have a great bunch of people I can rely on and who give me lots of inspiration for stories. This story is for Trish and our nights out together! Finally, as ever, I thank my Mam and Dad for giving me a life-long love of books and Jason for always being there. X

Chapter One

Friday, 16 December

'Don't be such a killjoy!' Kelly yelled from the dance floor. 'The music's brilliant now. Grinch – get up here and dance.'

The strobe lights lit up her friend's face and Kelly saw Rowan sigh then fold her arms indignantly. Kelly shrugged a "suit yourself" and sashayed back into the centre of the tightly packed crowd. She felt high on life tonight and no one was going to bring her down. She knew Rowan would rather have stayed in the city centre but this old printing press on the edge of Helmsforth might look a dump but was a great space for clubbing and what the heck, her friend needed to learn to live dangerously once in a while. Taking risks had never done Kelly any harm. The DJ really knew how to work his audience. He put on another floor-filler and the crowd whooped, jumping into the air in time with the beats. Kelly joined them very well aware that the short hemline she was rocking was being eyed up by many of the men gathering around her. She spotted one with his mouth hanging open and when he raised his gaze to meet hers, Kelly simply winked at him and wished him a Happy Christmas before swirling round and continuing to dance.

Suddenly her movement was restricted and she felt her hemline being tugged. She turned round angrily expecting to shake off that man but instead it was Rowan, trying to hold her dress down.

'What on earth are you doing?' shouted Kelly over the noise.

'You're not leaving much to the imagination,' replied Rowan pushing off a drunken guy who was trying to drape a length of tattered tinsel around both of them. 'This lot look like a pack of hyenas ready to pounce.'

Kelly took hold of her friend's hands and started spinning her around.

'You're like some Victorian governess sent to protect my modesty,' she called out. 'Relax, have a bit of fun for once.'

Rowan pulled her hands away and Kelly could see she'd offended her friend. Rowan was about to leave the dance floor but as she did, the opening chords to a well-loved anthem lit up the room. Kelly cheered; this was one of the songs they always danced to together at university and Rowan surely couldn't refuse to stay and dance to this. Kelly reached out and dragged Rowan into the centre of the floor.

‘Come on, we love this one,’ Kelly shouted. ‘You’ve got to dance with me – it’s our song.’

Rowan raised her eyes skywards in mock despair but Kelly held her hands and the friends danced and belted out the well-known chorus along with the rest of the crowd. They soon attracted the attention of a couple of men who hovered around them trying to make it a foursome. Kelly winked at Rowan then turned towards the man trying to flirt with her and pressed her body against his as they gyrated together. The guy attempting to get Rowan’s attention tried to press himself on her, evidently hoping for the same treatment but Rowan pushed him off and tried to drag Kelly from her dance partner. Kelly shrugged Rowan off and very soon both men were dancing with her. She laughed and performed a couple of sexy dance moves then put her arms around both of them while they ran hands over her slinky dress and down her thighs. Rowan shook her head and left the floor. She went over to the bar and sat on a stool, shoulders dropped.

The DJ declared he was taking a break so Kelly gave each of her dance partners a kiss on the cheek and stumbled back to the bar.

‘You ready to go?’ Rowan leaned in and yelled in her ear as Kelly raised a hand to try and get the attention of the barman.

Kelly checked her watch and frowned at Rowan as if she’d just said something completely ridiculous.

‘No way – it’s far too early to go home,’ she shouted over the hubbub. ‘I do love you Rowan but nowadays you can be such a party pooper. Come on, it’s Christmas – let your hair down.’

Before Rowan had the chance to reply, Kelly’s dance partners approached with big drunken grins on their sweaty faces. They were now carrying strands of battered tinsel that they’d probably stripped from the grubby walls.

‘Can we buy you ladies a drink?’ one of them shouted, draping the tinsel around Kelly’s neck.

Kelly put her arms around both her oldest and her newest best friends, pulling the group together in one big hug and shouted, ‘Shots!’

The guys were delighted and leant over the bar to order the drinks. Rowan tossed Kelly’s arm off her and gathered up her bag.

‘I’m going to the loo,’ she stated firmly. ‘Then I’m going home and I want you to come with me.’

Kelly took hold of Rowan’s hands. ‘One more dance, go on, please. Just you and me, I promise.’

Rowan yanked her hands free and shook her head. 'Kelly, it's past two. We've been out since four o'clock this afternoon and I'm knackered. I've got work tomorrow even if you haven't. Come on, I'm not leaving you on your own.'

Kelly's knights in casual armour arrived back with the shots and handed them round. Kelly took hers and downed it in one, getting a whoop of applause and then she took another. Rowan refused the brightly coloured liquid she was offered.

'We were just going,' she yelled at the bloke who raised his eyebrows at Kelly.

'No way,' he said. 'Not when the party's just getting started.'

Kelly shrugged then downed yet another shot.

'I need to get back. I'll order an Uber, though God knows how long we'll have to wait,' Rowan tried to reason.

'You'll be fine,' slurred Kelly. 'It's the Friday before Christmas. There'll be millions of taxis. You'll be perfectly safe.'

'I was thinking of you,' replied Rowan. 'You're the one downing shots.'

'Don't worry about your friend,' one of the guys interrupted. 'I'll look after her.'

He stood in front of Kelly as if trying to prevent any further conversation with his target for the evening. It worked. The music started back up again and Kelly downed her drink, cheered then started dragging both guys back onto the dance floor. One of them looked back at Rowan with a triumphant look on his face.

Rowan made one last attempt and shouted after them, 'Kelly, I'm going now – come with me. How will you get home?'

'Oh I'll tuck her in nice and snug,' yelled the guy. 'Might not be her bed though.'

He pulled Kelly close and dipped her, ballroom-style in the centre of the floor. She shrieked with delight then curtsied to the crowd, wobbling over as she did. Rowan held her hands up in despair. She headed towards the loo and took a glance back at Kelly who was laughing and acting as coy as a drunk person can when she's in too far.

The toilets were disgusting as might be expected on the last party night before Christmas. Half empty glasses smeared with lipstick decked the sink area, the floor was carpeted in sodden paper towels and there was a distinct stench of vomit coming from somewhere. Rowan used her foot to tentatively push open the doors of several cubicles before finding the least offensive. She locked herself in and felt a moment of calm. It was actually cool and quiet in here compared to the bar and as Rowan sat on the loo she kicked the door in anger. Nights out with Kelly increasingly ended like this – with her feeling like the one in the wrong, the killjoy. They'd been friends for six years, since meeting in Fresher's Week and though they might seem like yin and yang – that worked for them. Kelly had been over the moon with something tonight, something she couldn't talk about. The celebratory champagne after dinner had gone down well but Kelly didn't know when to stop and she was a nightmare when she'd had too much.

Rowan opened the cubicle door and headed to a clean-ish wash basin. As she dried her hands she looked at herself in the mirror and a haggard woman stared back. That was the other huge difference between her and Kelly – their appearance. Kelly looked every inch the party girl whereas she, well she looked like the respectable retail manager that she was. Rowan sighed and combed her thick chestnut hair then pinched her cheeks a little to make her complexion look a little more festive. She realised she had frown lines from glaring at Kelly all night and Rowan mused that seeing a little less of her friend would probably takes years off her looks. She raised her eyebrows and opened her mouth wide attempting to smile and wipe the anger from her face. She couldn't let it get to her. Kelly had decided to stay here and she was old enough to make her own decisions.

'And so are you,' Rowan said to her reflection. 'So quit whingeing and go home.'

Rowan left the cool of the Ladies, holding the door for a group of women who staggered in. She returned to the heat and noise of the bar where the chaos greeting her just served to reinforce her decision to leave. She looked through the crowds at the dance floor but Kelly wasn't there. Rowan felt a tiny glimmer of hope; maybe Kelly had decided to come home with her after all. She rummaged in her bag for her cloakroom ticket and handed it in to the attendant. As the attendant rummaged along the rail, Rowan noticed that Kelly's very distinctive snow leopard faux fur coat wasn't there. She must have collected it. Rowan turned again to look around the club; the friends often joked that Kelly's coat could probably be seen from space but Rowan couldn't see it anywhere. Had Kelly left without her?

'My friend had a black and white fur number hanging up,' said Rowan as the attendant handed her the sensible down jacket she'd arrived in. 'When did she collect it?'

The attendant shrugged and said she was just back from a break. Rowan sighed, walked back to the bar and leaning over it, yelled into the barman's ear, 'Did you happen to see my mate leave?' she asked. 'She's got greenish-blue hair and was drinking shots a little while ago?'

'Yeah,' he shouted back. 'She staggered out about five minutes ago. If you hurry you'll catch her – she wasn't exactly going in a straight line.'

Chapter Two

Saturday, 17 December

Professor Maxie Reddick ploughed up and down the pool. Her heart was pounding both from the exertion and the anticipation, just eight more lengths and she'd have achieved the New Year's resolution she'd set herself back in January – to continue her swimming lessons and complete one whole mile, sixty-four lengths by the end of the year. She knew she was neither fast nor elegant in the water, she had only mastered breaststroke and wouldn't even attempt that sleek flip turn after each length but she was dogged and tenacious. Maxie slowed down, making each stroke count, careful not to run out of strength or energy and as the water parted with each stroke her mind drifted back to the awful Friday evening she'd had yesterday.

Maxie lectured in Criminology at the local university and had used this expertise to branch out into other areas. Not only did she run the ACU – the Applied Criminology Unit which partnered with the police researching methods to improve detection techniques, she also had a regular podcast. On Friday after work, she'd headed into the studio to record her podcast *Criminal Thoughts* with her co-presenter Craig Johnston. Every week they discussed an area of Criminology and linked it with well-known cases. Yesterday the topic had been Unconscious Bias and they'd had a fabulously interactive show. Maxie had been making the point that everyone makes decisions about other people based on their appearance or their accent or even name and that because of this the justice system cannot be truly equitable.

'We all do it,' she'd said. 'And we may hate ourselves for it but it's there. Tell me, which of these mothers would you be more likely to suspect of child neglect – the married one who is home when her kids get back from school and has a few glasses of Chardonnay to relax each evening or the single mum who comes in late after working two shifts at the local taxi rank and has a bit of cannabis when the kids have gone to bed?'

'Well only one of them is illegal,' Craig had replied.

'True, but they both render you senseless after a few and only one would have you described as a drug-taking single parent.'

They'd posted images and recordings of different types of people online; all races, accents and classes were covered. Craig and Maxie listed some crimes and asked listeners to head to the website and state which person was most likely to commit each crime. The results showed the natural biases and the discomfort people felt.

"I want to say that the black guy was the one most likely to have been to prison for assault with a knife but I know that's racist so I'm picking the white guy with the tattoos – even though I also know that's another stereotype."

'The problem,' Maxie had explained, 'is that we look for evidence that supports our natural bias and ignore anything else. If I now tell you that the wine-drinking mother got pregnant at fifteen, she's at home because she was sacked for always being drunk on the job and the husband has left her? The single mum owns that taxi firm, she's single because she's widowed and the cannabis is medicinal. Now you have a completely different view and although you still don't know which is neglectful, your opinion has changed. It's the narrative that the jury are told which makes the difference.'

There had been so much interest and discussion that they'd promised their listeners to come back to the subject in a later edition – but last night Maxie had to leave on time. She had a date. A blind date.

The irony of presenting a show on unconscious bias prior to meeting a man she'd selected on the basis of appearance hadn't escaped her and she hoped she could hold back any opinions on the poor soul until they'd at least got through dinner. The dating site hadn't been her idea at all; she'd split up from her now ex-husband over a year ago and some of her colleagues from the university had decided she needed to get back out there, signing her up for a free trial.

'We said you were a teacher rather than a professor,' they'd told her.

'Heaven forbid that a woman should present herself as intelligent,' had been Maxie's retort.

'It's intimidating,' they'd replied. 'It will put people off. Also – we've said that you like a good laugh and are only looking for friendship at this stage.'

Maxie protested but when the app pinged and a rather handsome looking forty-something appeared asking to meet up, they'd begged her to give it a go.

'Just once,' they said. 'You might even enjoy it.'

Since her marriage breakdown, Maxie hadn't had any male company outside of work and she did miss it. She'd decided to give it a go – after all with pepper spray in her bag and a detective sergeant in her contacts list, she was ready for any scenario. They'd messaged each other and agreed to meet in a bistro Maxie knew well. She'd determined not to buy anything new and having fretted over every piece in her wardrobe, eventually settled on a deep damson coloured wrap-around dress. Maxie checked herself out in the mirror and thought it said everything she wanted it to – classy but fun. She thought she had a little too much cleavage on show so discreetly pinned the wrap up to show only a respectable décolletage and simple gold pendant. She was ready to go.

The bistro was tastefully decked in silver and blue Christmas decorations with a very contemporary white twig tree giving the place a winter wonderland air. Maxie arrived first and was shown to the table and when her date walked in very shortly afterwards, Maxie watched as he strolled towards her and mentally gave him an eight out of ten. His profile picture was pretty accurate; she'd probably describe him as craggy when her colleagues asked – a bit like Liam Neeson and they'd be impressed by that. As an actor he always seemed to play the hero who would rescue women in distress rather than murder them on cold winter nights and surely that had to be a good sign. He kissed her on both cheeks and said he was sorry he was slightly late. Maxie replied that she was simply glad he'd turned up at all. They both laughed and having broken the ice, they sat down and ordered wine. They were both a little over polite to begin with but as the initial nervousness eased, the conversation flowed along with the wine; they discussed the things they loved and loathed about Christmas, their mutual terror of online dating and the plotline of a series they both watched on Netflix. They managed to avoid any controversial subjects and by the time they ordered a dessert to share, Maxie realised she'd relaxed and was actually having a good time. Then, as she shifted in her chair, the pin that was holding her wrap-around together came loose and Maxie noted her date's eyes fix on her cleavage.

'Oops,' she said as she found the pin and fastened it back up. 'I thought I'd locked the girls in for the evening. Sorry about that.'

'Don't apologise on my account.' He grinned salaciously. 'Surely it's wrong to keep such beauties in confinement.'

He scooped up a spoonful of ice-cream and reached over the table, feeding it to Maxie. She suddenly felt uncomfortable with his words, that grin and now this gesture. She couldn't refuse to eat or she'd have a scoop of melted ice-cream down her front but as soon as she'd swallowed it, she made a point of checking the time.

'I'm really sorry but I have to go.' She attempted a regretful smile. 'Have to be up early in the morning.'

'Want someone to bring you coffee in bed?' suggested her date, reaching out and stroking her hand. Maxie pulled it away quickly and jumped up out of her chair. She took her purse out of her bag and placed some money on the table.

'We did agree to go Dutch didn't we?' she said signalling to the waitress for the bill.

'Next time it'll be on me,' replied her date. 'Maybe I'll cook for you at my place.'

Maxie pulled on her coat and excused herself as politely as she could. She hadn't been sure whether she'd read the signals wrong. He'd been fun right up until the moment her pin popped and then it all seemed to go very sleazy. Did he think she'd done it on purpose? Was he just responding the way he thought she wanted him to? Maybe that's how people flirt these days? She'd felt ridiculous but knew she had to get out of there.

He'd sent a text while she was in the taxi, thanking her for a lovely night and hoping they'd see more of each other soon. Maxie's mind went onto overdrive and she hadn't been able to stop herself from wondering whether that had a double meaning – see *more* of each other? More frequently or more flesh? Was she reading too much into it? Maxie had shuddered and decided that no matter what her colleagues thought, she wasn't doing this again. She'd responded to the text by thanking her date for his company and had purposefully not mentioned another meeting.

Sleet was beginning to fall as Maxie rushed from the taxi into her apartment building. She hadn't dared to breathe until she was safely inside with the door locked. Her phone pinged with a message so she'd picked it up and without thinking waited as an image downloaded. Then screaming she'd thrown the phone on the sofa and wiped her hands down her dress as if she'd touched something dirty. Grimacing she'd approached the phone slowly in a state of disbelief at what she was sure she'd just seen. She looked again at the image her date had sent her and there it was. His erect penis.

Maxie gagged as she swallowed some of the swimming pool water. This was not a memory she wanted to hold onto so for the final length she gave it all she had and ploughed her way through the water, kicking her legs out as fiercely as she could, imagining they were aiming right at that guy's crotch. As she touched the side breathless but having achieved that mile, her face broke out into a huge smile. She lifted the goggles from her eyes and looked up at the clock on the wall – it had taken her just a little over an hour. Fair enough, she shrugged, her next target would be doing that same distance in fifty-nine minutes or less.

In the changing room, Maxie dressed quickly. She always thought this was the worst part of her Saturday afternoon swim – having to struggle out of a wet swimsuit back into clothes. The way the fabric seemed to stick to her skin as she pulled it over her body made her feel as if she'd swallowed the contents of the pool and grown two sizes. She had one leg in her tights and was hopping around the changing room when her phone rang. She'd blocked her date and had also cleaned the phone with a disinfectant wipe but that sound made her jump. It was completely irrational but she knew she'd feel vulnerable answering the phone in this state of undress so ignored it while putting on the rest of her clothes and once fully clothed, cautiously looked at who had called.

On seeing DS Andrew Dawson's name she sighed with relief and called him back as she walked through the leisure centre. The piped music overhead urging everyone to rock around the Christmas tree was far too loud to listen to a call properly so she headed for the exit where the automatic doors slid open and she stepped out into the cold, dark and wet December day.

'How was your swim?' asked Andrew.

'I did it,' replied Maxie. 'I swam the mile. I made one New Year's resolution for this year and that's it ticked off and just in time. But I'm guessing you didn't call to ask me about swimming?'

'You guessed right. I need the help of the ACU,' said Andrew. 'We've had a missing person reported and the couple reporting it apparently know you – a George and Patricia Hendry.'

'Mrs Hendry? She was one of Karl's teachers at secondary school. Blimey, it's a long time since I've seen her. Text me the address,' said Maxie throwing her sports kit into the boot and climbing into her car. 'I'll get there as soon as I can.'

Chapter Three

Maxie drove past the sign telling her she'd now entered Helmsforth and took in her surroundings. It was a place that had changed so much over the years. Although it was a district on the outskirts of the university city of Lonsdale, it was very different. In the nineteenth century it would have been the industrial heart with it's canal, impressive Victorian mills and rows of terraced houses. Then for a while it was unfashionable as the city centre itself attracted all incomers. As the city became too expensive for younger people and families though, they began migrating towards Helmsforth and developers and entrepreneurs followed. Helmsforth didn't look much to any outsider but it was becoming more fashionable.

Maxie continued along the narrow streets that ran parallel to the canal and right now, beside one of the locks, a group of carol singers from the local rotary club were in full swing under the town's enormous Christmas tree. Around them an audience looked on, joining in when they found a chorus that they knew; fathers with children perched on their shoulders, couples wrapped around each other for comfort and warmth, old friends in mittens and bobble hats – all enjoying a moment of festive cheer before heading home after an afternoon's shopping.

When she reached the address she'd been given, Maxie thought the row of neat stone terraced houses looked like something from a Christmas movie set. Each house was decked out in strings of multi-coloured lights which flashed on and off cheerfully under a black sky – all it needed was a blanket of snow to make the picture perfect. It was only late afternoon but nearing the shortest day of the year, it could have been midnight. These villages were pretty by day but being nestled at the foot of the hills as they were, as soon as the sun went down, they bore a coldness that chilled deep to the bone. Maxie was wrapped up well after her swim but mused that all the layers she possessed wouldn't be enough to warm her here.

She recognised Andrew's car just ahead of her so parked up behind him and, tugging her hat down over her ears, got out of the car and walked up to meet him.

'We got a call at the station to say a young woman was missing and an investigating officer came out earlier,' explained Andrew as they walked. 'It turns out that the woman has simply not turned up for afternoon tea so the officer suggested that they wait for an hour or so to see if she appears. They're not happy about that and asked to speak to the detective who works with Professor Reddick. I've turned into the Robin to your Batman.'

'Glad it's not the other way round,' replied Maxie. 'Your costume is awful.'

Together they reached a house with a very neat garden. Even at this time of year, holly bushes were neatly trimmed while winter pansies and cyclamen flowered in well-tended pots. Maxie looked at the other houses in the street as Andrew rang the doorbell and saw the changes that had happened in Helmsforth reflected in them. Maxie could pretty much guess the inhabitants of each house just from the gardens and decorations. Those covered in lights with "Santa Please Stop Here" signs on the lawns were obviously new families with children, the more elegant strings of white or gold probably belonged to young adults eager to demonstrate their style and taste and this house? She knew the age of the occupants of this house but even if she hadn't anyone could see that it belonged to an older person. She imagined the Hendrys were still keen on gardening but probably not steady enough to get up a ladder and hang lights.

The door opened and Maxie's guess was confirmed. An old man smartly dressed in slightly baggy corduroy trousers, a checked shirt and knitted waistcoat introduced himself as George and invited them in. Maxie followed Andrew through the narrow hallway into the small lounge where the blast of heat from the roaring fire nearly melted her on the spot. She felt her cheeks redden almost instantly and began unpeeling some of her layers.

'That's some fire you have,' she said to George. 'I can never keep one going.'

'The trick is not loading it up too much at the start,' replied George reaching for a poker by the fireplace and giving the logs a prod to position them better. A sprightly looking old lady walked in wiping her hands on her apron and Maxie recognised the woman who'd taught her son a few years back. Mrs Hendry had been close to retirement back then and although her face bore signs of age, her eyes were as bright as ever.

'Professor,' she exclaimed. 'Thank goodness you're here. You don't look a day older. How is that son of yours doing?'

Maxie explained that he'd decided against university and was working in a gaming company and loving every minute of it. Pat clasped her hands together in happiness and replied that she was pleased to hear he'd found his passion. She asked if they'd like tea which Maxie and Andrew both accepted. George invited his guests to sit down while Pat left the room to make tea, returning only a few moments later with a tray containing a teapot and cups as well as a large iced fruitcake.

'We got all of this ready for Kelly coming,' explained Pat as Maxie expressed delight at the offering. 'She never misses tea with us before she goes out on the town and Kelly normally brings the cake but she said she loves a fruit cake at Christmas so I told her I'd get it in this week.'

'Don't worry, she won't mind us starting it without her,' added George. 'Live for today – that's her motto.'

The elderly couple chuckled at that and while Pat cut slices of cake and poured tea which George handed round, Andrew began questioning them.

'So Kelly is the person you told the investigating officer about earlier?'

'That's right,' replied Pat. 'Kelly Ingles – that's her full name. We told her she should be called Kelly Jingles with all those bangles up her arm. They make a right racket don't they love?'

Her husband nodded and shakily raised a cup to his lips.

'And why do you think she's missing?' continued Andrew.

'Kelly comes to see us every week,' said Pat. 'Always on the dot of three.'

'She is,' added George. 'Missing. I could set my clock by her. No matter what, she's here full of her stories about the week she's had. Kelly has some stories doesn't she Pat? She's always up to something or other, giving the boys the run around. She makes us laugh.'

They chuckled again and reminisced over a couple of the stories this missing girl had told them. Andrew interrupted their gentle conversation. 'So I understand from the officer's notes that she comes here every Saturday afternoon and today she hasn't? You originally reported her at three-thirty and it's now six o'clock, so she's three hours late and that's out of character. Have you tried calling or texting?'

Pat explained that her fingers were far too thick and gnarly to text so she preferred to call, to talk to someone. She'd done that and there was no answer. Andrew took a note of Kelly's number and tried it himself. It went straight to message.

'Have you tried her home? Do you know where Kelly lives?'

'On Mountview Road, but I don't know the number I'm afraid,' replied Pat. 'Her friend Rowan lives a few doors down from here though. That's how we got to know her isn't it George?'

'It was,' replied her husband. 'I was bringing the shopping in one Saturday and I'm not as young as I was, so I had to put one of the bags down – to catch my breath. Next thing I know, this young woman comes bounding up offering to help.'

'We thought she was going to rob us at first,' continued Pat picking up the thread as if together they'd told this story many times. 'She had all those metal bits in her nose and bright red hair – well you would wouldn't you? But no, she carried everything in and so I offered her a cup of tea for her troubles. She stayed over an hour didn't she George? And we hadn't laughed as much in ages.'

Maxie watched as Pat reached out and squeezed her husband's hand. Everything in this room bore the signs of many years of love: the photographs on the walls and dresser – from the faded black and white wedding picture to the colourful studio portraits of children who were most likely grandchildren, the artificial tree now slightly threadbare but decked with home-made decorations and topped with a star that had lost some glitter. There were gifts beneath the tree wrapped in cheerful snowman paper and ready to give out. Maxie wondered if any of these were for Kelly. The old couple did seem to care about this girl very much.

'She sounds lovely,' said Maxie. 'You mentioned that she has a friend down the road? Rowan? Have you asked her if she's seen Kelly?' Maxie knew that was the next obvious port of call and wanted to get going without seeming to rush these lovely concerned people.

George shook his head. 'She works on a Saturday and might not be home yet,' he explained. 'She's a manager at the supermarket in town. They'd have been busy today.'

'I hope we were right to ask for you, Professor,' said Patricia. 'I listen to your podcast – well we both do – and when you talked about that unconscious bias, I was afraid that's what would happen here.'

'You were afraid the police would be biased against Kelly?' asked Maxie.

'Well probably they will be, but I meant us,' replied Patricia. 'They see an old couple and they think we've lost our marbles. That's bias isn't it?'

Maxie said it certainly was but reassured her that the police took everything seriously no matter who reported it. She guessed it would be believed coming from her. Andrew stood up and thanked the couple for making the report. He told them they'd try Rowan's door to see if she was home then let them know how it went. The couple nodded along at his words.

'Does Kelly have a boyfriend or girlfriend?' asked Maxie as she walked to the hallway with Andrew.

'Oh she likes the boys,' replied Pat shaking her head with a grandmotherly concern. 'But she doesn't like to be tied down that one.'

Back on the street, the cold stung Maxie's face as if trying to punish her for having escaped it for a few moments. She hunched up her shoulders and rubbed her arms.

'What do you think?' she asked.

'I know the investigating officer did the right thing by suggesting we wait an hour or so,' said Andrew. 'I think this might be a waste of your time and mine.'

'Do you think Kelly has just forgotten today's visit?'

'Probably, or she's tied up with shopping, sleeping off a hangover, gone out with friends. There could be a million reasons at this time of year but let's keep your friends happy and go see if this Rowan knows anything.'

They walked towards the house Pat had pointed out noting that the couple were still standing at the window watching them go. Maxie waved at them and they both waved back.

'Checking up on us?' asked Andrew.

'No,' replied Maxie. 'I think they're genuinely concerned. They both seemed to really look forward to those afternoons.'

The door they knocked at said "young professional" with its décor; it was painted a fashionable grey colour and had brushed steel door furniture where a tasteful silver wreath now hung. An exhausted young woman opened it, still dressed in her coat and scarf. She didn't look pleased to see them.

'Yes?' she asked curtly. 'Can I help you?'

Andrew held up his police ID and introduced Professor Reddick. Rowan frowned at them, looking puzzled but saying nothing.

'We're making enquiries about Kelly Ingles,' explained Andrew. 'I believe she's a friend of yours?'

'Kelly?' said Rowan. 'What about her?'

'She's been reported missing,' replied Andrew. 'Can we come in?'

Rowan stepped to one side to let both Andrew and Maxie in. The house was identical in layout to the one they'd just left but that's where the similarity ended. Maxie noted the lack of family photos across every surface, the clutter of plates and glasses left abandoned in the kitchen, a scent of plug-in air freshener rather than home baking and the coldness of a central heating system that had just been switched on.

'Sorry it's such a mess,' said Rowan. 'This is the busiest week of the year at work. Do you guys want coffee or something?'

Both Maxie and Andrew shook their heads and Rowan looked relieved. She cleared the small kitchen table and invited them to sit down.

'So who says she's missing then?'

Andrew explained the visit to the old couple down the road and Rowan nodded along.

'Yeah, she does visit them every week. Does their shopping every now and then but they only see one side of her.'

'What's the side they don't see?' asked Maxie.

'She's a party animal,' replied Rowan. 'And the last time I saw her she left me in a club on my own and I had to get a cab back alone.'

'When was that?'

Rowan explained the events of Friday – that they'd had a Christmas meal with Kelly's work colleagues then the rest of their party went into Lonsdale for the clubs while she and Kelly stayed and went to The Printworks. Andrew took notes.

'So the last time you saw or heard from her was last night?' he asked.

'Well technically this morning. It was after two.'

'And you haven't called each other since?' continued Andrew.

'Honestly, I haven't had time.' Rowan sighed. 'There were no cabs so thanks to her I got back here at four and I had to get into work at seven. I've just finished a ten-hour shift and I'm ready to crash. Quite frankly I don't want to hear from her for the rest of the weekend.'

Andrew asked for a photo of Kelly, and Rowan dug out her phone. Maxie looked at it and thought back to Pat's words, how they'd thought she was going to rob them when they first met. Maxie wasn't surprised. The green-haired woman on the photo seemed to have piercings and tattoos in every place visible; she didn't look the type to sit and have fruit cake with an elderly couple.

'Your neighbours said she had red hair,' said Maxie.

'Oh it changes all the time.' Rowan shrugged. 'That cut's new too.'

Maxie looked again at the asymmetrical bob thinking only the young could get away with a style like that.

'Does Kelly have a boyfriend?' Maxie continued.

'Moot point,' replied Rowan. 'But that's where she'll be if she's anywhere. He's stupid enough to take her back no matter what she's done.'

Rowan dialled a number and asked the person if Kelly was there as the old folk thought she was missing and there were some police in her house asking questions. Whoever was on the other end of the line was evidently more concerned than Rowan as she fired back a series of answers to questions.

'I don't know – I'm not her bloody mother.'

'Well she didn't stay here.'

The call ended abruptly and Rowan looked up at her unwanted guests with a furious expression.

'Luis thought she was staying with me. He wants you to go round there if you can.'

Andrew said he thought that would be a good idea and Maxie asked whether Rowan would come too so they could take the statements together. She wanted to watch the relationship dynamics between these two – someone, judging by the tone of the call, who sounded concerned about this missing girl and someone who seemed glad to see the back of her.

Chapter Four

Luis stood in the doorway as they pulled up outside the house. Maxie gauged that he was taller than her own son Karl, so this guy had to be over six foot tall and had muscles on top of muscles. With his broad shoulders and wavy jaw length black hair, he looked like an angry matador and although Luis completely filled the space of the small doorway, he still managed to pace impatiently as his three visitors made their way up the drive.

While Andrew made the introductions, Rowan barged past Luis into the house. They all followed her into the lounge where an easy-maintenance black leather sofa and chairs, magnolia walls and plain curtains suggested to Maxie that the house was rented. However, it didn't lack warmth – on shelves and walls were photographs of a dark-looking family – very probably Luis's. Pictures of small children were encased in photo frames bearing the words "best uncle" and more artistic poses by Kelly in simple black frames took pride of place. A small real tree stood in a stand by the window but no one had switched on the lights. Maxie and Andrew sat down but it was Luis who began the interrogations.

'How could you leave her on her own in a place like that?' he shouted at Rowan in an accent that confirmed his Spanish looks. 'It's a complete shit-hole.'

'I didn't leave *her*, she left me,' Rowan shouted back. 'And the last time I saw her, she wasn't alone.'

'Did she leave with someone? Did you see her go?'

'No, I didn't.' Rowan sighed, putting her head in her hands then dragging her palms down her face. 'I promise I have no idea who she was with. I went to the loo and thought she'd still be on the dance floor when I came out but she wasn't. The barman said she'd gone and I was furious with her.'

A tear formed in the corner of her eye and Rowan wiped it away. 'Sorry,' she said sniffing. 'I'm exhausted. I just wanted to get home. I never really wanted to go there in the first place. I'm so sorry.'

Maxie watched Luis as he moved to sit alongside Rowan and put his arm around her.

'No, I'm sorry,' he said to her. 'I shouldn't have shouted. It wasn't your fault and I know what she can be like.' He looked up at Andrew and Maxie. 'So what do we do now?'

‘First of all,’ said Andrew. ‘I’d like to establish both of your relationships with Kelly and the details leading up to when you last saw her.’

Rowan went first, listing all the pubs and clubs they’d been to on Friday and explaining that they’d been friends for six years, ever since meeting in the first year of university.

‘It was her works do,’ she explained. ‘It was the only night off I could get from work so she invited me along. We started at Greenwell’s then when everyone else left, we did pretty much every bar in the high street before ending up at The Printworks.’

‘Did you share digs or study the same subject?’ asked Maxie as both Luis and Andrew seemed to be taking notes.

‘Both,’ replied Rowan. ‘We both did Business Studies and had a flat together.’

‘So you went into retail management,’ continued Maxie. ‘What does Kelly do?’

‘PR,’ replied Luis. ‘She makes terrible brands trendy but she loves it.’

He rolled rr’s in “terrible” making the word sound the complete opposite.

‘You’re Spanish?’ asked Maxie.

Luis nodded. ‘My parents moved here when I was eight years old. They own the tapas bar in town.’

‘Do you work there?’ asked Andrew.

‘No, they used to make my brother and I wait tables to earn our pocket money when we were sixteen. After that I never wanted to see another dish of patatas bravas in my life. I’m a carpenter by trade but I make set designs most of the time now.’

Andrew then asked Luis how long he and Kelly had been together.

‘Six months,’ replied Luis letting his head hang.

‘But they’re considering their options right now,’ added Rowan.

Luis lifted his head and glared at her. ‘What a stupid expression. Kelly just needs time.’

‘Time for what?’ asked Maxie.

‘The owner of this place is selling it next year and I asked Kelly if she wanted to buy it and move in together.’

‘And she wasn’t sure about that?’ continued Maxie. Luis just shrugged and Rowan rubbed his arm sympathetically.

‘So if you weren’t with Kelly on Friday night where were you?’ asked Andrew.

'At a pub with my friend Harry – the King's Arms and we left at around eleven-thirty. You can check, they know us there,' replied Luis.

'Kelly still lives here though – while she's considering these options?' asked Maxie.

Luis replied that she did.

'So presuming she should have come back here to sleep at some point in time and given that it's after six, why haven't you called the police?'

'I've just got back from work. Six o'clock is hardly late – besides, she sent me this text last night,' replied Luis getting out his phone and showing them: *With Ro.* 'I assumed she was staying at Rowan's. She asked me to give her some space – that's what I'm doing.'

'She wasn't staying with me,' said Rowan emphatically.

'So who was she staying with?' demanded Luis.

'I don't know!' Rowan shouted back.

'I presume Kelly is on social media,' said Maxie interrupting their argument and getting a nod from both Luis and Rowan as they calmed down. 'Have her accounts been updated today?'

'Yes.' Rowan shrugged. 'But they're scheduled posts – she sets them up in advance so she doesn't need to look at them over a weekend.'

'That's unusual isn't it?' asked Andrew.

'Her whole work life is social media so she tries to give herself a break,' replied Luis. 'Before she started scheduling them she was never off her phone, it was a nightmare. I don't use that rubbish and I asked her to stop.'

Luis ran his fingers through his dark hair and sighed. 'She can't be missing,' he said. 'It hasn't even been a day. If she wasn't with Rowan maybe she got a hotel for the night?'

'Anyway, on TV they say you don't even need to call the police until forty-eight hours are up,' added Rowan. 'When you're sure they're really missing. Isn't that right?'

'That depends on their usual behaviour,' replied Andrew.

'Let me tell you some of the statistics around people who go missing,' said Maxie softly. 'The police get nearly three hundred thousand reports of missing people every year.'

'That many?' said Luis. 'How come we never hear those numbers?'

'Well, two-thirds of them are under eighteen and they're just running away from home,' continued Maxie. 'The good news is that over ninety per cent of cases are resolved one way or the other within the first forty-eight hours.'

'One way or the other, what does that mean?' asked Rowan, taking hold of Luis's hand.

'The majority are found safe and well,' replied Andrew taking up the delivery of this information. 'Although those true crime stories focus on people who vanish for years, that's not typical. However, a minority have willingly left their homes and we have no authority to force them to go back.'

Andrew made this final point slowly and purposefully, looking at Luis directly.

'You think that's what's happened here?' asked Luis, his nostrils flaring as he looked to be trying to control his frustration. 'She's walked out on me?'

'That's not what the detective sergeant was implying,' said Maxie. 'But I think you'd rather know all the likely outcomes wouldn't you?'

Both Luis and Rowan nodded so Maxie continued in a calm and soothing voice.

'Most missing persons are men. It's highly unusual for a mid-twenties female to go missing but Christmas is different. Numbers peak in December because people get drunk and fall asleep somewhere, or they lose their handbags and have an accident. They're safely in a hospital bed but there's no ID to contact relatives. The police check all the places a young girl might be sleeping off a party as the first port of call.'

Maxie didn't add that after the eighteen hours that had now passed, a person was more likely to be found having had a tragic drink-related accident. This town had a canal and a river flowing through it and in a place like this, that's where the December missing were often found having stumbled over the edge. They were known as "water-babies" which sounded far cuter than the bloated corpses that ended up in the morgue. If Kelly was not in the hospital or morgue right now then after the forty-eight hours had lapsed, the police would be assuming the disappearance was voluntary or suspicious. And the boyfriend who'd just been dumped would be the first suspect they'd pursue.

'Shall I start ringing the hospitals?' asked Luis taking his mobile out of his back pocket.

'I could try the club to see if they know anything,' added Rowan.

'Let us do that,' said Andrew. 'I know Kelly hasn't been missing for long but it was cold last night which makes her a high risk. We will begin the official investigation which includes tracking her phone and calling hospitals. They will have to respond to our enquiries. Don't worry we'll get back to you as soon as we hear from them.'

'Could I possibly look around?' asked Maxie. 'Just to get a feel for Kelly?'

Luis shrugged and explained that most of Kelly's clothes were in the spare bedroom as she used it like a dressing room but Maxie was welcome to "snoop", as he put it, as much as she liked. Maxie left Andrew taking more details and headed upstairs. She opened the door to the double room Kelly and Luis obviously shared; the bed was unmade, men's clothes were strewn on the floor one side and a woman's on the other. The bedside tables also revealed who slept on which side of the bed with the pile of novels on one side of the bed being in Spanish. Maxie opened the wardrobe door and as Luis had said, there were no female clothes. She left that room quietly and opened another door just down the hallway. It was smaller but still contained a double bed and was tidy. The bed was made and the dressing table was empty. Maxie recalled her own, with make-up and hairbrushes strewn all over. She imagined a young woman like Kelly had far more than she did but there was very little here. Maxie opened the wardrobe door and here hung Kelly's clothes although Maxie did think it looked a little sparse for a party-loving woman. At the bottom of the wardrobe were some unused charity bags – the type that Maxie got shoved through the letterbox every week. Was Kelly having a clear out? Maxie took a couple of pictures with her phone and left the room as she found it.

'Does Kelly have a passport?' she asked on returning to the living room.

Luis muttered an 'of course' and got up to open a drawer in a dresser. He rummaged around, calmly at first and then frantically as he evidently couldn't find it.

'And an overnight bag?' asked Maxie. Rowan nodded and said she had a designer wheelie thing. Maxie asked Luis if he could fetch it down and again he returned empty-handed. Luis looked angry, confused and upset as he pulled his phone from his back pocket and stabbed out a number.

'Kelly – where the hell are you? Call me now.'

Luis threw his phone against the wall. It fell apart.

'Great, now I need a new phone too. *Idiota.*'

'Come on now,' said Andrew. 'We know this is hard but there's no need for that.'

'Don't pretend to have sympathy for me,' replied Luis. 'I know what you're really thinking. My girlfriend just walked out on me. She'd rather get blind drunk and flirt with some bloke in a sleazy pick-up joint than come home to me.'

'They don't think that,' said Rowan gently. 'They can see you care.'

She picked his phone up and checked to see it was still working: it was. She took the cover off her own and wrapped Luis's phone in it. She handed it to him.

'To keep it safe – for when Kelly calls.'

He took it and nodded his thanks as Rowan rubbed his arm. Then he looked up at Andrew and Maxie with anger still in his eyes.

'Shouldn't you be out there looking for her?' he asked.

Maxie and Andrew stood and confirmed they'd be in touch as soon as they had any news.

'Just one more thing,' said Andrew. 'Do you have the details of Kelly's next of kin? Her parents?'

'It's just her mum,' replied Rowan. 'Not that she gets on with her. I have her address somewhere in the house.'

'I can take you back home now,' said Andrew.

Rowan looked up at Luis. 'Do you want me to stay with you?' she asked.

Maxie noted the doe eyes she'd used but seemingly Luis hadn't.

'No,' he said sharply. 'I want to be alone.'

Luis walked straight to the front door and held it open. Having been unequivocally dismissed, Andrew and Rowan headed to his car and drove off while Maxie hopped into hers and took her phone out of her bag to record some thoughts.

'Remind Andrew to check flight bookings – also local charity shops. Either Kelly has cleared out or Luis is getting rid of her things.'

She put her phone into its hands-free holder on the dashboard and as she did, Luis's front door opened. Dressed in a leather jacket on top of a black hoodie pulled over his head, he got into a small van parked on the street and drove away.

'Now where on earth are you going?' Maxie said to herself as she hurriedly turned the key in the ignition and began to follow.

Chapter Five

Maxie memorised the shade of Luis's dark blue van and the last three digits of the registration plate so she could let him get a few cars ahead of her and still be able to follow him. The van stopped at the traffic lights at the end of the road and Maxie slowed right down. When they changed to green the cars between them turned right so Maxie found herself directly behind Luis as he turned left onto the main approach into the town centre. Drops started falling on the windscreen; large fleshy raindrops that wanted to be snow but couldn't quite gather the energy. Maxie went to flick on the windscreen wipers and flashed her main beam into Luis's line of sight.

'Damn,' she murmured as she tried the other stalks on the steering wheel.

The wipers found, she alternated between manic speed and sloth-like before finding the right level. Why anyone needed all these speeds was beyond her; only one of them ever seemed to be effective in any weather she'd ever come across. The Jeep had been her gift to herself after her divorce and being brand new and in pristine condition, it would be easy to recognise if Luis had been curious as to who was flashing him.

If alerted by her headlight error, Maxie would have expected him to stop and confront her but there was no reaction and the van continued to drive purposefully through the streets away from this old part of the town. Luis took roads and lanes that Maxie didn't know so she kept as close as she could without attracting any more attention. Within twenty minutes they were in the town centre and Luis had slowed down. He stopped and parked up while Maxie waited until she was sure he was getting out of the car before doing the same. She parked far enough away for him not to notice another car pulling up but close enough to be able to catch up. If he walked at full pace, the considerable difference in their leg lengths would put him miles ahead.

The centre of Helmsforth was busy which took Maxie by surprise until she remembered it was the last Saturday before Christmas. The crowds criss-crossed the roads in front of her, laden with shopping bags and their shoulders hunched up against the cold. It brought back memories of battling through brightly lit department stores to find gifts for her son Karl and her ex-husband Philip. In years gone by, she would have been doing exactly the same thing as this crowd; Philip and her would split up to buy each other's presents then get back together for an early supper before heading home. The restaurants looked busy so perhaps this tradition was still going, for some people anyway. Nowadays, her typical Saturday evening revolved around a glass of wine with cheese and biscuits rather than cocktails and olives. But then, with Karl simply wanting cash rather than a gift, she had no one to shop for.

Maxie pulled on a hat and gloves before beginning the tail. She needn't have worried about being able to keep up with Luis as he walked slowly in front of her, checking the pavement which glistened under the streetlights and kicking piles of rubbish that had blown into the gutters. Maxie guessed he was heading towards Greenwell's – the first place Rowan had mentioned and realised he was searching the streets as he went, hoping for evidence that Kelly had been here. She could have told him he was wasting his time.

Luis reached the first bar Rowan had said they'd visited after Greenwells and Maxie stood outside watching through the window as he showed his phone – presumably the picture of Kelly – to the bar staff. They each looked at it, some shook their heads and then one nodded, giving Luis some information. He appeared to thank them and then come back out onto the street. Maxie waited again until he began walking, stopping at a taxi rank just a little way ahead. She watched as Luis went from car to car stooping and talking to the driver and once again showing them the photo on his phone. Maxie saw his shoulders drop as he evidently failed to get the answer he was looking for. Luis then left them to walk further up the street, peering into each alleyway as he did so. Maxie followed. She got to the taxi rank and asked the lead car what Luis wanted.

'I'm working with the police and he's a person of interest,' she told them.

'Showed me a picture of a girl and asked if I'd seen her,' the driver told her. 'I hadn't and neither had any of the other guys.'

'What about him?' Maxie asked. 'Have you ever seen him before tonight?'

The driver shook his head. Maxie thanked him and hurried towards Luis. She peered into the side streets as he'd done and grimaced at the rain-soaked debris and litter that had gathered. She thought about all those times she'd heard about rain "washing the streets clean" and wondered why it hadn't tonight. Instead it had soaked through the trash, the discarded food wrappers and empty beer crates piled high ready to be collected. It created a black papier mâché which would now be trampled into every hotel, bar and home around. Winter filth spreading everywhere on the soles of people's shoes – not something you see on many Christmas cards. Whatever he was looking for, he wouldn't find it in there.

The evening turned to night and Maxie noticed shopping bags being replaced by tiny handbags as the crowds changed from shoppers to revellers. Many of them looked the same age as her students and with term now finished they could party every night of the week. No doubt some of them would be heading home next week and this was their last night out together. Maxie found herself wondering what Karl was up to tonight and while distracted, she very nearly blew her cover as she ploughed forward, head down against the cold. Luis had stopped, dead in his tracks and stood staring across the road. Maxie, who had narrowly avoided barging right into him, followed his line of gaze and saw he was watching a group of girls dancing and singing in the street. They accosted a couple of men and draped tinsel around their necks. A good natured cancan followed and then they parted blowing kisses and shouting their undying love. The girls laughed and then teetered up to the taxi rank. They stumbled into the first one and it drove off. Maxie noted the rise and fall of Luis's chest as he sighed. She wondered what he was thinking. Whether he was wishing Kelly had left when Rowan asked her to? Neither of them would be here right now if she had.

Luis shook his head and the tendrils of his sodden hair rained droplets of water into the light of the street lamps. Maxie watched as he squeezed the moisture from his curls as if he'd just noticed they were wet. He pulled his hair back, took a beanie hat out of his pocket and pulled it as far over his head and face as it would go. He then tugged at his scarf to cover up the rest of the exposed flesh and started walking again. Maxie followed at her safe distance watching him sift through the debris of the night still hoping to find something. He stopped at a metal railing which bore discarded odd gloves on top of each point like some latter day executioners spike. He took time to check them but evidently found nothing of interest. As she stood behind him, she watched his shoulders drop slightly and seeing a sign for The Printworks just a few yards ahead, she knew that's where he was heading and presumed from his stance it was the last place he wanted to go.

Maxie couldn't follow him in unnoticed. In that place she'd stand out as much as she would at a supermodel convention. Nope, she had to stand out here and wait near the doorway in the freezing cold. It wasn't long before the security guys on the outside door held their earpieces with some urgency and then rushed inside the building. Five minutes later they reappeared and bundled Luis out into the street. He yelled something at them in Spanish then marched off kicking a black plastic bag as he went. The bag spilled its guts and smeared the pavement with leftovers from fast food containers, and bottles which rolled down the road. Luis targeted a bottle, kicked it again and watched it smash against the building. The bouncers started towards him but he ran and was faster than them. While the bouncers were distracted, Maxie went inside and made her way to the bar.

Later on tonight this place would probably be transformed by the lighting and music into some kind of pleasure dome but right now it was still a dingy beer-soaked hole with last year's decorations double-Sellotaped to the walls. It was a huge empty space befitting its former use as a printing press but now it was designed for groups and dancing. Industrial air ducts and metal pillars tried to say grunge but the rest of the place simply said grime. The floors had just been mopped and the smell of disinfectant fought with the years of human odour drenched into the stained velour booths and spliff-trodden carpets to mount an attack on Maxie's senses. Bags of trash stood just beside the door ready to be thrown out, the novelty hats tattered and torn at odds with the Hollywood image of the season that everyone still tried to believe in. It was hideous.

On the wall was a huge monitor which flashed through photos from previous nights; Maxie watched as the images faded in and out. She'd seen the photos Rowan had taken but they didn't capture the whole sordid scene. These images were like a real-life Hogarth cartoon. In the foreground of one picture, two women steadied themselves pouting for the camera while in the background blokes had their shirts off and were locking bellies sumo-style. In another someone looked upset, with mascara down her face as she was being propped up by friends. Maxie stood at the corner of the bar and watched. If alcohol didn't warp your memories and people could see what they really looked like after a few then they probably wouldn't do this, she thought wondering what she must have looked like back in the day. The miracle of Christmas, she mused, wasn't that Santa Claus existed it was that anyone actually survived it.

'Not pretty is it?'

Maxie turned to see the barman wiping down the surfaces.

'Is it like this every night?' she asked.

'Most weekends but it's a bit worse at Christmas. You get all these people who aren't used to drinking and of course they've been on the wine all afternoon at their work dinners before they even get here which doesn't help. What can I do for you?'

'I'm a consultant with the police,' she replied quickly, flashing the barman her university ID, hoping he didn't look at it too closely. 'I've got a couple of questions about the guy you've just thrown out. And could I get a coke please?'

The barman served Maxie her drink and asked another guy to cover him while he spoke to her. 'What do you want to know?' He signalled Maxie to come into the back room. It obviously doubled as an office and a place for staff downtime as a microwave and sofa fought for space with a PC and swivel chair.

'The guy you just threw out, what was he asking about?'

'A woman who was in the bar last night and apparently hasn't come home yet. He had a picture of her.'

'And did you remember her?'

'God yeah, she's in one of those photos somewhere. She was in a bit of a state, draped over some guy and downing shots.'

'Do you know who he was? Was he a regular?'

'Nope, I think he was part of the stag do that was in here. God knows why you'd want to get married at Christmas but there were a few of them in, from Golston way I think. They had a minibus.'

'And you told him all this?'

The barman nodded.

'So why was he thrown out?'

'I only said she looked a right one.' The barman laughed. 'A proper little cock-tease and then he just went for me. I know it's a bit harsh but call a spade a spade eh?'

Maxie took a deep breath and hoped Luis had at least managed to land one punch on this sanctimonious jerk.

'Did the woman in the picture leave with this stag party?'

'No idea but we do have CCTV on the exit – we could have a look if you like.'

Maxie might assist with police cases but she had no authority to ask to see any footage without Andrew there. Still, if it was going to be offered to her then who was she to refuse? The jerk might be useful for something after all. He swivelled the chair round to the PC and started skimming through images until he found what he was looking for: Kelly tottering out of the bar. There were only a few seconds of footage.

'Is that all there is? Do you have any other angles?' asked Maxie.

'No, that's it. The cameras are focussed on the bouncers in case we get sued. The owners don't care what happens when the punters are off the premises.'

Maxie asked him to play it again. There wasn't much to go on. Kelly was definitely drunk and definitely leaving the bar alone but just before she vanished from the camera's line of vision, she also definitely waved to someone across the street.

Maxie told the barman that the police would probably call in to take a copy of the recording and the club's pictures of the evening, then she left the bar. She walked back to her car and noticed that Luis's van was still parked up. She approached it and saw he was inside with his head lying on the steering wheel. Maxie tapped on the window and he looked up. His eyes were bloodshot and his face was drained white as he wound down the window and looked up at Maxie.

'Where did she go?' he said. 'Where?'

Chapter Six

Sunday, 18 December

Andrew called Maxie and told her that he and the investigating officer were going to see Luis with an update. She was already dressed and waiting so immediately leapt into the car and over to Helmsforth.

'Morning,' said Andrew as he and the junior officer got out of his car at the same time as Maxie. 'I hope you got some sleep and weren't up all night thinking about this case.'

'You know me too well,' replied Maxie. 'Actually I spent the evening in town following Luis. After you left he took it upon himself to start his own investigations. We ended up in The Printworks – you should know that they have CCTV which shows Kelly leaving just after two and they have images of the guys she was dancing with. It was pretty much as Rowan described.'

'Thanks. What do you think about Luis's actions? Returning to the scene of the crime? The officer here checked with the bar he said he went to on Friday. Him and his friend left around eleven-thirty so there was plenty of time for him to get into town afterwards,' said Andrew.

Maxie shrugged, having not made up her mind on this one. It was a fallacy played out mainly on TV screens that criminals returned to the scene of the crime when generally they didn't do this. Arsonists were the main exception; they loved to watch their work. Research showed that they took great pleasure in seeing the power and beauty of the flames destroying their chosen target. Although Maxie's old family home had been destroyed in a fire she could still understand this fascination – there was something awe-inspiring about fire. However, she also knew that the other exception to the rule concerned crimes of passion. They usually happened on the spur of the moment, driven by an unexpected word or deed so the perpetrator hadn't planned the crime at all and might return to the scene for a number of reasons. The crime usually took place in highly disorganized chaotic circumstances so a person might not believe their own recollection and would return just to confirm that the crime had actually happened. Or the perpetrator might be completely cognisant of their actions and would return out of regret or fear that they'd left something incriminating behind. Maxie had watched Luis searching for something last night and therefore could have been checking that he hadn't dropped anything or that none of the bar staff recognized him. The tears in the car might have been a realisation of what he'd done rather than acceptance that his girlfriend was gone. Maxie knew there could be a number of reasons for Luis's actions and was planning on staying close to him until she could learn more about him.

Luis opened the door to them and they headed into the lounge where Rowan already stood. The little room was crowded with five people, every one of them taller than Maxie.

'Have you found her?' asked Rowan as soon as they walked in.

Andrew asked if he could sit down which was a signal for them all to do the same. As had happened on the previous visit, Rowan took a seat beside Luis on the sofa and put a hand on his arm. Andrew indicated that the officer could begin the update.

'We've called Kelly's mother and she hasn't heard from her daughter but wouldn't have expected to. The last location her phone could be traced was outside the club around the time of the message she sent. We've also contacted all the local hospitals, shelters and hostels and no one matching Kelly's description has been admitted recently,' said the officer.

'That's good isn't it?' said Rowan. 'It means she's not … dead.'

Luis glared at her and shook her hand away. 'How could you even think that?' he snarled.

'I'm sorry,' replied Rowan. 'But why else would she still be out there?'

Luis got up and started pacing the room. 'What happens next?' he asked.

'I know you care very deeply about her,' said Maxie. 'But the police need you to be completely honest about a few things that will help with their enquiries.'

'Like what?'

'Does she ever take drugs?'

'No never,' snapped Luis.

Maxie looked over to Rowan but she just shook her head to confirm Luis's answer.

'Okay, I'm just asking because if she did take them, maybe unwittingly, they could wipe out an entire weekend. I've seen it happen to my students.'

'Has she done this type of thing before?' pressed Andrew following Maxie's lead. 'Stayed out all night with someone she might just have met?'

That was it. Luis punched the mantelpiece and turned, squaring up to Andrew as if looking for a fight. The junior officer jumped up and stood between them, urging Luis to be calm.

'We have to ask these things,' said Maxie gently, patting the arm of the chair indicating to Luis to sit down.

They all returned to their seats and the room fell silent until Luis calmed down, rubbed his eyes and sighed.

'I'm sorry about that,' he said leaning forward with his arms on his knees and his head drooped. 'Kelly gets drunk, she flirts and she's a nightmare at times. But she's also gorgeous and funny and whatever she has done, wherever she is, I need to know. Just because she likes a party doesn't make her any less of a human being.'

'Of course it doesn't,' replied Andrew. 'We all like a party.'

He asked Luis whether Kelly would be expected at work in the morning.

'Yes,' replied Luis. 'She doesn't finish until Christmas Eve.'

'And if she loves her job as much as you've said I imagine she'll make an effort to get in, even if she is hung-over somewhere right now?' asked Andrew.

Luis nodded.

'Okay,' said Andrew. 'I'd like you to give the officer here a formal photo of what she looked like the last time you saw her and a full description of what she was wearing.'

'It was a black dress.' Luis shrugged.

'It was a figure-hugging black jersey mini with sequins round the neckline and hemline.' Rowan sighed as the officer took notes. 'She also had a glitter clutch bag, suede platform heels and a fake snow leopard fur. The shop has a website – I'll send you links to the exact outfit.'

Andrew thanked her and continued to tell them that the officer would begin house-to-house enquiries but they still believed that she would be in touch with one of them soon. 'Please be assured,' he said, 'that we'll be taking this very seriously.'

Andrew, followed by his officer, stood up and walked towards the door.

'What can we do now?' asked Rowan. 'Should we do one of those missing person posters on Facebook or something?'

'My advice is to refrain from that right now,' cautioned the junior officer before anyone else could get a word in. 'There is still a good chance that Kelly is just sleeping off a hangover at another friend's house and she'll be home soon in time for work and craving junk food.'

'So by all means ask a couple of her closest friends but hold on from making any big announcements,' added Andrew. 'Get the takeaway menus ready, then wait for her to come home and tell you she'll never do it again.'

'That sounds like her,' said Rowan with half a smile.

'If she does contact either of you,' Andrew told both Luis and Rowan, 'even if Kelly thinks all this is a waste of time, you must let us know.'

They both nodded and the police left.

'I have to be at work,' said Rowan to Luis. 'Will you be okay?'

Luis nodded and gave a slight wave as she headed off. He raised his eyebrows at Maxie. 'Don't you have somewhere to be too?' he asked.

'I was hoping I'd be able to help you,' replied Maxie.

'How?'

'I run a facility at the university called the ACU – the Applied Criminology Unit. I look into ways of making policing more effective and the reason I'm here is that I want to find ways of supporting the relatives of missing persons better. I personally don't believe it's helpful to advise you just to sit and wait for Kelly to turn up.'

'I'm with you on that one,' said Luis. 'But what can you actually do, apart from follow me around town that is?'

'Well, I could help you look for Kelly in ways that won't get you thrown out of bars or arrested.'

Luis snorted at her dismissively. 'Sorry, I didn't mean to do that,' he said, 'but I'm going through the worst time of my life and Miss Marple turns up offering to give me some private detective tips – no offence.'

'None taken,' smiled Maxie. 'At least Miss Marple always gets her man. Do you think I could have a coffee?'

Luis shrugged and nodded in the direction of the kitchen. He followed her as Maxie took the lead and flicked on the kettle.

'So it's just over thirty hours now since she was last seen isn't it?' asked Maxie as she handed Luis a coffee.

He nodded. 'And the police have nothing useful to tell me.'

'You know that's not the case. Everything the detective said is true. December is a nightmare month for missing persons but they're very rarely missing. They just get drunk and fall over somewhere. For the first forty-eight hours, they'll keep working to the assumption that she'll turn up of her own accord. She could know that she's offended you and not want to face the music yet.'

'You think she's scared of me?' asked Luis, his nostrils flaring slightly.

'Maybe scared of hurting you,' replied Maxie. 'And if you don't mind me saying, in the pictures she did seem pretty close to those guys she was dancing with. I can't imagine that won't cause a row or two after you've got over the initial relief of having her back.'

'You don't mince your words do you?' replied Luis.

'I don't have to and I don't think you're the type who'd want me to.'

Luis gave Maxie a slight nod then looked up at her as if a light bulb had gone on. 'Those guys – the barman said they were there with a stag party. Now I know Kelly doesn't take drugs but what if they spiked her drink? Where did the barman say they lived?'

'Golston I think,' replied Maxie.

'That's it,' declared Luis. 'I cannot work out why she still hasn't come back but if she's been drugged, then it all makes sense.'

'Tell me what you're thinking,' said Maxie watching as a very animated Luis started rushing around the house picking up his keys, phone and jacket.

'They had a minibus,' continued Luis. 'What if she got on board with them?'

'The police will check that lead and find the minibus company,' replied Maxie.

'Eventually maybe – after they've wasted more time with a house-to-house,' replied Luis. 'And you've said yourself, I cannot just sit here. I can picture her being dragged onto that bus, maybe it felt like one big party to begin with. But let's say the drugs started to wear off and she got very disoriented during the journey – she told them to let her off and might have asked to be dropped off somewhere she thought she recognised.'

'Go on,' said Maxie.

'But what if it was miles away? So now Kelly is out there in the sticks having to make her own way back. What if she's lost her phone, her purse and has no money, what would she do?'

'Call you or Rowan,' replied Maxie. 'You have a van and she'd know you would pick her up. There are still a few phone boxes knocking around.'

'Maybe not where she is and besides, the numbers are programmed in, she probably doesn't actually know them. Or she doesn't want us to know that she was stupid enough to get herself stranded somewhere. You said it yourself – she doesn't want to face the music.'

'I'm sorry but where does this theory leave us?' asked Maxie.

'It means that the police search isn't wide enough – Kelly could be anywhere,' replied Luis. 'We have to find this stag party and see if my theory is right, find out where they dropped her off. Unless you think the police will search this widely?'

Maxie knew that Andrew wouldn't follow this theory up yet while there was still a chance of Kelly coming back in time for work tomorrow. It was a fairly random line of enquiry but if it made Luis think he was doing something positive then who was she to stop him.

'I think you're right in that they'll be focussing on the door to door today,' she replied.

'Which will get them nowhere,' said Luis. 'Don't they think my neighbours would tell me if she was shacked up with them? I know they won't bother to take this seriously until she doesn't turn up for work and by that time, I might have her back.'

'I guess anything's possible,' said Maxie. 'What would you like me to do?'

Luis held up the results of a phone search to her. 'Look, it says there are around eleven churches in Golston – he's probably getting married in one of them. That club has a Facebook page and when I looked, there was a picture of that group of guys with Kelly. I'll download it and then I reckon I should be able to get round all of the churches in one day.'

Maxie took the phone from him and looked at all the little crosses marked up.

'So if you're as keen to help as you say,' Luis continued. 'How do you fancy a road trip?'

Chapter Seven

'I'll drive, you navigate,' said Maxie steering Luis away from his van and into her car.

Maxie had calculated that if she was the one behind the wheel she could control the day's events a little better. She didn't particularly want to spend the day disrupting church services around the county but she was the one who'd barged into Luis's life offering help so she couldn't really back out when he called her bluff. Besides which, this is why she'd wanted to be involved in a missing person's case – to understand the emotions and resulting actions of the family left behind. Several criminology research papers mentioned the state of limbo they experienced – how not knowing where your loved one was, left them frozen somewhere between grief and loss. If they'd had an argument as their last interaction, families were burdened with incredible guilt. People reacted in different ways to finding a loved one missing – some froze, unable to comprehend how it could have happened while others, like Luis were filled with a frenzied need to take action. Maxie felt that the police procedures in place failed to spend enough time on the family and friends of the missing person. She was hoping to demonstrate that actively involving the family in the search could alleviate not only these emotions but could help the reconciliation when the missing person was found and potentially reduce police time.

It wasn't just the academic in her that was piqued right now. Maxie wanted to find Kelly safe and sound. Luis's behaviour last night could be regarded as suspicious or simply desperate and she needed to know whether all of these frantic searches he seemed set on were the result of feeling helpless or guilty about something. Studies had shown that if you watch people's behaviour when they're traumatised, it can reveal a great deal. Maxie could definitely see this case forming part of the curriculum next term. Not only could her students discuss the adequacy or otherwise of the current missing person's procedures but they could also put themselves in the shoes of those people, like Luis, left completely in the dark. They could role-play each position and establish what the force could do to help more effectively? Were current liaison practices enough? How would they hide their own tracks or start looking for their own friends? Does a missing person even warrant police attention? Should they stay away until there is evidence of a crime? As Kelly was around their age, they'd be able to relate to her case. It could be quite an interesting debate.

'You stay on this road for the next six miles,' said Luis jolting her from her thoughts. Maxie nodded as Luis continued talking. 'So tell me about your work, the things you mentioned.'

'I undertake academic research which might help the police in their line of duty. Missing person cases are difficult for family liaison officers because they don't know whether the person has left the family unit voluntarily, has been harmed by that same family or has been taken by a third person. Until the person is found, they don't know whether or not they're supporting a criminal. The family may want to help the case but what if the information they give or the actions they take are false or distractions?'

'You think this journey is a distraction?' growled Luis.

'Of course I don't,' replied Maxie placating her passenger. 'Whether we find any leads or not, we're following up the only information we have. It's a practical thing for you to be doing. Can I ask how you're feeling right now?'

Luis let out a huge sigh and turned his head to the window as if thinking about the question.

'I don't know how to describe it,' Luis eventually replied. 'I feel … as if none of this is real. I want to scream but it feels as if no one would be out there listening anyway. You can't just vanish from the face of the earth. There must be someone who knows what's happening but they're not saying. And that's what's killing me – knowing that there could be a person out there who does know where Kelly is and I don't even know who they are.'

'What made you head out last night?' asked Maxie.

'I wanted to be where she'd been. I thought I might find a clue to tell me where she was, maybe someone who'd seen her. But no chance, then I lost it with that barman at The Printworks when he said what he did. It was like a blind rage came over me and I wanted to hit him. He would have deserved it but it didn't exactly help my case – I look like a violent man now don't I?'

'I think I would have wanted to hit him too,' replied Maxie. 'But you have to watch that temper of yours.'

Luis sighed. 'I know but I've never been in a situation that I couldn't just sort out. That's what I do, fix things and make them better but last night you could say I nearly made things a whole lot worse.'

He lay his head against the side window looking truly miserable. As he breathed the window steamed up and he drew a little "K" with his finger then rubbed it out.

'At least I found out about that stag party,' he said sitting up straight. 'So I guess I did find a clue.'

'Hence the road trip,' added Maxie.

'Look I do realise this is a bit of a crazy mission but what would you want me to do? If it were your daughter who'd gone missing? I have to try everything. I need to know what's happened.'

Maxie realised that Luis probably didn't hold out much hope of success this afternoon but needed to do this whether he believed in it or not. They were coming up to the six mile mark since his last instruction and the traffic in front of them was starting to build up as they neared the approach to an out-of-town shopping mall. No matter what was going on in anyone's lives, this was still the last weekend before Christmas and the roads were chaotic. It's always strange, Maxie thought to herself as she looked into the cars around her, being among hundreds of people doing ordinary things when the life of the person sitting next to you has been turned upside down. Somewhere in this throng there'll be a woman whose husband has just died, a man who has just found out he's a father, or a child who's just been diagnosed with leukaemia. Yet here they all were, crawling along at ten miles an hour so they could wrap up gifts, eat too much food and pretend that for one day of the year at least, everything was okay.

They ploughed on and Luis worked out the most efficient route around all of the churches. Their bodies were stiff from driving as they eventually pulled up outside the first of them. They both stretched as they got out of the car then Luis leaned down to tidy his hair in the reflection of the window. He smoothed down his jeans and buttoned up his coat. Maxie watched him and he caught her eye.

'I was brought up a good Catholic boy,' he explained. 'I can't go into a church looking scruffy.'

There was a service finishing so they waited for the priest to finish saying his goodbyes to the congregation (which took an *excruciatingly* long time in Maxie's view) and then approached him with their question and a photograph of Kelly and the group of men she had been dancing with. The priest knew nothing and had no weddings in his church until after Christmas but he was very jolly and wished them luck in their "valiant quest".

'This isn't *The* fucking *Da Vinci Code,*' muttered Luis as they left. Maxie gave him a dig in the ribs.

'He was just being nice. Try to be less surly. They're hardly going to help you if they think you might punch their lights out for giving the wrong answer.'

Luis told her he was sorry and that she was right. Then with every other priest or vicar they approached, Maxie noticed him smiling politely before asking the question. Although everyone he spoke to was sympathetic and pleasant, it didn't help. No one had seen any of the group and seemed to be sure that the man in the photo wasn't marrying in their church any time soon. Unfortunately, none of the ministers would give them the details of any weddings that were happening either so the trail stopped there.

'If Kelly isn't back tomorrow,' said Maxie as Luis kicked a gravestone in frustration, 'we can ask the police to get those details and follow up.'

The sky now settled into indigo having tried on a deep violet and before then a ghostly green. The air outside the car was calm and fresh in contrast to the despondency they would go back to inhaling inside after this fruitless day. Maxie took a deep breath and stretched her arms up and around her head. She yawned and rubbed her eyes.

'Sorry for wasting your time,' said Luis as they headed back to the car.

Maxie shook her head. 'It wasn't a waste. You had an idea and followed it up. I'm glad you did and as you said, it's better than sitting at home doing nothing.'

They sat silently as they began their drive home. There had been no call to either of them from the police or Kelly throughout the whole day and now the darkness of the night and the mood in the car threatened to make for an awkward trip home so Maxie made small talk.

'How did you meet Kelly? I never asked.'

She was pleased to see the corners of Luis's mouth rise very slightly as he thought about it. 'Through a friend,' he said. Maxie could see that his eyes had moved up to gaze at the roof of the car in indication that he was recalling the details of that night.

'It was Rowan's birthday,' he continued. 'I didn't know Kelly then but she was in charge of organising a wine tasting for her. We were all supposed to learn to tell our Cabernet from our Carménère – or at least that's what the invitation said. I still can't tell the difference. My friend

Harry said I had to come along with him. I really didn't want to but when I got there and saw Kelly, we both knew how the night would end.'

'Love at first sight?' asked Maxie. 'For both of you?'

'Ah, she shone like a fiery sun,' replied Luis. 'I knew that the other guys had noticed her but she looked at me too and with that one glance we were only waiting for the room to clear.'

Maxie could feel the hairs on her arms tingling as she listened to Luis speak. With his slight Spanish accent and faraway tone, it sounded like an epic love story. Maxie simply hoped it wasn't going to end up as a tragedy.

'After that,' said Luis, 'we moved in together. Kelly had been sharing with Rowan but that arrangement was never going to work. Kelly doesn't exactly keep her voice down while making love.'

Luis laughed at the memory but Maxie was feeling slightly awkward now. She cleared her throat loudly and Luis looked across at her. 'Too much information for your research?' he said seeming to enjoy her discomfort and continuing while keeping his eyes fixed on her. 'It wasn't fair on Rowan in the end. She would come home from work and find the latch bolted on the front door while we were making love in the living room. I may not have known her for long but I do know every inch of her.'

'Now that definitely is too much information,' said Maxie imagining she sounded very prissy. 'I think you can skip straight to the part where you're considering your options or whatever you young people call it.'

'There's not much to say.' Luis sighed. 'I rent my house and she moved in with me then a couple of weeks ago I found out the owner was selling it. She got some money from her grandfather when he died so the deposit would have been okay.'

'Do you know how much she inherited?'

'A few thousand,' said Luis. 'Not a huge amount but it was enough and between us we could afford the mortgage so I bought a bottle of champagne and that night I asked her to move in with me. She said she needed time.'

'What for?'

'She said she wanted time to think. She'd been very busy with work stuff but nothing out of the ordinary.'

'How did you feel when she reacted like that?'

‘A bit down I guess,’ replied Luis. ‘We’re good together. I want to spend the rest of my life with Kelly, have a family with her. I thought we wanted the same.’

Luis laid his head back against the window and Maxie could suddenly picture the chasm between this gentle giant and the firecracker he’d fallen in love with. Maxie couldn’t help but wonder what Rowan would say about Luis and Kelly’s relationship if she were questioned alone. Maxie doubted that Rowan would have turned him down.

Chapter Eight

When they got back to Luis's house, Rowan was already there knocking on his door. She rushed up to Luis when he got out of the car and wrapped her arms around him.

'Where have you been?' she asked. 'I've been calling you. Do you have any news?'

Luis shook his downcast head and disentangled himself from her grip to open the door. Rowan turned her attention to Maxie.

'I've googled you,' she said. 'You're not just a professor – you have a true crime podcast with that reporter Craig Johnston. You are genuinely here to help aren't you? Not just to get a story?'

She stood with her hands on her hips not letting Maxie pass until Luis took her by the shoulder.

'Leave it Rowan,' he said. 'Maxie's been helping me.'

Rowan narrowed her eyes and Maxie felt them burning into her back as Luis signalled for them all to come in. Once inside, the professor decided to go on the charm offensive to win Rowan over.

'I can understand your concern and if my friend were missing, I'd be equally suspicious,' she said. 'But I am officially supporting this case in my role as Head of the Applied Criminology Unit and with the blessing of Detective Andrew Dawson – who you met. However if you're uncomfortable with me being here I'll go. I don't want to cause either of you any more distress than you're already experiencing.'

'No, stay,' said Luis. He hugged Rowan and looked down at her with sad eyes. 'We need all the help we can get don't we, Ro?'

Rowan visibly relaxed against him and nodded. 'So where were you today?' she asked, snuggling further into Luis and not letting go.

Before Luis had time to answer, the doorbell rang. Maxie walked over to the window and pushed aside the curtains to see who was there. It was Andrew and the investigating officer. Maxie offered to go and let them in and Luis nodded at her. Maxie led them into the lounge and like practised performers on the stage all knowing their positions, they all sat down in the same places they'd been before.

'It's over forty hours since Rowan last saw Kelly,' said Andrew. 'My officers have made all the usual preliminary enquiries but without success. I'm taking it that none of you has heard anything from her either?'

Everyone in the room shook their heads.

'Mr Caballero, if anything really *bad* had happened to Kelly, we'd have found her in our initial searches.' Andrew's emphasis left them in no doubt as to what he meant. 'I have spoken to Kelly's mother and from tomorrow morning, if she doesn't turn up for work, Kelly will be officially entered onto the missing person's database where cross searches can be made both nationally and internationally.'

'You think that's why she took her passport?' asked Rowan.

'We have to acknowledge that Kelly has had time to go anywhere she wants,' replied Andrew. 'Now I need to understand if there are any reasons why she might choose to leave of her own accord?'

Luis looked as if he was about to explode but Rowan grabbed his hand to calm him.

'It's important that you tell us as much as possible, and that you're completely honest, no matter how uncomfortable it is,' said Andrew. 'Going missing voluntarily really is the most likely scenario now.'

Maxie knew that Andrew was keeping Luis and Rowan onside with this comment because from now on he'd be running a twin-track investigation and the other scenario he would be considering was a suspicious death. At this stage Luis looked every bit the devastated boyfriend but Maxie could tell there was something else going on here. There were skeletons in the closet somewhere.

'What exactly does voluntary disappearance mean?' Rowan was asking Andrew. 'That she's run away from us?'

'Yes, a person could elect to give up all contact with their current life without telling anyone,' replied Andrew. 'So we'd like to start by considering the top reasons people decide to leave of their own accord and seeing if they apply to Kelly. Did she have debts or money worries?'

'No.'

'Problems at work or with her family?'

'No.'

'Arguments with friends or anyone threatening to harm her?'

'No.'

'A history of mental illness or a recent breakdown?'

'For God's sake, no!' yelled Luis. 'She's just a normal happy-go-lucky person. I'd have told you from the beginning if she were unstable. We were … we are happy together.'

'They can see that,' said Rowan taking Luis's hand and holding tightly onto it as he tried to pull it away.

Maxie was watching Luis and Rowan as Andrew continued his questioning and the officer took notes; Luis's face seemed to drain of colour with each one asked. He swallowed and his Adam's apple bobbed in his throat,

'You said that you do find most people though?' he croaked. 'Please find Kelly.'

'We'll all do everything we possibly can,' said Maxie. 'Can I ask you about these past couple of weeks? It made Kelly uncomfortable when you suggested moving in together?'

Luis nodded reluctantly.

'She had some money you said? Is there a chance that Kelly has looked for and found somewhere else to live?' asked Maxie. 'Have there been estate agent calls or property details popping up on her phone?'

Luis looked genuinely surprised at the question. 'I don't check her phone,' he said. 'You think she's just moved house and not said?'

'Rowan,' said Maxie without answering the question. 'What about you, have you noticed any calls that Kelly didn't want to take in front of you? Or any other out of character behaviour?'

Rowan frowned and thought about it. 'She has been taking more work calls,' she said. 'But I just assumed that was because of Christmas.'

'Okay,' said Andrew. 'Well we can look into that tomorrow.'

'Is now the right time to start the social media campaign?' asked Rowan.

'Yes,' replied Andrew nodding. 'From tomorrow, as soon as we've established Kelly hasn't returned to work, then get the word out.'

'Don't worry, I'll take care of that,' Rowan said to Luis. 'I know you hate all that stuff.'

Luis clenched his fist and raised it as if ready to punch something then thinking the better of it spread out his fingers and sat on them.

'No – surely we can wait for that stuff … We'll look completely stupid when she just breezes back. We'll ask people ourselves just don't … don't advertise it yet.'

Andrew looked at Maxie raising his eyebrows and she could see he had his suspicions about Kelly's boyfriend.

'Luis, you may not have a choice,' said Maxie. 'Not being married, you're not Kelly's official next of kin and the police will have to take the approach that her mother wants. She may want a huge social media campaign and surely you're better off having someone you know, like Rowan, running it?'

'Kelly's mother will want lots of attention,' said Rowan quietly. 'I've only met her a couple of times but from everything Kelly said about her, she's the type to like a drama.'

Luis nodded slightly. 'And they didn't get on,' he added.

'We need to take some of her things back with me today,' said Andrew. 'Can we have her laptop or tablet, a better photograph and something for a DNA sample – a tooth – or a hairbrush? If Kelly turns up tomorrow then I'll return them but it will save time to collect them now.'

Luis walked out of the room into the kitchen next door and came back with an iPad which he handed to the investigating officer.

'Does it have a password?' asked Andrew.

'It's just "p@ssword" with an ampersand,' said both Luis and Rowan in unison.

Everyone shook their heads in despair but Andrew voiced their thoughts. 'She didn't take any form of security seriously then?'

Rowan took the officer upstairs to the bedroom to select the other items and now, having collected what they needed, the police left promising to get back with any news.

Luis slumped into the sofa.

'What do you want to do about work?' asked Rowan. 'Should we try and call her boss before tomorrow? Harry will have his number – we could give them the heads up about what's happened.

Luis raised his hands to his face and screamed out. 'Why is this happening? All these people knowing our business? They will look at me with sad eyes but they don't really care. They're all going to think she's left me aren't they? Oh they'll act all concerned to my face but behind my back they'll be saying they're not surprised, that I wasn't right for her. I was too boring for her. She's better off without me.'

'I'm sure they won't say that,' said Rowan. 'If anything they'd be thinking you're the one who's better off.'

'How on earth could you say that?' Luis scowled.

'*I'm* not saying it.'

The pair sat in silence for a few moments until, still staring straight ahead, Luis asked, 'But what if this is it? What if she's really gone?'

Maxie was sitting silently watching the dynamics between these two people. She could see they were actually very much alike – both calm to Kelly's storm. Their mutual friend had brought them together like a beacon promising warmth and light but now that glow had gone they both looked as if they might just crash on the rocks.

'What if she really has just upped and left us?' Luis continued, repeating himself as the potential reality of the situation seemed finally to dawn on him. 'But why would she? Was it me? You would know wouldn't you? Did she say anything about wanting to leave me?'

'No,' Rowan reassured him. 'She said nothing to me – nothing.'

Luis looked up at Maxie. 'You must have read about cases where people just walk out of their lives and are never seen again.'

Maxie nodded in reply. 'Alas, it happens,' she said. 'And unfortunately sometimes their families never find out why.'

'Now it's happening to us and it doesn't seem real,' continued Luis. 'I cannot believe she would disappear without saying anything just because she doesn't want to live with me.'

'I have to admit,' said Maxie, 'that from what you've both said, Kelly doesn't seem like the type of girl who would be afraid to tell you directly.'

'She would ask me to tell you,' said Rowan looking gloomily at Luis.

After a few more moments of silence, Luis asked the women to leave saying he needed time to think.

Outside in the freezing cold air, Maxie offered Rowan a lift home which was accepted.

'So you think Kelly's mum might kick up a fuss over this?' asked Maxie as they drove out of Luis's street.

'Just a bit,' replied Rowan. 'Wait till you meet her and you'll see what I mean. She wouldn't exactly win parent of the year – that's all I'll say.'

'I can tell all of this is going to be hard on you,' coaxed Maxie. 'Absolutely none of it is your fault.'

'Try telling that to Luis, or Kelly's mum or her workmates.' She picked at the skin on her fingernails. 'When this gets out they'll all ask how I could have left her alone. I can just see her bloody mother working it for the cameras telling them she'll never forgive me if anything's happened to her. She'll probably conveniently forget all the uni holidays that Kelly stayed with me rather than go home and face her mum's drinking.'

'You've been looking after Kelly for quite some time then?' said Maxie. 'Do you have a theory as to where she might be?'

Rowan paused as if unwilling to say what was on her mind.

'I thought at first she was trying to teach me a lesson,' she finally said. 'That maybe she was hiding out somewhere trying to punish me for leaving the club even though I hadn't and was still in the loo. I thought maybe she was waiting long enough to worry people and when she was sure that people had suffered enough, she'd reappear and we'd all be so grateful to have her back.'

'Would she do that kind of thing?' asked Maxie.

Rowan nodded adding, 'As you'll see, her mother likes the dramatics and you know what they say – the apple doesn't fall that far from the tree.'

Chapter Nine

Maxie hated driving at night so the journey home took longer than it would do normally and her body was stiff with tension by the time she pulled up at her apartment building. Despite the fact that the students were all on holiday right now, university employees were still working and although it was a Sunday evening, her weekend had been hijacked by Kelly's disappearance so she still had some papers that needed looking at tonight. As soon as she'd double-locked her front door and kicked off her shoes, Maxie stood under a hot shower unable to stop thinking about Luis and Rowan and this other person in their lives. Kelly. A person she'd never met but felt she knew. After drying herself, Maxie put on some cosy pyjamas, poured herself a glass of red wine and settled herself on the sofa with the laptop on her knee.

Having stopped rushing around, she was famished and realised she hadn't eaten today. She opened up the delivery app on her phone and flicked through the range of restaurants on offer. Perfect – her local Thai was offering a takeaway banquet for one. Just what the doctor ordered. The app told her the delivery would take forty minutes and that was just enough to get through her work.

She flicked through the emails vying for her attention; she guessed the majority of these had been hurriedly dispatched as their senders left for Christmas breaks. She ignored any that wished her a Merry Christmas knowing that even if she did respond to them, they wouldn't be read until the new year. There was one task she really did have to attend to before tomorrow morning's final faculty meeting of the year. The university was attempting to secure funding for a new online fraud facility to meet the growing demand from international students and every day the awards body who would give them the grant to create the department seemed to send more questions and more forms to complete. Maxie desperately hoped to find an email which simply said "funds agreed" but instead each one began "request for information". She wanted to be able to walk into tomorrow's meeting having dutifully responded to all the points, so she did just that and sent it flying to the procurement department handling the proposal. She guessed they would be keen to get all the answers to the company before the Christmas break and she was right. Even at eight o'clock on a Sunday evening, she received an email response by return thanking her.

Further down the list of emails was a keynote speaker request from the Society of Female Directors. Maxie had been to a few of their conferences and enjoyed the debate with other women so instantly agreed to speak. Taking a moment to consider what she'd talk about, Maxie settled back into her "thinking" position, leaning back in the chair, arms folded behind her head seeming to stare up at the ceiling but with her eyes closed. Whenever anyone new joined the Criminology department and saw her like this, they assumed she'd just nodded off. They'd tiptoe into her office then jump out of their skins when she yelled a "What can I do for you?" at them without moving a muscle. Colleagues and students soon got used to this unusual contemplative style and when she was in this position, everyone knew that the cogs were definitely whirring.

She was in this position when her phone rang, making her jump. She'd started nodding off after all. It was Andrew.

'Just checking you got home okay,' he said.

'Yes thanks,' replied Maxie. 'I gave Rowan a lift home and had a good chat with her.'

Maxie could hear hesitation in Andrew's voice.

'What's up?' she asked.

There was a moment's silence before Andrew replied, 'Oh it's my new DI. He's not that keen on "teachers" as he calls you, being involved.'

'He does know that his boss, Chief Inspector McAlister launched the ACU doesn't he?' asked Maxie.

'Yep,' replied Andrew. 'And he says nothing in front of her but he thinks academics have a habit of reading too much into a situation.'

'Meaning?'

'That sometimes a runaway is just a runaway – his words not mine.'

'It's a bit early to be jumping to conclusions like that,' said Maxie. 'Do you want to know what I found out?'

'Is it anything new?'

'I was told that she inherited a bit of money but apart from that nothing new,' replied Maxie. 'But I think your DI is wrong – none of this feels quite right to me.'

'I guess that's how it feels with missing people,' replied Andrew. 'This is the state of limbo you mentioned.'

'I guess so,' replied Maxie. The line went silent before Maxie eventually asked, 'Do you think you'd *like* Kelly if you met her in different circumstances?'

During the official investigation Andrew was confined to giving the party line but Maxie knew that in their informal conversations, he'd tell her what he really thought. Besides which, she'd be able to tell if he were lying.

'Maybe,' he answered. 'I can't imagine going out with her now but probably would have spotted her in my twenties, on a night out with my mates. We'd likely have tried it on a bit, said she was a bit of a go-er.'

Maxie tutted. 'What a delightful turn of phrase.'

'You asked,' said Andrew. 'What about you? Could you see yourself as Rowan?'

'Not as Rowan,' replied Maxie. 'But a few years back, I was Kelly. I was the party animal out all night. If we'd been twenty in the same decade, you and your mates would have been flirting with me. Now there's a thought to put you off your supper.'

Andrew roared with laughter at the other end of the phone.

'Just teasing,' continued Reddick. 'The thing is, no matter what trouble I got into, I always found my way home as soon as I could. I infuriated boyfriends and flatmates every weekend and even though I knew they'd give me a hard time when I got back, the lure of my own bed and a packet of paracetamol was too hard to resist. I'd never have stayed away this long.'

'I know what you mean. But it wouldn't be the first time someone has abandoned a relationship rather than face a tough conversation.'

'I know,' said Maxie before taking a deep breath and putting on a more cheerful voice. 'But let's wait until tomorrow and hope that she simply breezes into work wondering what all the fuss is about.'

'Here's hoping,' he replied. 'It's a big day tomorrow. Her mother is coming in and I imagine you'll want to meet her?'

Maxie said she definitely did.

'No doubt she'll want an explanation when there is none,' continued Andrew. 'I hate that bit. How do you explain to a parent that their child has gone missing for no obvious reason?'

'Just be honest,' replied Maxie. 'It's what most people want.'

With that Maxie's intercom rang. 'That's my takeaway,' she said to Andrew. 'Try not to think about this until tomorrow.'

'You too.'

Maxie hung up and buzzed the delivery driver up. She checked his ID with the safety chain still on before opening the door fully and accepting the bag of little aluminium containers. She took them over to her dining table and taking the plate out of the warming drawer, set herself a proper dinner place as she always did in an effort not to feel and look like a sad single person. Having topped up her wine, Maxie unfolded a napkin and placed it on her lap.

'*Bon appétit,*' she said to herself, raising the glass in a toast.

Maxie opened the takeaway cartons and took a spoonful of prawn curry from one, some jasmine rice from another and some spring rolls from a third. As she raised her knife and fork to eat, her phone rang again. Her heart danced in her chest to see it was a video call from her son Karl.

'That looks good,' he said as she moved her phone around to show him the feast.

'If you visited one Sunday, all this could be yours,' replied Maxie. 'Or even better, I could cook for you.'

'I thought you were trying to encourage me to come round not put me off for life.' Karl laughed.

'Just as well you're miles away with comments like that,' replied Maxie.

'Well actually, that's what I'm calling about,' said Karl. 'I'm making a trip up there tomorrow.'

Maxie squealed and picked up the phone to leap around the room with it. 'It's a miracle,' she shouted out. 'Son comes home to mother at Christmas!'

'Steady on, I don't want you having a coronary before I get there.'

Maxie sat back down and listened as Karl explained his itinerary. Her heart was pounding with nervous anticipation as he spoke. He'd moved to Manchester last year and after meeting his current girlfriend there, he'd spent last Christmas with her family. Maxie could only hope that it was her turn to host this year, but as he continued, she realised that wasn't to be.

'The plan is to spend Christmas Day at Olivia's and then we're heading down to London for New Year,' he said. 'So I thought I'd come over and have like, an early Christmas with you if that's okay?'

'Of course it is,' replied Maxie, holding her voice steady. 'I can't wait to see you. And I'm guessing that there are clothes that need washing and ironing too?'

'I always knew you were a mind reader,' said Karl.

He continued to tell his mum when he'd get there. Maxie listened, now knowing that she'd be alone at Christmas yet again but she wouldn't lay a guilt trip on Karl. Her marriage had broken down and that wasn't his fault. He was twenty years old for goodness' sake – he was entitled to a life. Her ex was now living close to London so although Karl hadn't mentioned him, she imagined that Karl would be seeing his dad on his trip down there. A tour of the country to accommodate estranged parents.

'I won't be cramping your style or anything will I?' asked Karl.

'No,' replied Maxie. 'But I might have to work during the days. The university is still open and police have asked me to help on a missing person's case. She's a young woman who was last seen at The Printworks in Helmsforth and hasn't come home.'

'Never been there,' said Karl. 'But I know it's a bit of a dive. When did she go missing?'

Maxie told her son the details that she had – it wasn't confidential and there would be a social media post about it in the morning. She could see that Karl was tapping away on his tablet as she spoke.

'What are you doing?' she asked.

'Just looking at The Printworks's Twitter feed from that night. What does she look like?'

Maxie described the green hair and short black dress.

'Is this her?' he asked holding up an image of Kelly sticking out her pierced tongue, a shot glass in either hand. Maxie told him it was.

She hadn't seen that particular image before but knew that when this case went public, Kelly would get a zero sympathy vote from the general public if this became the defining image of her.

'Looks a bit of a party animal,' said Karl, his words confirming her thoughts. 'Are you sure she's missing? Friday's not that long ago. It might just have been an almighty bender.'

'But if your boyfriend or girlfriend was expecting you home, wouldn't you at least try to call them?' asked Maxie knowing her son probably had more insight into Kelly's generation than she did.

'If you were thinking straight, maybe,' he replied. 'But she could be completely out of it. Maybe tried something she hasn't had before – that could last a weekend you know.'

'That's what I thought,' said Maxie. 'None of her friends have mentioned that she'd taken anything although the idea that her drink may have been spiked did come up. But let's say it's not drugs, what other reasons would someone like Kelly not come home? What would keep you from calling Olivia and telling her you're safe?'

‘Nothing would stop me from calling Olivia,’ replied Karl, his voice softening as he spoke of his girlfriend. ‘But if the relationship isn’t that great, sometimes you just don’t want to speak to them.’

Maxie sighed thinking back to the times before her divorce when she’d felt exactly like that.

‘Like,’ continued Karl, ‘you know people will be worried but wherever you are, maybe with friends, on your own or with someone you’ve just met, it’s just *easier*. They don’t expect you to explain or to take sides, you’re just free for a few hours and you don’t want that time to end.’

Maxie’s heart seized a little on hearing this. Her divorce had nearly destroyed their relationship. When Karl moved to Manchester it was partly to get away from their arguing. It had been his cry for help, a cry to say that anything, even ditching all of his childhood friends was better than staying near them. Maybe Kelly was crying for help too, wanting to show people that her life wasn’t as perfect as it appeared.

‘But at Christmas?’ asked Maxie.

‘Especially at Christmas,’ replied Karl. ‘All those people pretending to like each other for one day. You’d definitely want to get away from all of it.’

Over in Karl’s flat, Olivia walked into shot and waved at Maxie.

‘Hi there,’ said Maxie. ‘You look lovely, are you heading out?’

‘Just to a friend’s house,’ replied Olivia.

‘Well I won’t keep you Karl, you get on and I’ll see you tomorrow,’ said Maxie. ‘I’m really looking forward to having your perspective on this case. One last thing – this Kelly seems to have really good friends *not* people she’d want to escape from. They’re worried about her and just want her back safely.’

‘Well take that with a pinch of salt,’ replied Karl. ‘Nothing is ever as good as it looks from the outside.’

Chapter Ten

Monday, 19 December

Today is going to be a good day, thought Maxie as she drove onto the university campus. The phone call with Karl had put her in a good mood all evening and she'd enjoyed talking the case over with him, getting his perspective. She'd also been quite reassured to hear him say that Kelly might still be sleeping off her night out; the knot in the pit of her stomach had eased a little when Karl said that. Her son would know how young people behave better than her and perhaps today Kelly would turn up at work as if nothing had happened. On that thought Maxie crossed the fingers on both her hands as they gripped the steering wheel.

Andrew would call her as soon as he'd been in touch with Kelly's employer but first things first – she had to focus on her day job. The morning faculty meeting would be little more than a check on outstanding issues and then a chat with her colleagues over mince pies and a little mulled wine. Maxie would then have a final tutorial with Leo Turner, one of the PhD students she was supervising and that would be it – she'd be free to focus on Kelly. Even if Kelly had turned up by then, and Maxie really hoped that the young woman would, she could interview her friends and family to establish the range of emotions they were experiencing. Other studies had found a mixture of relief and confusion as to why the person had gone missing; Maxie suspected there would also be anger and recriminations greeting Kelly's return.

Maxie got to the car park and found an available space at least two feet closer to the entrance than she normally got. It was all good karma for the day to come. She nodded at security then ploughed through the swing doors, the warm poncho she was wearing billowed out as purposefully as she strode along. Maxie stopped by her desk and picked up the neatly stacked papers and agenda that had been dropped off for the meeting. It went well and was over quickly. With a plate of mince pies in her hand, she went to find Leo. He was in the study room watching a story that had just been reported.

'Have you seen the news?' he said. 'There's a little old lady missing in Lonsdale. She wandered out of her care home just before breakfast was served.'

He moved to one side so Maxie could see the rolling news report on his laptop. The sweetest looking old lady was smiling out from the screen.

Maxie's shoulders dropped as soon as she saw her. Although it felt incredibly cruel to even think it, she knew there was no way Andrew would get the chance to concentrate on Kelly today. Not with this lovely old lady missing too. This was it, the Christmas case that everyone would get behind, the one that would now take up a disproportionate amount of his time. There was always one and the victim was always photogenic.

'Apparently she always gives sweets and presents to the other residents,' said Leo. 'They call her Mrs Claus.'

Maxie exhaled loudly and ran her fingernails through her hair feeling their sharpness. Mrs Claus? Well that was definitely it, she thought. The media would be all over this. There'd be a hashtag – #FindMrsClaus – and the picture of this charming white-haired old lady would be everywhere. If Kelly was still missing, the media certainly wouldn't be fired up about finding the pierced, shot-drinking Kelly now. Not when they had an angel to rescue. Maxie left Leo and rang Andrew.

'I've just seen the news,' she said. 'Do you need any help?'

'Oh thank God you asked.' Andrew sighed. 'They're going all out on this one. I've had to leave a message with Kelly's office. They don't start work until ten but that's when the press conference by the family of this missing Mrs Claus is scheduled for and the DI is going to promise that we'll have her back home by the six o'clock news. It'll probably go national and they're saying that this force has to show what it can do for a change. Apparently we need a "Christmas miracle".'

Andrew gave her the address of the care home and filled her in on the details as she drove to meet him. Mrs Claus was a resident in a local private residential home where she had intermittent dementia symptoms and had been missed as the carers were getting people ready for breakfast. She was fully dressed and had taken a large umbrella from the hall but wasn't wearing a coat. It didn't take Maxie long to reach the home. She parked up alongside Andrew's car and joined him at the entrance.

Instinctively, Maxie held her breath as she walked through the doors of the residential home. Her own father had spent his final years in a home and she remembered visiting him, standing at the doorway, waiting for that stench of illness and decay to hit her. This place, however, was nothing like her father's home. Times had definitely moved on for the better. It was incredibly warm and in the beautiful, bright reception, an enormous real fir tree took pride of place. Smartly dressed nurses buzzed about and most importantly for Maxie, the home smelt of good quality air freshener rather than disinfectant. An elegant headmistress type character greeted them and showed them into her office. The headmistress reiterated the modicum of facts they already had. They took family details and promised to stay in touch before stepping back out into the very welcome cool December air.

'Blimey it was hot in there,' said Andrew tightening up a scarf that he'd previously loosened off.

Maxie thought about the numerous studies which had researched the merits of using tracking devices on dementia patients. Of course they'd all noted the ethical issues of such an action but if they were ever the norm, they would certainly know where to find Mrs Claus. Maxie stood in the grounds and looked around wondering where an old lady might go from here. Opposite the home, a bright LED display for the bus stop shone out, wishing everyone a Merry Christmas between the timetable messages. It was almost too merry to ignore. Maxie pointed towards it.

'Come on, that's where she'll have gone.'

They walked into the shelter and looked at the timetable. If Mrs Claus had left at the time the home said she had, there was only one bus within fifteen minutes and that would provide her direction of travel. This was the end of the line and the bus went one way – into the centre of town. The idea of their sweet old lady being caught up in the frenzy of shoppers sent a wave of dread through Maxie. The next bus arrived and Maxie grabbed Andrew. 'Let's get on.'

Maxie knew the research on dementia and guessed the old lady wasn't actually heading for somewhere she knew but for somewhere that just looked welcoming. Mrs Claus would be living in the moment and they had to try and recognise anything that might catch her eye: a bright shiny sign, a friendly driver or an empty bus with comfy seats for a bit of warmth and a sit down. They could all look very enticing for a bit of a day out.

'Can't we drive into town?' asked Andrew.

'No we have to see this journey through Mrs Claus's eyes,' replied Maxie.

The first stop wasn't inspiring at all, just past a salvage yard with graffiti covered walls – she wouldn't have got off here.

'The transport guys might have some CCTV footage,' said Andrew picking up his phone.

'It'll just show her sitting happily on a bus,' replied Maxie still staring out of the window. 'And I bet we can tell where she'd have got off before they come back to us.'

‘Maybe, but it’s worth trying. They’re still searching for anything about Kelly on the night she disappeared so I’ll ask them to look at this route too and find out who was driving the bus.’

‘I doubt you’ll find anything,’ said Maxie looking up at the route. ‘I know there isn’t a night bus on this route and I can’t see her waiting out in the cold for three hours until the first morning one at 5am.’

They reached the next stop and Maxie took a look at the ordinary looking street outside the window and decided once again that an old lady wouldn’t venture out of the nice warm bus here.

Two stops later Maxie saw what she’d been looking for: a scene to tempt anyone out of the cosy coach, especially someone with a penchant for giving out presents. Directly in front of the bus stop was a square filled with the wooden stalls of the ubiquitous Christmas market. In every town and city around the world ornate candles, chocolate covered waffles and reindeers fashioned out of pine trees were being sold as artisan crafts. Not for the first time in her life, Maxie cynically wondered whether all these artisans actually worked out of a factory in China. Nevertheless, the scene was perfect for Mrs Claus, lights twinkled, carols played over the loud speakers and the aroma of roast chestnuts enticed you in. She nudged Andrew and together they stepped off to start a methodical search of the stalls.

Andrew’s phone buzzed to tell him the press conference had taken place so he pulled the video up. He and Maxie watched as Mrs Claus’s blonde granddaughters looked into the cameras and pleaded with people to find their gran. It was a smart move to get two angelic looking little girls to ask the public to help. The briefing finished with a close-up on the photo of the elderly lady with the headline – #FindMrsClaus. It would be in the lunchtime edition of the local newspaper and in every online feed within two minutes. Maxie knew this kind of thing rallied communities. You might not know this lady but you wanted her to be found and when she was, you’d celebrate as if she were your own. Maxie heard the voice of Andrew calling her to a stall.

‘This guy says she tried to buy some chocolates from him.’ He guided her towards a cuddly-looking guy in a pinstripe apron.

‘She was looking at these chocolate penguins,’ he told them, ‘but she didn’t have any money. I didn’t know who she was or I would have given them to her free of charge obviously. She seemed very nice.’

I bet you would have, thought Maxie. That was one PR opportunity you messed up.

‘Did you see where she went next?’ asked Andrew.

The stallholder shook his head and then started looking behind them. Maxie turned to see a couple of reporters with cameras and mikes approaching them. Quickly she grabbed Andrew and walked away, head down. The stallholder, on the other hand, combed his hands through his hair, straightened his apron and walked towards them.

‘I guess he’s going to miss out the bit where he turned her away,’ mused Maxie.

Away from the gathering furore, Maxie studied the surrounding buildings around them. ‘Where did you go next Mrs Claus?’ she murmured before setting her eyes on the cinema opposite. A Christmas tree in the foyer twinkled and a retro banner declared that it was showing *It’s a Wonderful Life* every day this week. Maxie nodded at Andrew and they walked towards it.

‘Dementia patients remember events from their distant past,’ she explained. ‘This film would have been in her era.’

The electronic doors opened to an empty foyer and they saw that the first showing wouldn’t start for another couple of hours. The box office wasn’t manned yet but in the distance, they heard the hum of a vacuum cleaner and they walked towards it. The young man brandishing the hoover had his back to them and his headphones in. His cleaning strokes matched whatever he was listening to, a couple of fast pushes then a wide circle accompanied by a swing of the hips. He was enjoying his work anyway. Andrew stepped forward and tapped him on the shoulder. The cleaner swung round with such shock in his eyes that you’d think he’d been caught masturbating not dancing. He turned off the vacuum and took the headphones out.

‘We’re looking for this lady,’ explained Andrew showing him the photo on his phone.

The cleaner smiled broadly and nodded for them to follow him. Quietly he led them through the doors to the screen. It was quiet, peaceful and somehow other-worldly, like seeing behind the scenes of your favourite TV soap. The cleaner pointed to the back row where Mrs Claus sat, her head nodding in her slumber. Her breathing was laboured but peaceful and she looked completely at home. Beside her stood a large cinema-sized cup with a straw in it.

‘She told me her daughter would be along to meet her soon but I guess I lost track of the time. She was a bit thirsty so I got her some lemonade and sat her in here,' the cleaner explained. 'I will pay for it, I promise. Don't tell my boss.'

That's why the meek definitely should inherit the earth, thought Maxie. They act first and think of the consequences to themselves later.

'I don't think they'll mind,' she assured him.

Maxie tiptoed towards Mrs Claus and gently shook her awake.

The old lady opened her eyes and looked around in surprise. 'Did I nod off? Is Catherine here yet?' she asked.

Maxie smiled taking her hand. 'She's waiting for you at home. Shall we get back?'

'It's so beautiful here isn't it?' said Mrs Claus. 'And that James Stewart is so handsome isn't he? I called my son James you know.'

Maxie just smiled and helped her out of the seat while Andrew called in to say Mrs Claus had been found. By the time the three of them had reached the exit, the cameras were there making the most of the film title and the old lady's adventure. Contrary to his usual nature, Andrew walked up to the media microphones to tell them that they had found Mrs Claus and that she was extremely well. He added that he would like to specifically note the kindness of the chap cleaning the cinema. Andrew pointed the media towards him and left the cleaner to tell the tale. A car soon arrived containing Mrs Claus's children and grandchildren. They embraced and the relief on their faces was overwhelming. Despite initially thinking this whole charade a massive inconvenience this morning, Maxie smiled. She was back to feeling pretty hopeful about life.

Chapter Eleven

Hailstones started pelting the car roof as Maxie and Andrew both pulled up at the police station. Maxie got out, holding her bag over her head.

'I wish this weather would sort itself out,' she shouted under the relentless noise of the golf ball-sized shower as they ran towards the entrance. 'We've lethal frost, horrible slush and now this. Every type of snow except the nice kind.'

Andrew's phone rang and Maxie stood beside him, shivering as he answered. 'Thanks for that anyway,' he said sighing. 'Send someone over to get her laptop, find out her bank details and take statements from anyone who was out with her that night and make us an appointment to talk with her boss as soon as he gets back.'

Maxie felt that knot in her stomach resurface but said nothing, just raising her eyebrows in question.

'We've heard from Kelly's employer,' said Andrew. 'She hasn't come in for work but her boss is away on business and won't be back till Tuesday.'

'Damn,' replied Maxie. 'I was still holding onto the hope that she was just going to breeze in there this morning.'

'Me too.'

'Do you want me to go over while you speak to Kelly's mum?' asked Maxie.

'No, the investigating officer can take the initial statements and I think you'll want to hear what Kelly's mum has to say. Come on'—he opened the door for her—'we've got twenty minutes before Mrs Ingles arrives. This is going to be a long day.'

Maxie checked her watch as Andrew took her on a detour via the canteen. Kelly's mum was due in soon but Andrew was right – they had a few moments to warm up. She hadn't eaten this morning either and all that running around had left them both starving but undeniably heartened by the whole experience. As Andrew walked through the corridors, his fellow officers high-fived him and called "nice one" as if he'd just reprehended a master criminal. Still, if finding one old dear who'd wandered off on a little day trip could conjure up the festive spirit here for a few days then it was worth it.

'Not often you get to find a missing person before lunch,' he said to Maxie as they rushed down their bacon butties. 'And you never know, with the media all excited about their part in it, they might just pull out the stops for Kelly when the time comes.'

'Or they might move on to kittens up trees,' replied Maxie. 'They move in mysterious ways.'

Just as they were finishing, Andrew got the nod that Kelly's mother had arrived and was being settled into the interview room. Maxie dusted down the crumbs which, as ever, had settled on her bosom, and made her way into the ladies. Looking into the mirror she brushed her hair and reapplied her lipstick; there was no need for anything else as the morning rush around the markets had actually done her a favour and she looked fresh and alert. Maxie took a brightly coloured silk scarf from her bag and tied it around her neck in a French knot. She hoped it said "got it together" at least from the waist up. She had to look sharp and professional because whether people admitted it or not, everyone was judged by their clothing. She knew Kelly's mum would be wondering what on earth a university professor was doing there and deciding whether or not she trusted her to help find their daughter. It worked both ways; she'd be trying to decide whether or not she looked like the type of mother you avoided at Christmas, which she mused was kind of ironic given her own son was spending the day elsewhere.

When Maxie walked into the interview room, the smell of cheap perfume and musky clothes almost overwhelmed her. Kelly's mother was sitting with a thickset man; they both had the haggard drawn skin that came with a drink problem. They held hands and looked as if they hadn't slept for weeks. Maxie hated herself for it but her heart sank on seeing them. She knew by just looking at the couple sitting at the interview desk, that the media would not be as friendly to them as they had been to Mrs Claus's family. She waited until Andrew had taken his seat and he'd checked that they were happy for Maxie to be in attendance. They nodded their agreement and Maxie sat down and waited for the conversation to start. Andrew first of all checked the identity of the man.

'Are you Kelly's father?' he asked.

Kelly's mum shook her head. 'This is Dave – my partner. Kelly never knew her dad. He scarpered before she was born.'

Her voice was coarse and croaky. On hearing it Maxie took a quick look at the fingers seeing the well-established nicotine stains which confirmed the reason.

'Are you a step-father to Kelly?' continued Andrew.

Dave shook his head.

'He's just here for moral support,' said Kelly's mum. 'Is that alright?'

'That's fine,' said Andrew. 'As you'll be aware, a couple who your daughter often visits raised an alert because she didn't make that visit. We contacted Kelly's friends who came home from a party that finished in the early hours of Friday morning. As of this morning, she still hasn't made contact and hasn't been into work so we now have to formally register Kelly as a missing person.'

Mrs Ingles started sobbing, wiping her nose on her sleeve and Dave put his big arm around her, pulling her into his chest.

'She should have been told earlier than this,' he bellowed, pointing a fat finger at Andrew. 'It's f'ing Monday. What the hell have you been doing about it all weekend?'

'Both her friends assumed she was staying safely with the other until late Saturday,' continued Andrew. 'Since getting the report we've progressed several lines of enquiry but in cases like this, nine times out of ten, the missing person comes home of their own accord by the end of the weekend.'

'So do you think something's happened to her?' asked Mrs Ingles looking at him through mascara-drenched eyes.

'Not necessarily.' Andrew had softened his voice. 'It's not unusual, particularly at this time of year, for people to simply feel it's all too much for them. They don't always tell anyone and they just go away by themselves.'

Maxie thought he'd put this very gently, as if Kelly had booked herself into a spa.

Andrew continued, 'Would it surprise you if Kelly had simply taken off?'

'Kelly's a law unto herself,' said Dave. 'She doesn't think the rules of life apply to her. She's got no time for her mum that's for sure. She wouldn't even help her out with a bit of money when she needed it.'

'I just needed it for groceries, not drink,' continued Mrs Ingles. 'Doesn't Connor know where she is?'

'Connor?' asked Andrew and beside him Maxie made a discreet note.

'Her boyfriend,' replied Mrs Ingles.

'No one has mentioned a Connor,' said Maxie. 'Her boyfriend is called Luis – he's Spanish.'

'That's news to us,' said Dave shaking his head. 'It was Connor the last time you saw her wasn't it?'

Mrs Ingles nodded her head slowly.

‘When was that?’ asked Andrew.

‘It was Easter,’ replied Mrs Ingles. ‘Her grandad died and she came up for the funeral. Kelly really loved him – she talked to him more than she talked to her own mother.’

‘Do you have a surname for Connor or know where he lives?’ asked Maxie, mentally calculating that Kelly had to have ditched Connor just before hooking up with Luis – or perhaps just afterwards. The couple in front of her didn’t have any more information about Kelly’s ex but Maxie guessed that Rowan would have to know where he was.

‘We only saw him the once,’ continued Mrs Ingles. ‘Big bloke with one hell of a temper. He threatened you didn’t he Dave? Had you by the throat.’

‘Really, what happened?’ asked Maxie noting that Kelly seemed to have a type when it came to men. She liked them large and strong.

‘Nothing,’ replied Dave puffing out his chest. ‘He wouldn’t have stood a chance.’

‘He told us to stay away from her,’ said Mrs Ingles. ‘He said she didn’t need the likes of us in her life.’

‘Do you think Kelly might have gone back to Connor?’ asked Andrew.

The couple didn’t know. Maxie listened as Andrew continued to ask the stock questions that had to be asked but she knew they wouldn’t provide them with any more information. Rowan had said that Kelly didn’t get on with her mum and now she could see that it went further than that – they simply weren’t in each other’s lives. It sounded as if the grandfather was the stable influence and it helped explain why Kelly had latched onto George and Patricia.

‘If she’s been gone for two days, why hasn’t there been a public appeal?’ Mrs Ingles was asking.

‘And a reward,’ added Dave. ‘For finding her or giving you lot some information like we have. You didn’t know about Connor did you? That has to be worth something.’

‘You’re right, we didn’t know about Connor so thank you for that,’ replied Andrew very calmly. ‘And there hasn’t been an appeal to date because it’s not always the best approach to take.’

‘What about the reward?’ persisted Dave.

Andrew shook his head. ‘I’m sorry, there’s no reward either. These are routine questions that we would expect to be answered freely.’

Mrs Ingles shrugged up at Dave and Maxie wondered whether he'd only come along on the possibility of earning something from it. There was no telling.

'You found that old lady within a couple of hours of the appeal,' said Mrs Ingles suddenly sitting up and slapping a hand on the desk. 'I want to do an appeal for Kelly on telly and get her picture out there. I want to ask for help finding her and put posters up.'

'And then someone might put up a reward,' added Dave. 'That happens all the time, the community comes together. Or maybe that company she works for – they're loaded. They must want her back.'

'You can't stop us can you – it's not against the law? She's my daughter,' said Mrs Ingles.

Andrew started tidying his papers into a folder then rested his elbows on the table and linking his fingers looked directly at the couple.

'You're right, I cannot stop you but I genuinely don't advise it yet,' he said. 'My team are currently questioning Kelly's work colleagues and we may have more insight into what happened after that. My wholehearted advice is that you wait to hear from me.'

Kelly's mum slouched back with her arms folded in a defiant stance.

'For twenty-somethings like Kelly,' said Maxie hoping to soften the adversarial mood that seemed to have developed, 'an appeal isn't always effective. My research shows that while the public really get behind stories about elderly ladies or young children, they're less motivated when it comes to healthy adults – rightly or wrongly. Often a social media campaign works better but even that can backfire. I do think you should hold off for now.'

'I'm going to assign you a family liaison officer,' continued Andrew as he stood to leave. 'We have to leave to continue the investigation but I promise you, we will do everything we can to find Kelly.'

He held out a hand to shake but it was refused so thanking them for their time, Andrew nodded to Maxie and together they left the interview room as the family liaison officer walked in.

'They were a piece of work,' Andrew declared once safely down the corridor.

'Well at least they gave us Connor,' said Maxie. 'Not sure why Rowan didn't mention him?'

'He might be very firmly in the past.' Andrew strode towards the door. 'But seeing as we can't talk to Kelly's boss yet, let's go and talk to

Rowan. I told you it was going to be a long day – I bet you're glad you had that bacon butty now.'

'You're right there,' said Maxie having to speed walk to keep up with him. 'Do you think they'll attempt this appeal?'

'If they believe there's money in it,' replied Andrew.

'That's what I thought,' said Maxie. 'And I can really understand the need to do something but I just can't see it working out well for them.'

Maxie knew that unconscious bias wasn't just about race or gender – class was also a hugely discriminating issue. Mrs Ingles and her partner were the personification of that horrendous expression – trailer trash. They were poor and they looked poor. However theirs was not the dignified poverty of a mother trying to keep her family together by working three jobs, theirs was the poverty of benefits squandered on alcohol while a daughter had to fend for herself. Neither the media nor the public would be kind to them. And the tragedy of it was that any appeal by the mother Kelly obviously avoided would rebound on the missing girl. Maxie knew that there could be some adverse publicity if some of Kelly's Facebook photographs got out there. On the whole, the public didn't like to see young women enjoying themselves like that and they'd probably say *"like mother like daughter"*. Maxie hoped the family liaison would be able to persuade them to wait, better than she or Andrew had.

Maxie agreed to take a lift with Andrew and come back for her car. As she nestled into the passenger seat, she thought about Kelly's parents and about how Kelly had simply cut them out of her life. True, they didn't seem to care too much about her but it was Kelly's decisive action that interested her. Kelly had a history of walking away from people – is that what she'd done here?

Chapter Twelve

Andrew switched on both their heated seats and Maxie sighed with pleasure as the warmth started to permeate her body. She took her phone out of her bag and switched the sound back on.

'Nine calls from Luis and one from Patricia Hendry,' she said to Andrew. 'I'll call them back.'

She did so putting her phone on speaker so Andrew could hear the conversation. The first call was to the elderly couple who were incredibly upset to hear that there was still no news. The little teary sniffs almost made Maxie cry too. She had nothing more to tell them but promised to come and see them at the end of the day to update them. Maxie's heart was full to bursting as they told her they'd have some tea and cake waiting.

'Dear Lord,' she said to Andrew after the call. 'I almost want to find Kelly more for their sake than hers. I really hope she hasn't just taken off. I don't think they could cope with that.'

Andrew cleared his throat and Maxie watched him keeping his gaze directly ahead and exhaling his emotions, looking as affected by that call as she was. She made the next call.

Luis picked up instantly, telling her what they already knew – that Kelly hadn't turned up at work. She assured him that she was with the detective sergeant right now, that statements were being taken at Kelly's office, that her details were now on the missing persons register and that they'd interviewed Kelly's parents.

'Did they know anything?' asked Luis.

'I'm afraid not,' replied Maxie. 'I didn't realise that you'd never met them.'

'Kelly told me she didn't get on with them,' replied Luis. 'I can't imagine that – my family are everything to me.'

Maxie didn't want to ask him about Connor so simply said they were on their way to follow up some new information and would tell him about it if it proved helpful. She could hear Luis breathing and guessed he was reluctant to hang up on the call. Maxie could well imagine that he would join them in this car, sitting on the back seat if he could. She told him that she had to go but would keep in touch then hung up before Luis could ask any more questions.

'What did you think?' asked Maxie. 'Is it genuine concern or guilt?'

‘Well you’re the expert in criminal psychology but we do know he has a temper,’ replied Andrew. ‘We both saw him throwing that phone and almost smashing it. Then there’s his visit to The Printworks. Who knows what he would have done to the barman if the bouncers hadn’t intervened.’

‘Anyone would have thumped that barman after what he said about Kelly.’

‘Just don’t get too close, Maxie. Not only is he quick to anger but he could easily have driven into town after leaving the pub. And don’t forget, the CCTV showed her leaving with someone she recognised and for all we know – that might have been him. What’s your opinion?’

Maxie sat quietly, thinking about the question. For her the jury was still out. Luis seemed very genuine but Kelly’s life seemed like a tangle of wires to her right now and she wasn’t sure which the live one was. When she had taken Andrew and his team through the reasons a person might return to the scene of the crime, they’d listened attentively and Andrew sent an officer back to the bar to check whether Luis had been seen either inside or outside The Printworks on the night Kelly disappeared. Andrew also had them check any available CCTV – which he knew was pretty scarce in Helmsforth – as he needed to establish whether Luis had actually gone there after the pub and whether he was the person she was seen waving to. Unfortunately, there were no useful cameras and the bouncers couldn’t say one way or the other. Maxie knew that their recall could be called into question any way if it came to trial. Their testimony would now be blurred by the fact that everyone knew who he was thanks to his attempted attack on the staff. Maxie now wondered whether that was actually what Luis was really doing there – to be seen and therefore cast doubt over *when* he’d been recognised.

‘Earth calling Mars,’ said Andrew breaking her line of thought.

‘Sorry,’ she said shaking her head. ‘In answer to your question, I don’t know. He seems to love Kelly but they’re not called crimes of passion because someone feels lukewarm about the other person.’

The car pulled into the crowded supermarket car park. All round them couples pushed enormous piles of groceries in wobbly trolleys towards family cars. Despite the jolly novelty jumpers many were wearing, the expression on most of the faces was anything but happy.

‘Ho, ho, ho,’ murmured Andrew as they watched a man push a trolley too fast, causing a bag to topple and a bottle of wine to smash to the ground. ‘He’ll be in trouble for that.’

Sure enough, the man's partner marched up to him with her hands on her hips. She looked down at the glass and started shouting at him. He bent down and started picking up the glass while she took the handles of the trolley and left him there. A supermarket assistant wearing a tinsel-trimmed beanie hat walked up to the man and put his hand softly on his shoulder. He took the collected glass from him and then picked up the rest. The assistant put a hazard cone beside the remainder and walked away, waving at the man and wishing him a Merry Christmas.

Andrew and Maxie got out of the car and walked up to the customer service desk. Andrew had to show his police badge to the line of customers who had begun grumbling at the couple who seemed to be jumping the queue. He asked to speak to Rowan and after having a conversation on the walkie-talkie, the assistant directed him to the fruit and veg aisle.

When they got there, Rowan was helping unload a wire trolley of potatoes into the fixture.

'They've just come in,' she said gasping for breath. 'It was all I needed, the week before Christmas and I've got no spuds to roast.'

She heaved a final sack onto the shelf and then left the assistants to it. She told Andrew and Maxie to follow her, which they did, dodging and diving through the motorway of customers and online-shopping pickers.

'I'd have thought people wouldn't be buying Christmas food until later in the week,' said Maxie now wondering if there'd be any left by the time she went shopping.

'Some will,' said Rowan. 'Others don't like to leave anything to chance – and it'll all last if it's stored well.'

They reached the warehouse at the back of the shop and found a quiet corner.

'So what news is there?' asked Rowan. 'Luis said she hasn't turned up for work.'

'That's right – she hasn't,' said Maxie.

'I have people in her office taking statements from work colleagues,' added Andrew. 'But after this length of time with no word from Kelly and no record of her in any hospital, we presume one of two scenarios – that she has left of her own volition or that she has been harmed in some way and cannot contact us.'

Rowan's expression was giving nothing away.

'There's no one else here so let's have the cards on the table,' said Maxie. 'We've just heard about Connor and were surprised that no one has mentioned him before now. You must have known him.'

Rowan nodded but pursed her lips tightly.

'Did she leave Connor to get together with Luis?' asked Andrew. 'Could she have gone back to him? Why has no one mentioned the guy?'

Rowan blew out an exasperated sigh but still said nothing. She stared downwards and started biting her fingernails.

'Come on Rowan,' urged Maxie. 'You're her best friend. You've known her longest and I simply cannot believe you have no idea where she is.'

Rowan raised her eyes and looked angrily at Maxie. 'I have absolutely no idea,' she snarled quietly. 'Trust me I wouldn't be covering for her if I did. I don't have time for those sorts of games. She left Connor about a week before meeting Luis – the two events weren't connected but it's typical of her to find a new bloke instantly.'

'It certainly doesn't work like that for me,' said Maxie trying to build empathy with the young woman.

'Me neither,' replied Rowan.

'Okay,' said Maxie, 'so you're on a night out together and she wants to party on while you want to go home. Now where would she go? Would she go off with another group? How likely was this stag party idea of Luis's?'

'Pretty unlikely,' replied Rowan, shrugging her shoulders. 'I suppose she might have gone if they'd said they were going to another club but Kelly likes her creature comforts. She doesn't care who she inconveniences so Luis or I would have got a call to fetch her as soon as she got bored. If she'd gone on somewhere for the night, she would have been back by now.'

'That's what I think too,' said Maxie. 'You couldn't keep me from my pyjamas for all the Prosecco in the world.'

Rowan gave a half-hearted laugh and added, 'Me neither.'

'But that's what makes it worrying,' continued Maxie. 'She hasn't inconvenienced you or Luis – so who else might she call? Does this Connor keep in touch with her?'

'Not any more,' said Rowan. 'He said all the usual things about them staying friends but then when Kelly started posting pictures of her and Luis on Facebook, it got a bit awkward.'

'How?'

'He started messaging me asking how long Kelly had known Luis and whether she was seeing him before they split up.' She sighed. 'He tried to blame me for not telling him about Luis but honestly, I had nothing to do with it.'

Maxie shook her head and sighed in sympathy. 'You get a lot of flak for Kelly's actions don't you?'

'Not really,' replied Rowan. 'I know it looks that way but she's a lot of fun usually and she might be a pain in the backside but I do love her to bits. I honestly think she'll turn up soon. I'm simply fed up with all this happening right now – and when I'm pretty much exhausted with work.'

'Just one last thing,' Andrew said. 'We saw during our first visit that Luis has a bit of a temper on him. Do you think he'd ever hit her, if perhaps he thought she'd been flirting with another guy?'

Rowan looked horrified. 'No, never. Absolutely not, he's one of the good guys. He wasn't just going to ask her to move in you know, he was going to propose.'

Wow, thought Maxie. That's new news.

'And what about Connor,' continued Andrew. 'We've heard he had a temper too.'

'Kelly has a type,' said Rowan. 'To quote her – she likes fire in their bellies and lead in their pencils.'

Maxie let out an involuntary snort of laughter. Andrew finished asking his questions and as a fresh delivery of mince pies arrived in the loading dock, they left Rowan to her work.

On their way out of the store, Maxie bought a large bar of chocolate to sustain them on the drive home. She opened the packet in the car and snapped off a couple of squares, putting them into Andrew's open palm. Then she broke off some for herself but managed to drop it into her lap. She fished around, finding the square but not before it had softened in the heat of the car and melted slightly on her trousers. She took out a tissue and wiped it off carefully.

'I should have left it there. It might help my dating profile if I put "Has chocolate-coated legs" in my profile,' she murmured aloud.

'What was that?'

'Sorry, nothing important. I've started online dating. What did you think of what Rowan said?'

Before Andrew had the chance to respond, his phone rang and he pressed the Bluetooth button to answer it.

‘Boss,’ said the voice. ‘Bad news – I haven’t been able to dissuade Mrs Ingles.’

‘You mean she’s going ahead with an appeal?’

‘Yes sir,’ replied the voice. ‘And her partner Dave has started a crowdfunding campaign to cover the costs of the search. They’re announcing that at the same time.’

Andrew blew out his cheeks then told the voice they were on the way back.

‘That won’t help will it?’ he said.

Maxie grimaced and shook her head.

‘I guess there’s nothing we can do about it right now,’ continued Andrew. ‘Let’s just focus – what did you think about the conversation with Rowan?’

‘We’re getting two views of Kelly aren’t we? On the one hand we have a young woman who has tea with an older couple every Saturday and on the other we have someone who flits through life without a care in the world,’ replied Maxie thinking through the opinions she’d heard. ‘But in both cases, when you’re in her circle, things are wonderful, magical but then when she shines her light somewhere else, you don’t know what’s hit you. I don’t think she knows the impact she has on people or how she makes them feel. She ditches her ex suddenly, is seen in a club with someone other than her current boyfriend and pisses off her best friend but I don’t think any of that would make her stay away from home. She knows she could charm her way back into any of their lives and they all say she’s too fond of her creature comforts not to give it a go. I don’t think she’s staying away from home because she’s too embarrassed to come back. This girl has bigger balls than Shrek.’

‘So what do you think has happened?’ asked Andrew.

‘Although I don’t think she’d stay away because she was flirting with someone, the marriage proposal worries me,’ replied Maxie. ‘What if Kelly guessed it was coming and wasn’t happy about it. Luis could only see it making her happy but what if it was likely to have the opposite effect and Kelly had to get away before it happened, after all we know she could afford to. She couldn’t face turning Luis down so decided not to face him again.’

‘So you think that could be the push factor? That she’s gone for good?’

‘Perhaps,’ replied Maxie. ‘If so then she has to have made some plans and maybe that’s why there are so few clothes in the wardrobe and her suitcase is gone. We'll know soon from your searches whether she's withdrawn any money or used any of that inheritance-recently so maybe that person she was waving to is part of the getaway plan. We need to talk to this guy Connor.'

Andrew nodded then Maxie continued, 'But we've never met her,' she said. 'We only have other people's opinions of Kelly. I think we can say that she stirs up emotions and not always in a good way. Let's say she did know about the proposal, in fact, let's say that Luis has already asked her. Maybe it was in jest while they were in bed, whatever the circumstances, he's asked her. To him it's the most important moment in his life. He's asking the woman he loves to stay with him forever. What do you think Kelly would do?'

'Probably laugh it off,' replied Andrew.

'That's what I think. It might trigger fears of being trapped, the end of her freedom. If she laughed at Luis, he'd have been extremely hurt. He might have lashed out.'

'This is all major supposition. You honestly think he's hurt her?' asked Andrew.

'I don't think he'd mean to but I really hope not,' replied Maxie.

Chapter Thirteen

'I don't think you need to worry,' Andrew said as they headed up the corridor of the police station. 'You know the stats better than me but I'm sure they say that it's far more likely that she's taken off voluntarily.'

'And you know that most academics have a problem with those stats,' countered Maxie. 'First of all we don't record the missing person for a few days waiting for them to come home, then a body turns up in the interim and it's recorded as a suspicious death not a missing person.'

Before Andrew had the chance to respond, a member of his team interrupted them to say that Luis was in the interview room. As they walked in, Luis leapt up, clutching a passport in his hands.

'I found it,' he called to them, holding it out as they approached.

Andrew and Maxie sat down and indicated for Luis to do the same as he handed over his precious cargo. Andrew flicked through it and sighed. 'This one is out of date,' he said, passing the document back to Luis. 'Is there a more recent one? Have you been on holiday recently?'

'Yes.' He folded his arms on the desk and dropped his head onto them. After a few moments he looked up and continued. 'We went to Spain in September. I didn't check the passport, I just presumed ...'

'So she must have the current one with her?' asked Maxie. 'Luis are you sure you didn't hear or see anything that would make you think Kelly was planning to go somewhere? You can tell us if she was leaving.'

'No – things were good. Where would she go?'

'Well you said she had some money from her grandfather so could easily have rented somewhere to live. We've also heard she has a recent ex-boyfriend,' said Andrew. 'Have you had any suspicions that he's back on the scene?'

Luis was furious – the flare of his nostrils gave that away – but he fought to contain it, crushing the passport in half. He said nothing and Maxie wondered whether he was angry because he suspected Andrew had spoken the truth or whether it was utter frustration and despair keeping him silent. She watched as he fought to get his breathing under control. He took a sip from the bottle of water in his pocket and eventually calmed himself.

'I want to go through Friday night again,' Andrew said. 'You were in the pub with your friend. He left you at around eleven-thirty and you stayed on for another half hour or so before going directly home – is that still your recollection?'

Luis thumped the desk. 'We've been through this a hundred times. It isn't a *recollection,* it's what happened. You know that. Harry told you the same.'

Maxie looked across the table at him, making and holding direct eye contact. 'Luis, you know the police are only asking all of this because they want to find Kelly. You know it's the procedure,' she said. 'You have to stay calm and be brutally honest with us.'

He nodded reluctantly and looked over at Andrew.

'You've got a bit of a temper,' continued the DS, 'which you've demonstrated to us a few times. I imagine with your temper and Kelly's carefree attitude, you often had rows while you were together?'

'We're still together,' replied Luis angrily. 'And every couple has rows.'

Maxie realised Andrew was going in strong to trigger a reaction from Luis and wondered whether he'd be able to hold it together. She leaned back in her chair to observe.

'If you were in our shoes, you'd want to interview you,' said Andrew. 'In fact I think you'd try and beat the answer out of us, never mind sit here politely in a warm station. You said that you and Kelly love each other but let's face it, she was dancing with another bloke that night. How did that make you feel when you found out? Humiliated? Did you do something to her?'

Luis inhaled deeply through his nose a few times. 'I would never hurt Kelly,' he said as calmly as he could. 'I love her. I adore her. I told you.'

'We've been told that you plan on asking Kelly to marry you,' said Maxie.

'*Sí,*' replied Luis. 'I thought if she knew that I didn't just want to live with her, I wanted to spend my whole life with her …'

How can I find out whether Kelly knew anything about that beforehand? thought Maxie, pretty certain that Kelly's reaction could go either way from what they knew of her.

'Then help us find out where she is,' continued Andrew. 'So on Friday, you came straight home from the pub? You didn't go into town? You didn't get a call from Kelly asking you to pick her up?'

'How could I? I'd had beer and whiskey,' Luis stated. 'I was in no state to drive.'

'And you went straight to bed?' asked Andrew.

'Most probably.'

'But no one can corroborate that?' Andrew continued.

'Of course they can't.'

They were going to get nowhere if Andrew continued his closed line of questioning so Maxie butted in and took over. 'Tell us about these arguments you have.'

Luis raised his eyebrows, paused for a moment and then began. 'They weren't really arguments – Kelly can be a nightmare to live with. She leaves stuff all over the place. Her washing is always all over the bathroom, her make-up all over the table. It's a mess. I'm always telling her off for it. I call her a slovenly witch and she calls me a neat freak. We yell at each other all the time but it's just our joke. Honestly, it's not serious and the make-up sex is fantastic.'

Maxie recalled the tidiness of that room – it wasn't as Luis described. The contrast in description bothered her more than the name calling. She knew that in relationships you give each other a name in private that would sound ridiculous or ominous in an incident room. She wondered whether it had ever gone beyond name calling and watching Andrew scribble notes she knew he would check this further. Luis looked at them both and seemed to have read their thoughts.

'Haven't I been the one trying to find her right from the start?' Luis said. 'Would I have done that if I'd harmed her in any way? Would I be here right now if I didn't want her back?'

Andrew shrugged and Maxie knew there had been so many cases where suspects tried to cover their tracks with manoeuvres like that. Maxie's phone beeped and she checked the message.

'I'm really sorry but I have to get back to the university.'

Maxie got up and shook hands with Luis, reassuring him that everyone was doing all they could to find Kelly. She nodded towards the door and Andrew followed her out.

'I'm so sorry but I have to go,' she said exasperated. 'The university has been trying to secure these sponsors for months and they're saying that if we can meet today we can confirm before New Year. It's a project that the chief inspector is very keen on too.'

'No worries,' Andrew said. 'I'll call you later and let you know how the rest of this conversation goes.'

'Keep him talking about his relationship with Kelly,' said Maxie. 'And see what you can find out about his previous relationships. If Luis is the trigger for her disappearance or worse, you might find out by asking about the other women in his life. And if you don't mind me teaching you how to suck eggs, remember to keep the questions open. He's very good at just replying with very short answers.'

'I noticed,' replied Andrew. 'Remember that appeal is on this afternoon – I'll get someone to message you when it starts.'

Back in her own domain, Maxie stood at the head of the conference room table presenting the credentials of the university to the senior partners of a legal firm looking to sponsor research into strategies for mitigating courtroom prejudice. This wasn't a new subject for the college or any other criminology department but it kept evolving thanks to the speed of change in societal behaviour and social norms. Sometimes, it was difficult to keep up with what society deemed acceptable.

'It wasn't so long ago that a jury would think a man more likely to be guilty if he held a blue collar job rather than if he were, for example, a respectable banker. Fortunately recent market crashes have changed that perspective for good.'

Her audience laughed.

'Nowadays, social norms are changing so quickly and although the mainstream media would like to present us as a liberal tolerant society, that isn't always or even usually the case. A juror may have been categorically informed that the fact a suspect or victim is transgender has no bearing on the case but that won't stop some people wondering about it. Not everyone lives in big cities where all walks of life integrate happily. You may have never seen anyone transitioning and it might look very odd to you. It might look suspicious and with that suspicion comes unconscious bias. This research aims to develop a methodology which will highlight any of these subconscious views and most importantly, the methodology can itself evolve as we will undoubtedly need it to.'

There was a knock on the door and Maxie's colleague popped her head round. 'The appeal is about to start.'

Maxie nodded and turned to the table. 'This is a case I've been helping the police with over the weekend. Would you mind if we broke to watch it? I think it's actually quite relevant to what we're talking about.'

The lawyers agreed so Maxie sat down and flicked on the large television screen which stood on a stand in the corner.

From the very start, it was obvious that this wasn't an official appeal. Maxie's heart sank when she saw the setting the local media channel had chosen for the broadcast – a Christmas grotto with Father Christmas perched in the background. Maxie noticed that Mrs Ingles had put on eyeliner and lipstick for the cameras but on her drawn and pallid face, she looked as if she were wearing a mask. Dave hadn't made any effort as he stood with his arm around his partner. Mrs Ingles held up several angelic looking pictures of Kelly: graduating in her mortar board alongside Rowan; sitting with her grandfather as he blew out the candles on a cake, and finally sitting on Santa's knee when she was obviously around four or five years old.

'She loves to dance,' said Mrs Ingles holding another picture of Kelly in a tattered tutu. 'She wanted to be a ballerina when she was young.'

'Help find our Kelly,' said Dave. 'The police are doing nothing so we've set up a social media page and a crowdfund website where the money will go to printing flyers and stuff.'

The TV presenter read out the website addresses as Dave urged everyone to give generously. The presenter asked Mrs Ingles if she had any final words.

'You found Mrs Claus,' she said, 'now please help us find our precious daughter.'

It concluded with the presenter turning towards a Father Christmas and handing him a letter.

'This is the only gift the Ingles want this year, Kelly safe and sound.'

It was so bad, it simply had to backfire. Maxie wanted to wrap Kelly's mum up in cotton wool until all this was over.

'That's the kind of girl the public will root for surely?' said one of the lawyers as the TV was switched off.

'We'll see,' replied Maxie. 'There is another side to the story.'

Then she told her rapt audience about the Kelly she knew.

'Who's there?' Maxie called out on hearing a noise as she walked through her front door after the meeting.

Intuitively she grabbed a brolly from the hallway stand and pressed her back flush to the wall. When the veins in her neck had stopped pumping adrenalin through her body, she realised she knew the intruder. It was Karl.

Taking a calming breath and putting down her deadly weapon, she walked towards the voice which took her into the spare room. She didn't know which she was more surprised by: that her son had actually come to visit as he'd said he would, that he seemed to have taken up residence in the bedroom she'd created for him or that he was now patting the bed beside him, inviting her to share this space. She tried to hide her excitement as she joined him in front of the open laptop. Despite knowing he'd leave as dramatically as he'd arrived, Maxie had to use all her superpowers to resist looking round to see if there were any signs that this might be a more permanent situation. There was a large sports bag on the floor with dirty clothes hanging out – maybe she could just take a very long time to do all the washing. Maxie forced herself to focus on what he was showing her. It was a social media page but not just any page – the page set up to find Kelly.

'What's happened?'

'It's being trolled, people calling her a slag, saying they'd like to get in her knickers if there wasn't such a queue. It's pretty bad, Mum.'

Maxie sighed. This is what she'd been dreading. Kelly was no Mrs Claus. She watched as Karl scrolled through the page. Mrs Ingles had posted the picture of Kelly in the tutu and looking at the reaction to it, Maxie thought it was probably their worst move.

'They're saying she looks like a stripper in this one.'

Karl pressed play on a post entitled "SLUT DROP" and there was Kelly now in the nightclub smiling and laughing as she performed for the crowd. A booty shake here and there, a coy look, rubbing against one guy after the other and then the eponymous move shot at an angle to leave nothing to the imagination. The video ended by cutting to Kelly's parents at the press conference telling the world that their daughter "loved to dance" and "wanted to be a ballerina".

'Oh poor girl,' said Maxie.

'And poor boyfriend. No wonder he didn't wanna go big on the public appeal,' said Karl. 'Imagine having a girlfriend like that.'

Maxie stood up and put her hands on her hips. 'Hold on a minute Saint Karl, she's not the only one in that club drunk or flirting. I didn't bring you up to have double standards.'

'I know, I know. I'm just saying that people are going to be taking the piss out of him whether they should or not. I wouldn't want to be in his shoes right now.'

Maxie reluctantly told her son that she got where he was coming from. She wouldn't want to be in any of their shoes, except Kelly's. Then she could have a look around and see where on earth she was and what was stopping her from coming home.

'There are lots of comments saying that a police force with such a bad record and so underfunded should be spending taxpayers' money on someone more worthy,' continued Karl, scrolling through the expanding list of derogatory comments.

Maxie shook her head in despair. 'You know, there's always a reason why it's okay to attack or victimise a woman, why somehow they're "less worthy". First it was skimpy clothing and now it's if she enjoys a drink. There's a saying "Alcohol is the new short skirt", that a woman must be game if she's had a few voddies.'

'This one has the short skirt and the voddies.'

'She's called Kelly and I'm not having it. Show me someone who doesn't like a drink now and then.' Maxie jabbed a finger at Karl as she spoke. 'Should I give up on you if you get plastered and go missing one night?'

'Point made, Mum.' Karl closed the laptop.

Maxie calmed down. 'I really want to help her, Karl. This just isn't fair. How can I make people see her as a person? A young woman worth finding?'

Karl shrugged. 'No idea but doesn't she work for some kind of PR company?'

Maxie's eyes brightened. She stood up and took hold of her son's head, planting a big kiss on top.

'You're not just a handsome face are you?'

Chapter Fourteen

Tuesday, 20 December

When Maxie opened her eyes after having just a couple of hours of restless sleep, it took a moment for her to remember why her heart felt so heavy. It was as if she'd been sobbing in her sleep or had a nightmare that seemed too real. Then she remembered – Kelly. Maxie had been unable to tear herself away from the social media site and those trolling Kelly. She hadn't dared to get involved and hoped with every passing minute that someone would start leaping to Kelly's defence. Maxie reached for her phone and went back to the page. To her relief, by now the comments were more balanced and while the level of abuse had toned down, there was still a wave of consensus that Kelly was probably just shacked up with someone and even if she wasn't, police resources were scarce and their time would be better spent on "innocent victims".

'Whatever that means.' Maxie closed the website. She wanted to find Kelly even if the young woman didn't want to be found – and after all this fuss who could blame her for staying in hiding. Although Andrew had been right and every statistic available told her it was highly unlikely, Maxie couldn't stop worrying that something had happened to this young woman. The stag party Kelly had been dancing with were questioned but had gone on to another club without her and had no clue where or even who she actually was. There was still the chance that this Connor would give them some clues but that seemed a long shot and Maxie knew that with no leads whatsoever, the police simply had nothing to investigate. Their experience would tell them that if she weren't found within the first week, she probably wouldn't be found at all. Those genuinely wanting to disappear tended to go to ground until the initial investigation was over. They moved only when people stopped looking and usually left their old lives behind for good. Maxie knew she had very little time before Kelly was just another lost soul on the missing persons database.

Maxie and Andrew had a meeting with Kelly's boss as soon as his office opened at ten o'clock. She was anxious to meet this man and hoped he would have a different perspective on Kelly – after all he employed her. Her phone alarm beeped to tell her it was time to get up so she got dressed quickly and threw her poncho on over several warm layers. The drive to the canal-side offices took longer than she'd expected; she was going to be late and she hated being late for anything. There was nothing she could do about it but take deep breaths until the cobbled road leading to the red brick mill conversions that now housed the media and PR companies of the town came into view.

Very nice, thought Maxie as they drove into a car park of trendy electric cars all plugged in and charging. She patted the dashboard of her jeep. 'I feel like an old dinosaur driving you.'

Maxie entered the building walking into a stark white foyer decorated only by the numerous awards displayed across the walls and the harlequin covered tub chairs. Andrew was already there and waved her over to sit beside him.

'At least they're not beanbags,' she said to him as she nestled her rear into the just about adequate seat space. A clear-skinned nymph from reception approached her and asked if she'd like some water while she waited.

'Could it be hot water with some caffeine in it or maybe tonic water with some gin?' Seeing the confusion it caused, Maxie just shook her head. 'Only joking, I'm fine thanks.'

Maxie turned to Andrew and asked, 'How did that car crash of an appeal go down at the station?'

'Nightmare,' Andrew said. 'The DI gave me a right going over for not keeping the case under control. He says it makes us look completely incompetent.'

Maxie said she was sorry about that, then they waited for another ten minutes in the churchlike silence of the reception, making small talk. Maxie checked her watch.

'This is ridiculous,' she said to Andrew. 'They can keep me waiting as long as they like but you're the police.'

Just as she was about to get up and start complaining, a handsome, smartly-dressed man bounced up to her.

'I really am so sorry to have kept you waiting. I'm not normally that type of person, I promise.' He grabbed her hand between both of his and shook vigorously, then did the same with Andrew. 'I'm Orlando. You think you're winding down for Christmas and then pow, up pops a new client. I just had to take his call, I hope that's okay. But it means it'll be a great start to the new year for the whole team.'

Orlando led them through the double doors and down an exposed brick corridor.

'Have you ever been in one of these old buildings?' he asked in a soft Scottish accent as both Maxie and Andrew shook their heads. 'Then let me give you the tour – they're really quite something. As you can probably tell I'm not even from around here but when I came down, I fell in love with the place.'

As they walked, Orlando continued talking. 'A lot of people assume these buildings used to be cotton or paper mills but this one is more likely to have been warehousing. We're right on the canal here, connected to the whole world via the industrial waterways. This building probably brought in coal and supplies for the local industry throughout its heyday and the one next door that we plan to extend into was probably storage for goods leaving factories. When I think about this canal structure I wonder what the guys who built it would have thought of today's transport system. Could you imagine their reaction to the bullet train in Japan?'

It was obviously a well-rehearsed narrative and Maxie wished they could just get on but Orlando didn't stop there.

'I like to tell my team that while we might not look as if we've a lot in common with the people who built this place, we have a duty to honour that heritage. We have to channel the innovation of those who created the canals, mirror the precision of those engineers and match the sheer hard graft of everyone who made it happen.'

'This is all very interesting,' said Maxie as Orlando led them into room after room decorated with black and white photographs of the old buildings. 'And on any other occasion, I wouldn't mind seeing the rest of the building as well as those cellars and canals but right now …'

'You're absolutely right,' replied Orlando. 'I'm sure you want to talk about Kelly now.'

Maxie nodded that they certainly did then followed Orlando into his spacious office and sat, as indicated, around his meeting table.

'So Kelly is missing I hear,' Orlando started the conversation. Looking directly at Maxie he asked, 'How are you involved?'

Andrew stepped in, showing his badge and explaining her work with the ACU – explaining The Applied Criminology Unit and how their research assisted the police force. Orlando looked impressed and opened his mouth to speak but Maxie cut him short.

'Were you at the office party on Friday?' she asked.

'To start with,' replied Orlando. 'The whole company had a meal together which I went along to, then I made sure the drinks were flowing and that everyone was having a good time. When the young folk separated to go clubbing, I left them to it. I don't have the staying power I used to. Or the inclination for that matter, I'm a bit too old for all of that now.'

He smiled and Maxie noticed the crow's feet wrinkles around his eyes. Women spent a fortune trying to disguise or get rid of their wrinkles and grey hairs but on men, they almost looked like an accessory. As if they were painted on to make them look wise or thoughtful. He had a touch of the George Clooney about him, Maxie mused as she studied his face. He smiled and raised his eyebrows in question, shaking Maxie out of her thoughts.

'What did you think when Kelly didn't turn up for work on Monday?' she asked hurriedly.

'I wasn't here,' replied Orlando. 'At this time of year I'm usually travelling the country taking clients out for dinner and that's where I was yesterday. It wouldn't have struck anyone as odd that Kelly didn't turn up so no one called me until later in the day. We work long hours in this business. We're at the beck and call of our clients morning, noon and night, so when it comes to the Christmas week, I'm not strict on attendance. We're open for business and if you've got a project to finish then you have to be in but if teams need a few hours or even a day to catch up on shopping, then I'm okay with that. It's always hell the first week of January so I've got to cut people some slack.'

'Are you surprised Kelly is missing?' asked Andrew.

Orlando rubbed the back of his neck. 'I am and to be honest, I can't quite believe it,' he said. 'Are you sure she hasn't just gone away for some winter sun?'

'Did she mention that she might do that?' asked Andrew.

'Not really,' Orlando said. 'But the young people here think nothing about jumping on a plane and if it were a last minute deal she wouldn't have had the chance.'

'Is Kelly good at her job?' asked Maxie.

Orlando nodded instantly. 'Definitely. She has real charm and charisma. In fact I think she got my share. The clients love working with her. It's like that old saying – the women want to be her and the men want to be with her.'

'That can't be the job though.'

'Part of it unfortunately.' Orlando shrugged. 'We have to make people feel good about staying with our company and they have to enjoy working with us. Obviously the main part is coming up with ideas to promote their products and maintain their brand integrity but Kelly is very good at that too. She's a creative girl, always coming up with campaigns and one-off activations. The only thing she absolutely sucked at was filing the contact reports but you can't have everything. Creatives can be like that.'

'And have none of these clients who love her asked where she is?'

'Not until yesterday when a few of them saw her mother's appeal. I've been handling calls about her since then.'

'What are people saying?' asked Maxie.

Orlando shook his head. 'It's polite concern at the moment but I can hear the undercurrent in their voices. If that trolling continues, they're not going to want to work with her when she gets back.'

'Damaged goods,' murmured Maxie wondering if anyone was going to cut this girl some slack. 'The problem is that no one is looking for her while they're simply throwing stones. Can't you do anything about it? If your company comes up with ideas to make a product or a person look good, couldn't you say some things online that might help Kelly's image right now? She could do with a bit of sympathy from the wonderful general public.'

'A few of her colleagues tried to defend her but the wave of opinion is stacked too high right now. I've sent out an instruction that no one is to comment on the website again. Even well-intentioned words can fuel a fire can't they? I was hoping that by keeping quiet the trolls would eventually move on to someone else.'

'It makes some sense,' said Maxie as that had been her intuitive reaction. 'Surely there's something more you can do to help her? You read about these celebrities falling out of nightclubs with prostitutes while their wives are at home looking after the kids. They seem to survive and some even make a career out of their … shenanigans.'

Orlando laughed at the word.

'It's not bloody funny,' fumed Maxie, suddenly exasperated by the place she'd thought could give her some help. 'Are you going to do something useful or not?'

Andrew placed his palm flat on the table next to Maxie as a sign for her to calm down. He checked that his team had taken everything of Kelly's when they visited yesterday and was told that they had. Then he asked if any of the employees had been at The Printworks and Orlando said that in his discussions with them, he believed Kelly had gone there with her friend but no one from work. Maxie sighed – they seemed no further forward.

Orlando looked at her and held out his hands. 'I'm sorry,' he said. 'I'm nervous and I feel stuck between a rock and a hard place.'

'How so?' asked Andrew.

'Rightly or wrongly,' continued Orlando. 'We have clients who would agree with those people online. They wouldn't want to be associated with a company who publicly endorsed her behaviour.'

'And yet you're the one responsible for that behaviour,' snapped Maxie.

'How on earth do you work that out?' said Orlando.

'Well did you organise taxis home for your staff after you'd hung around to get the drinks flowing?' asked Maxie.

'No, they all made their own way home as they usually do.'

'So you helped young girls get blind drunk in the centre of town and left them vulnerable to the elements.' Maxie glared as she stood and gathered her composure. 'I wonder how those holier than thou clients of yours would feel about that?'

'Hold on a minute, I think it's probably you acting all "holier than thou" right now,' said Orlando. 'Are you saying you *never* buy your team a drink at Christmas? Do you get them taxis home? Do you warn them not to talk to strangers? We're talking about adults here you know – they have to take some responsibility for themselves.'

They were now both standing up glaring at each other and not backing down. They held their positions for a moment until Andrew urged them both to sit down.

'Sorry,' said Orlando.

'Me too,' added Maxie.

'I'm not the waste of space you have me tagged for,' Orlando said. 'I run a business which relies on image but of course I want Kelly back safely. Tell me what happens now in the investigation and I'll explain how this business works and maybe together we can think of a way to help.'

Andrew kicked off by explaining the missing persons' process and Orlando talked through PR and image building. Two hours later, Maxie stretched her arms above her head and yawned. She now knew more about Kelly and the type of work she got involved in. She also now knew that Orlando wasn't married and had put everything he had into this business. The recent recession had hit them hard and he'd had to make redundancies and cancel contracts with local suppliers – which broke his heart. That's why he was so concerned that Kelly's disappearance would adversely affect him.

'I know that sounds incredibly heartless,' he said. 'And I'm sorry.'

In return, Maxie outlined the workings of a criminology department and the ACU. She told him how painting a false picture of Kelly, as her mother had done was bound for failure. And talked through the concept of "double deviance" – how a woman can be treated more harshly by both the public and the criminal justice system when they deviate from the gentle, submissive role they are supposed to play in society.

'And that's in all walks of life,' said Maxie. 'Apparently men would get nervous if I put professor on my dating profile.'

'I think it's quite sexy,' said Orlando.

Andrew cleared his throat loudly and stood up to leave.

'Let us know if you think of any other information,' he said walking towards the door. 'And if you have any ideas for helping to find Kelly then please do run it past us before starting.'

Orlando promised that he would and walked Maxie and Andrew back to the reception. Andrew shook hands with him and left immediately but Orlando put his hand on Maxie's arm to delay her.

'I'm sorry about the way I was back there,' he said. 'I was thinking about myself and I shouldn't have been.'

'You were a bit of a jerk,' acknowledged Maxie.

'I know,' said Orlando hanging his head. 'Look, tell me more about how I could tackle this bias thing.'

'The key is to confront people,' Maxie said. 'Don't shy away. Say "I'm fat", or "I'm old" or "I'm a drunk" – but I'm also a person. At the very least it gets people thinking "well I'm fat too – does that mean I'm worthless?" And of course the answer is no. Help people to see the woman.'

Orlando nodded and said he could work with that. He asked for her number and promised to work on some ideas and call her in the morning.

Maxie gave him her number and they stood for a moment in an awkward silence before Maxie said she really had to go now. Orlando walked Maxie out, placing his hand gently on her back. The cold night air seemed to tickle and stir every one of Maxie's senses. She turned to shake hands with Orlando and the clouds of their breath mingled between them.

'Till tomorrow,' she said hurriedly getting into the car before she did anything stupid.

As she drove away, Maxie willed herself not to look at him in the rear-view mirror. She counted to ten and took a discreet glance. Orlando was still there, in the freezing night waving goodbye.

Chapter Fifteen

As she sat at a traffic light, Maxie could feel the heat rise in her cheeks. It was impossible to remove her poncho while wearing a seat belt so she'd just have to suffer – it would serve her right; she felt thoroughly ashamed of herself. She'd gone into that office wanting to shake down the company boss and force him to do something to help find Kelly but she'd left feeling like a schoolgirl at a prom with the only promise from Orlando being that he'd think of something and call her in the morning. Maxie shook her head, berating herself. A car behind tooted loudly making her look up – the lights had changed to green. She waved an apology in the rear mirror and started off.

This was not the time for self-indulgence. She had to focus. Aside from the completely inappropriate but undeniably pleasant stirrings, she had gained something from the meeting with Orlando. She'd found out that Luis's friend Harry wasn't just a drinking buddy who could provide an alibi but a photographer and supplier to Orlando's company and a good friend of Kelly's. Andrew had interviewed Harry and verified the time Luis had left the pub that night but Maxie now wondered whether there was any other light this man could shine on this mystery. Maxie turned left into the next street that came up and looked up Harry's firm. She found the number and called him, insisting that they meet up today.

'I've got nothing more to say,' Harry said when they spoke on the phone. 'And I heard about that ridiculous road trip around the churches with Luis. I'm too busy at this time of year to play amateur detective.'

Maxie let the insult she'd heard many times before wash over her.

'Don't you want to find your friend?' she asked.

'I'm sure the police have more resources than I have for that particular task,' he replied. 'And I do *not* want my name or company associated with that car crash of an appeal.'

Maxie told Harry that they had strongly advised Mrs Ingles against it but she'd taken no notice. As the words came out of her mouth, Maxie felt a cloud of despair settle near her heart. She'd failed to find Kelly, failed to stop the appeal which had made things much worse, failed to stop herself flirting with Kelly's boss and now it looked as if she was about to fail in her efforts to speak to Harry. She let out a deep, deep sigh and pleaded with him to meet her. He sounded reluctant but gave Maxie directions to his office and told her she could have his attention between two and three when they'd be taking a break on the shoot – but no longer. After ending the call, Maxie gave herself a gentle slap on the cheeks.

'Come on girl,' she said to herself. 'You can do this.'

She arrived at ten to two and waited until the exact hour before announcing herself. The outside of the steel-panelled warehouse looked like every other one on this industrial estate at the edge of the river but when she walked inside, Maxie stood open-mouthed, amazed at the scene before her. An Easter photography shoot was well underway and the room was an abundance of spring: blossom trees and a field full of daffodils that would have Wordsworth fooled and most excitingly, to Maxie at least, wheelbarrows full of chocolate eggs – hundreds of them. Harry was summoned from his position and he walked towards Maxie without a hint of emotion on his face but with his hand outstretched in a professional greeting nonetheless.

'Wow,' said Maxie turning on all the charm and flattery she could muster. 'This place is amazing. I'd been expecting something that looked like a dockside iron works when I walked in, not Willy Wonka's chocolate factory. I have to say, your place of work is a lot more interesting than mine.'

The corners of Harry's mouth turned upwards – very slightly – as he led her through the building.

'This place is always at odds with the season outside,' he explained. 'To get your Easter eggs into the magazines, the photos have to be with them three months in advance – hence the shoot right now. We photograph Christmas in July so while it's baking hot outside we have a warehouse of fake snow.'

'Are they real?' asked Maxie pointing at the Easter eggs lying in the spring scene.

'No, not those ones. Chocolate would melt under the studio lights,' replied Harry. 'But we've some real ones in the fridge for the close-ups later. Sorry but there are none spare.'

'Don't worry, I wasn't hinting,' replied Maxie. 'Can we talk about Kelly?'

Harry nodded and led her to a cramped room off the main warehouse where he picked some boxes off a couple of chairs which had seen better days. He invited Maxie to sit down.

'We keep the main space free for filming which as you can see is in full swing. This will have to do.'

Maxie nodded. She'd met with two businessmen who knew Kelly today and they couldn't be more different. Both self-assured and guarded in their own way but one going out of his way to impress and the other seemingly intent on doing the absolute opposite.

Once they'd settled themselves into the space, Maxie asked him to take her through the events of Friday night. Harry shook his head which suggested both exasperation and boredom. He protested that he'd already told the police the entire sequence of events but then trotted out the timelines that Maxie knew. They confirmed Luis's account as she knew they would. One of Harry's assistants brought in some coffees and Maxie hugged the little mug of warmth – it wasn't just cramped in here, it was bloody freezing but he wasn't going to get rid of her with a bit of cold. She took a sip and let the heat flow through her body.

'Have you known Luis and Kelly for long?' she asked, having defrosted her lips with the hot drink

'Yes.'

Maxie could see he was goading her but she'd just done exactly what she'd advised Andrew not to – asked him a closed question. Maxie gave him "the look" – eyebrows raised as if she were staring at him over school ma'am glasses. Harry shrugged his surrender.

'Okay, I met Luis about two years ago when I needed someone to build a set. We got on together and became friends after that but I've known Rowan for longest. We went to the same secondary school and she was pretty much my best buddy. We came here to uni together and I still look out for her – which by the way, you need when you're under Kelly's influence.'

'You're not a fan then?'

'No, it's not that. I do actually like her and it was Kelly who introduced me to Orlando so I get lots of work from her company,' he replied. 'It's hard not to like Kelly. She's always been a good laugh and up for absolutely anything. When we were younger at uni, she was brilliant fun to be around and you really were guaranteed a great night out if she was there. Rowan just needs to get from being under her influence and start being her own person.'

'We understand you introduced Luis to Kelly?'

Harry snorted. 'That's not what I'd planned at all.'

'Tell me more.'

'It was Rowan's birthday party and I'd been asked to bring along some guys I knew. Rowan works all hours but isn't allowed to form relationships with anyone at work and she's too shy to just start flirting in a bar. Luis was newly single and I thought they'd make a good couple – they're both very loving people and they'd have been perfect together. They still would. I didn't account for Kelly though. She took one look at him and that was it, she completely monopolised him.'

'You said Luis was newly single? What happened in his previous relationship?'

'I never knew her but I think he said she just upped and went travelling,' Harry said.

Maxie filed this piece of information mentally and wondered whether Andrew had found out any more; it was potentially another woman who had potentially vanished from Luis's life.

'Did Rowan know or guess why you'd brought Luis along?' asked Maxie.

'I didn't say anything but I do think she would have been interested in him,' said Harry. 'It won't last though, Luis and Kelly – two firebrands like that eventually burn each other out. Rowan would have been a better match.'

'So you and Rowan were never an item?' she asked.

'I'm gay and before you ask, no, I'm not interested in Luis,' he replied in a mocking tone. 'I haven't bumped off Kelly to get to her boyfriend if that's what you're thinking.'

Harry laughed and Maxie could feel anger and frustration rising but she was determined not to get riled by this man. She stood up and started pacing around the tiny room, noticing that Harry was watching her. Maxie looked across at Harry and held his gaze for a few moments. He didn't flinch. He looked back at her without a trace of emotion on his face. The silence between them became uncomfortable and eventually Harry looked away and began fiddling with his watch. Maxie let him fester in the silence for a little longer before asking, 'Are you surprised by what's happened?'

Maxie knew that after an awkward silence, many people try to lighten the atmosphere. They spurt out something they later regret but not this guy. Harry regained his composure and took his time before answering.

'She's a law unto herself,' he said calmly. 'You never know what she's going to do next and that's what makes her exciting but unpredictable. I'm sure you've heard that she also walked out on her last boyfriend, Connor? Just packed her things, told him it was over and that she didn't like long goodbyes.'

'Nice.'

'I don't think she's ever intentionally mean, she just has no idea how much of an impact she has on people. She doesn't think about other people's feelings. And they can't even see it. To be honest, you almost have to be on the outside looking in to see it. That gaze of wonderment guys get when she flashes them a smile. No wonder she's brilliant at her job – she has them hypnotised.'

'So you think she might just have walked out on Luis?'

'I don't know but if she has then good riddance to her.'

'But if she had, where would she have gone? Is there someone else on the scene?'

'I'm just pleased she hasn't come crawling back to Rowan asking for her old room. If she does, I hope Ro has the guts to say no this time. Kells left her in a right state.'

'How?'

'It's going to sound trivial now but it wasn't at the time.'

'If it helps us find her …'

'I doubt it will but last year Rowan got a bonus from work and decided to use it as a deposit and get on the property ladder. Still the only way Rowan could do it was if Kelly would rent a room to help her out with the mortgage. It was cheap rent so everyone was a winner and Rowan took the plunge. True to form, a few months later Kelly ups and leaves to move in with Luis. Rowan really struggled for a while so I helped her out – not that I minded, she's like my little sister.'

'She's pretty broken by all this,' continued Harry. 'Maybe she blames herself or something. She told me that when Kelly gets back, she's applying for a transfer to a supermarket in a different part of the country. She knows she needs to get away from here, away from Kelly but I'll miss her.'

Maxie took in the news. She understood how Rowan felt, after all isn't that exactly how she'd felt when her marriage broke down – just the need to escape and work everything else out later? The closest friendships aren't that far from marriage. You share everything, have a secret language and turn to each other first in a crisis. Maxie could see that Rowan needed to divorce Kelly to be able to have a life of her own. A complex web of relationships was emerging – a boyfriend who was trying to hold on too tightly and a best friend who was trying to escape. Maxie would have to pay Rowan another visit as soon as possible just in case there was anything Kelly's best friend had omitted from her account of that night.

'How do you think Luis would react if he found out Kelly was about to ditch him like she did her last boyfriend?' asked Maxie. 'After all, he was about to propose and it would be the second time he'd been abandoned too.'

'Yeah, I heard about that,' Harry said.

'You don't sound enthusiastic.' Maxie got a shake of the head in response.

'It would never work but in answer to your question, he'd be absolutely gutted. And I'm sure he'd try and follow her to make her change her mind. But if I got to him first, I'd hold him back. They're not right for each other. He's a typical Spaniard at heart – wants to build a home, have kids and she … she's just not ready to settle down with anyone. They're both good people but they shouldn't be together.'

One of his assistants came into the room and asked him to sign off the set for the shoot.

'I have to do this. Are we good to walk and talk?' Harry asked Maxie.

'Of course, lead the way.' Maxie was keen to get out of this little room and return to the hope and magic of the Easter scene. 'So Luis builds sets for you? Did he build any of this set?'

'Yes – he did that five-bar gate over there,' replied Harry. 'He was here most of Friday before we went to the pub.'

'Were you together the whole day?' asked Maxie.

'Not the whole day as I told the police. We had to pick up the props from storage and the crates to make the gate. We were back and forwards all day but we were working flat out.'

'Did you use Luis's blue van at all?'

'Obviously, this lot doesn't get here by magic.'

Maxie nodded her thanks and said she'd leave him to get on with his work. Harry guided her out with his arm at her back as if he were marshalling an unruly crowd.

'Thank you for your time,' said Maxie as they reached the outside of the warehouse. 'I'll let you know if the police find anything.'

'Whatever,' he said before banging the door shut.

Maxie stood looking at the firmly closed door, knowing that it was blocking out more than the cold. Harry was clearly telling her that her time was up and he'd prefer it if she didn't come back.

Maxie got back into her car, took out her phone and switched on the recorder to commit her thoughts.

'Harry,' she said. 'Strange guy. Seems to like Kelly but certainly likes Rowan and Luis more. I can very definitely imagine Harry believing in the principle of the "greater good". I think he would have no problem lying to me – he doesn't take me seriously at all. But I also think while he'd not necessarily lie to the police, he'd keep shtum if not asked a direct question. I think he'd also deceive his best friends if it meant they got to live their lives Kelly-free …'

Maxie paused the recording and looked over at the warehouse again before continuing.

'The question is,' she said with the phone close to her mouth. 'Would he go any further than just lying to achieve his goals?'

Chapter Sixteen

The dark mood that had started to take grip when she left Orlando began to hover again, like a murmuration of starlings swooping and diving around her head. Driving with one hand on the steering wheel, she pulled down the sun visor and looked at herself in the mirror. She rubbed at the frown lines on her temple, pondering why none of Kelly's friends or family had any idea where she was and how a perfectly healthy young woman could possibly just vanish into thin air? And, although it had seemed and been a bit of a waste of time, only Luis had actually searched for her. Rowan and Harry were getting on with their jobs. Was it just because they really did know her best and were assuming she'd turn up when it suited her and not before?

Maxie slammed on the brakes as the car in front of her screeched to a halt. The shock brought her back into the present moment. She put both hands back on the wheel and willed herself to focus for the rest of the journey.

She needed to think, to be somewhere calm and peaceful and so headed for the university. When she reached the eerily quiet campus, she dumped her poncho and bag in her office and strode purposefully to the library. Every research study completed by the faculty was available online but she didn't want to sit behind her own desk. She needed to be in a different space to be able to see things differently. She needed to hold and smell paper, to read the words written and feel their significance flow from the page. The library somehow managed to be even quieter than the empty halls and study rooms. Maxie's shoulders dropped as she walked through this chamber of knowledge. It wasn't an old library, ornate with carvings and heavy with history, rather it was a new purpose-built facility with state-of-the-art computers. Maxie didn't want these today; she ran her finger along the shelves and they stopped at a book by a former professor about crimes of passion. What Maxie did know about Kelly was that she definitely stirred passions one way or the other. The professor thought about her conversations with Luis and Harry and could very well imagine their frustrations with Kelly manifesting themselves. She took the book out and walked over to a reading pod. The author was not telling her anything she didn't already know but Maxie found it helpful to read aloud the words that he'd written to define the crime, as she contemplated this case.

“A violent crime, especially homicide, in which the perpetrator commits the act against someone because of sudden strong impulse such as sudden rage rather than as a premeditated crime.”

Maxie knew that most people believed it to be a crime committed between lovers but that wasn’t the case. The author rightly stated that anyone, given the right circumstances, could commit a crime of passion and often it was only the location that prevented it happening. It was impossible to tell how many crimes were avoided simply because the sudden rage happened in a crowded space or because there was no access to a weapon of any kind. Maxie had liked what she’d seen of Luis but she’d seen for herself that he could be prone to bouts of rage. If he had gone into town after the pub and had seen Kelly – the woman he was about to propose to – flirting with those men then understandably, he would have been furious. Maxie imagined that with his strength he wouldn’t have needed to be near any weapon, his hands could do untold damage all by themselves.

Although she could imagine him launching into a rage, Maxie could also imagine him being wracked with guilt if he harmed a hair on Kelly’s head. She thought back to the day they spent touring churches, his desperation to find his girlfriend and the wild goose chase around churches. Was it all pretence? She knew there was another possibility but it was so rare it was usually only the stuff of TV dramas – *dissociative amnesia.* She’d given a talk on the subject a few years back at a conference and knew that it was now one of the most watched clips on the university YouTube channel. Undergraduates were always fascinated by this type of work and although the bulk of their studies would surround the procedures of policing, it was the nuances of the criminal mind that always attracted students to the course. Maxie put the book back on the shelf and walked over to the multimedia centre. She found the clip and because the library was empty, didn’t bother with headphones as she listened to her younger self. She’d begun by telling the audience the basic statistics – that there were many instances of offenders who claimed total or partial amnesia for violent crimes, including murder or attempted murder. Amnesia seemed particularly prevalent during domestic and sexual abuse.

“*A dissociative state is an altered state of consciousness associated with a traumatic experience,*” she’d said. “*And dissociative amnesia is the inability to remember important personal experiences and events after a traumatic experience of psychological origin.*”

She watched herself taking questions from the audience, most of who seemed to regard the condition as very convenient and equally unbelievable as a defence. Maxie remembered enjoying the debate and calling for quiet as the room became more animated.

"*How many of you have ever been mind-numbingly drunk?*" she'd asked as a murmur of laughter went around the auditorium. "*I mean so drunk that you wake up the next morning with a complete stranger in your bed, with your mates telling you what you did and showing you pictures you have absolutely no memory of? Anyone had any one of these experiences?*"

The video panned to show a large proportion of the audience with a hand up.

"*What if later that day, you get a knock on the door and police are standing there. They're telling you that while you were off your head, you punched a guy for looking at your girlfriend? There's CCTV proof, he's dead and you're now wanted for manslaughter. You've committed a crime of passion and you have absolutely no memory of it.*"

'Is that what you think has happened?' The voice behind her made her jump. 'Do you think I've hurt her and just can't remember?'

Seeing Luis standing there she hurriedly tried to switch off the clip.

'Don't bother,' said Luis slumping on a chair beside her. 'I've been watching it for a while.'

'How did you know where I was? And how did you get in Luis?' asked Maxie. The library had barriers and a pass system.

'I followed you from Harry's,' replied Luis. 'And I just jumped over the barriers.'

'I guess they're not really a barrier for someone your height are they?' said Maxie. 'Why are you here?'

Luis shrugged his shoulders then cupped his head in his hands. 'I don't know,' he murmured. 'To see if you'd found out anything?'

Maxie swallowed and looked around her to see if there was anything she could use in defence if Luis were about to turn his frustrations on her. There was nothing. She had to keep Luis calm even if that were the opposite of the way she felt.

'Tell me how you're feeling,' she said resting a hand on his shoulder.

Luis rubbed his hands over his weary face then murmured, 'Part of me can't believe this is actually happening.'

Maxie simply nodded and let him talk.

'When I woke up this morning, for just a second all was well with the world and I couldn't remember any of this nightmare. I mean, I knew something had happened but for a millisecond, it could have been anything. Then it sinks back in, the emptiness, the big black hole. You wouldn't have thought that someone *not* being there could take up so much space but it does.'

Maxie thought about her apartment. Before moving there she'd lived in a noisy family home with her husband and son so she knew exactly what Luis was talking about. She felt it every time she locked her front door at night.

'I know you told me that some people walk out on their lives,' continued Luis. 'But I don't believe she would have just left me like this. If she was sick of me, she'd have told me about it – that's for sure. She'd probably have thrown *me* out of my own home.'

Luis smiled half-heartedly, evidently imagining that scene. 'It's so quiet without her.' Louis looked directly at Maxie, his palms upturned in question. 'Where is she?'

'No one knows – yet.'

'Someone has to know!' he shouted.

He stood up, grabbed the remote control that Maxie had put down and switched the video clip back on.

'Do you really think this is possible?' He waved the remote at the screen. 'People commit these crimes and genuinely forget that they've done them?'

Maxie's heart picked up a beat as Luis seemed to get more agitated the more he watched. She didn't know whether or not he was dangerous but the simple facts were that she was alone in a deserted building with a distressed man who had at least twice the body strength she did. Her phone was in her bag so she couldn't reach it and call someone for help. Luis caught her downward glance to her bag and switched off the video.

'I'm not here to hurt you,' he said.

'I didn't think you were,' Maxie said, trying to keep the tone of her voice level and natural. She decided that the sensible move would be to walk to somewhere more public and added, 'You look freezing. Come on, let's go and get some coffee. The canteen will still be open for the research staff and might even be serving mulled wine today – highly diluted of course.'

She walked off, hoping she looked more confident than she felt and to her relief, Luis followed her lead. Maxie relaxed a little as they left the library and headed down the corridor to the canteen. She was particularly relieved when they encountered some of her PhD students.

'We're going for mulled wine in the canteen if you fancy joining us?' she said to everyone she passed. They all declined but that hadn't been the point; people knew where she was at least.

'Have you seen all the social media stuff,' asked Luis when they got into the bright glare of the cafeteria and sat down with mugs of coffee rather than mulled wine. Maxie took her phone out of her bag and placed it on the table so she'd have easy access to it then told him she'd seen some of it and was truly sorry he had to see it.

'I hate all that stuff,' said Luis. 'Keyboard warriors – that's what they're called isn't it?'

'The people writing those things don't seem like warriors to me,' stated Maxie. 'They're more like cowards.'

'I agree,' said Luis. 'Those websites stop people doing something useful, makes them lazy. You could help the environment by not buying lots of crap that you really don't need, but no, why inconvenience yourself when you can share a picture of a dolphin instead.'

He shook his head in disdain then looked up at Maxie. 'Why do they hate Kelly?' he asked. 'She's hardly the only person in this world with piercings and tattoos.'

'They don't hate her,' replied Maxie. 'I think they were responding to the way Mrs Ingles presented her more than anything. I think the bias may be against her and her partner more than Kelly.'

'Yeah, that really didn't help,' said Luis. 'So how come people aren't saying "I drink, have sex, tattoos and piercings and I'm no less of a human being – I'll help search for this woman"? No, instead they just let a really ugly picture go viral and that's what everyone thinks of Kelly now. They hear her name and they just see that image.'

'Please just stay away from social media, Luis. It won't help.'

'What can I do? What will help?' he asked. 'And don't say nothing because that's not an option. I can't sit at home and do nothing – you even said that to me.'

Maxie nodded and Luis continued.

'When you left after we'd been to the churches, I drew up this map of the town with a circle ten minutes in each direction from that bar. I've walked it every night to see if I can find anything like her bag or something that she was wearing. There's been nothing but maybe you could come with me? We could do that again together – get out there looking.'

'It's been four days, Luis.'

Maxie's phone rang and she saw Andrew's name on the screen.

'I have to take this,' she said, walking away from the table. After taking the call she returned to Luis.

'That was DS Dawson,' she told him.

'Telling you I punched another self-righteous prick for saying that Kelly would go to hell no doubt.'

Maxie nodded and told him the DS was on his way.

'It was worth it. I felt better afterwards and I'm sure Kelly will approve.'

They sat silently until Andrew, along with a uniformed officer, walked through the doors.

'Your luck's in again,' he warned Luis. 'They're not going to press charges either.' He instructed Luis to follow his colleague to the car where he'd be taken home.

'And please stop thumping people from now on,' called Maxie as he left.

'*Lo prometo*,' said Luis in his smoothest Spanish accent, flashing his beautiful brown eyes. *I promise.* Not for the first time Maxie concluded that if he'd fronted the public appeal, there'd have been far more positive coverage. If only she could rule out his involvement.

Chapter Seventeen

As soon as Luis had left with the uniformed officer, Andrew asked what they'd been discussing.

'Dissociative amnesia,' said Maxie, grimacing as she guessed rightly what Andrew's reaction would be.

The detective sergeant threw his arms up in the air. 'Brilliant. Just brilliant. Now, should we ever find that he had something to do with this, the boyfriend with the temper and the opportunity now has a defence given to him by a professor of criminology. My DI will be thrilled about this one.'

'Come off it,' said Maxie. 'Anyway, I didn't do it on purpose. He sneaked up behind me when I was reading.'

Maxie knew discussing it with Luis hadn't been her brightest move but it was a difficult defence to prove so if the case against Kelly's boyfriend stacked up, it wouldn't really make any difference. She guessed Andrew was just frustrated by the case.

'I'm sorry but this case is bugging me – we don't have a single lead,' said Andrew confirming her thoughts. 'We checked her bank details and nothing seems amiss. She has a few thousand in savings which I'm assuming is her inheritance.'

'Had any been withdrawn recently?' asked Maxie.

Andrew shook his head. 'Nothing withdrawn from either the current or savings account since her disappearance but we don't know how much the inheritance was in total so can't say if she kept any back for herself before opening the account. I also found Luis's ex-girlfriend – alive and well. She says he falls in love too quickly but other than being a bit intense, claims he's lovely. My DI has already decided that a woman who's seemingly taken her suitcase and passport *and* has walked out on her previous boyfriend without looking back has simply done the same again. This time Kelly has had to walk further but the DI thinks she's just lying low until the coverage dies down.

'I've followed up every scrap of evidence and every bogus call. There's no useful CCTV, nothing. The DI has now hinted that he isn't convinced continuing the search is a good use of our resources.'

Maxie knew that the crime of "wasting public money" would be bearing down hard on Andrew's boss and the public opinion of Kelly would factor in his decision-making. She could go above the new DI's head and speak to her old friend DCI McAlister but that wouldn't help Andrew and besides which, a good DCI would back up her team's decision. The police would be damned if they investigated this disappearance much longer and damned if they didn't. The weight of these external factors was rarely considered in any academic studies and yet they very definitely affected both the individuals in the force and the decisions they made.

'What about Rowan? Don't you think she might know more than she's said?'

Andrew shook his head. 'I doubt it. The barman clearly remembers her being ditched at the club. She's as much a victim here.'

'But maybe she didn't tell us *everything* she knows,' pressed Maxie.

'You're thinking of going round there again aren't you?'

Maxie nodded.

'Okay,' said Andrew. 'We'll give it one more shot – I can't imagine she'll be pleased to see us again.'

A call to the supermarket informed them that Rowan was at home so they hopped into Andrew's car, set the satnav and were soon in the road of neat terraced houses where Rowan and the elderly couple lived. This time as they approached, there was a "TO LET" sign attached to the outside. Andrew expressed surprise but Maxie filled him in on the information she'd received from Harry – that Rowan had applied to be transferred to a different supermarket.

'She's definitely putting all this behind her,' said Maxie as they parked up. 'And a lot sooner than I'd imagined.'

'Seems odd,' replied Andrew. 'You'd think she'd wait until we had news of Kelly.'

He strode up to the door with Maxie following him and knocked. His phone rang as he waited.

'Really? Good work, get both the home and the work address and we'll go over there tomorrow. No alerts, let's just go.'

Rowan peeped her head around the door, the security chain still on. She didn't invite her visitors inside.

'Can we come in?' Maxie had to ask. Rowan hesitated before unhooking the chain and opening the door. All the doors off the corridor were closed and she led Maxie and Andrew straight into the living room. In Maxie's experience, when people first met the police, they tended to be polite and helpful – eager to make a good impression. Then as time went by they grew wearier of the visits and the same old questions. Rowan was definitely at the weary stage. She made no effort to make her guests welcome. Maxie took it upon herself to sit down and Rowan reluctantly followed her lead while Andrew remained standing, aiming to appear in charge of the conversation.

'I see you're letting the house,' he said. 'So where are you off to?'

'Is it relevant?' Rowan asked.

'Not really, we're just interested,' Maxie said softly. 'Is it the transfer you applied for? Harry told me about it. We know that this has been very hard on you.'

'That's the understatement of the year.'

'From what I've learned about Kelly, she's a bit like marmite – you either love her or hate her,' continued Maxie. 'Does that sound about right?'

Rowan smiled sadly. 'Not really, as I said, everyone starts off loving Kelly. She wouldn't have it any other way. If she senses indifference, she'll make a beeline for you, find out your interests and talk to you until you like her. That's what makes her good at her job. You could be the world's biggest bore and you'll come away thinking she was fascinated by your love of engine parts or whatever.'

'So what goes wrong?'

Rowan raised her hands in exasperation. 'Well take this place. The rent was as low as I could make it and much lower than she was paying so it worked for both of us. For the first time since I'd met her it felt like we were on an equal footing, doing something for each other – but that couldn't last could it?'

Maxie knew all of this but it was news to Andrew and anyway, interesting to hear from Rowan's perspective.

'What happened?' Andrew asked.

'She met Luis and started shagging him all over the house. It didn't feel like my home any more. I'd try to open the door and the chain would be on so I couldn't get in or worse, I'd get in and she'd be running from the kitchen, clutching her clothes. I'm not a prude but I didn't want someone else christening every room in my house.'

'Neither would I,' said Maxie.

'Luis was lovely. He was the one who apologised. Kelly started spending more and more time at his place and then one day she was just gone.'

'That must have been a relief and a worry,' prompted Maxie.

'The thing is there is never any malice at all in anything she does. She brought me a bottle of Prosecco and some chocolates so that I could celebrate having the place to myself and she meant it. She simply breezed off into the sunset as usual.'

'So where are you going?' asked Andrew.

'My company have been great. Being associated with Kelly right now and all those images online could have been horrendous for my career, especially as I was there with her, but they've protected me,' said Rowan. 'I told them that I simply needed to get away and they've agreed. I'm covering maternity leave for a store manager over in Liverpool and it's a much bigger store so it's good for my promotion prospects. If I let this place, it'll more than cover the mortgage. I just need a fresh start.'

'Liverpool?' Andrew commented pointedly but Maxie didn't understand the significance of his tone.

'So how will you feel when Kelly reappears from wherever she's gone?' she asked.

Rowan thought about it for a while. 'Honestly? I don't know. Angry that she's led us all on this dance but at the same time relieved that she's safe … but I genuinely can't imagine that she isn't safe anyway. And I'll be glad that it's over – the dramatics. There's always dramatics around Kelly so I'll be relieved that I can say goodbye once and for all, then get on with my life. Harry thinks the only way I'll ever actually have a life of my own is when I get away from Kelly. I didn't believe him but I can see now that he's probably right.'

'He cares a lot about you doesn't he?'

Rowan smiled and nodded. 'I love him to bits. If he weren't gay he'd make my ideal husband. He's like my big brother now and he's always shoving all these guys he meets in my direction.'

'Like Luis?' asked Andrew

Rowan shrugged. 'Harry thought we'd be ideal together and that we'd hold lots of dinner parties where he'd be the guest of honour.'

'But Kelly intervened?'

Another shrug and a nod of the head from Rowan. Maxie smiled sympathetically.

'Who needs friends eh?'

'I wouldn't change any of the past though. Kelly and I had some hilarious times but you just know when it's over don't you?'

'You do.' Maxie certainly knew that feeling. 'And there's something about this time of year isn't there? You can't contemplate waking up in the new year with exactly the same worries hanging over your head.'

The two women sat silently, each deep in her thoughts.

Andrew cleared his throat and pulled back his shoulders. 'Oh, and just to let you know, we've found Kelly's ex – Connor,' he said. 'You may be surprised to know where he's living now.'

An almost imperceptible glance upwards gave Rowan away and Maxie suddenly knew what Andrew was about to say.

'You won't be surprised, will you Rowan?' Maxie asked. 'Why not call him down?'

Rowan opened her mouth briefly as if to protest ignorance but then dropped her shoulders and trudged to the bottom of the stairs. 'Connor,' she called. 'Come down. They know you're here.'

Heavy footsteps trudged down the stairs and a tall, sandy-haired man with blue eyes walked into the room. Maxie had to hand it to Kelly – she certainly seemed to pounce on some good-looking guys. And if Harry had been the one to find Connor then perhaps she should ask him to start fixing her up when this was all resolved.

Connor walked towards Maxie and Andrew with his hand outstretched. 'Pleased to meet you,' he said in a soft Irish accent. He sat down on the sofa next to Rowan. Maxie looked at them thinking that they made a good couple.

'Not half as pleased as I am to meet you,' said Andrew. 'Now can you tell me what you know that could be pertinent to this case and please, don't miss anything out – we haven't got a lot of time.'

Connor confirmed that he worked in an accountancy firm which managed Harry's accounts. He dated Kelly for around eighteen months but as a junior in the firm, he always had to work late and was tired when he got home. If Kelly was actually there, she found him very boring. He wanted to settle in with a bottle of wine and she wanted to dance.

'Some opposites attract, some don't,' he said.

They'd split up just before Rowan's birthday party and he wasn't going to go but Harry asked him to and at the last minute, he'd decided to pop in and say hello to the birthday girl.

'I guess at some level, I was hoping to see Kelly and thinking that we might get back together but when I got there, she was completely pissed and draped around her latest victim. She'd moved on. I went home and tore up every photo I had of her.'

‘I didn’t know you’d seen that,’ said Rowan, stroking his arm. ‘I’m really sorry.’

‘Nothing you could have done about it,’ said Connor. ‘More fool me for thinking I was someone special.’

‘You are,’ said Rowan holding his hand tightly.

‘But why didn’t you come forward when the news broke of her disappearance?’ asked Andrew.

‘I called Rowan,’ replied Connor. ‘Mainly to check she was okay but I wasn’t there so I couldn’t help.’

‘Kelly’s mum remembers you from a funeral you attended,’ said Maxie. ‘Apparently you held her partner by the throat.’

Connor shook his head. ‘He deserved it. Kelly had just lost the only person she cared about in that bloody family and he asked her – *at the graveside* – if her grandad left any money.’

‘It seems to be his main preoccupation in life,’ said Maxie.

Connor put his arm around Rowan’s shoulder. ‘Coming forward wouldn’t have helped. Kelly hasn’t been in touch with me and I have no idea where she is. Honestly.’

‘So now you two just plan to ride off into the sunset together?’ asked Andrew.

‘It’s not like that at all,’ Rowan said angrily. ‘Connor’s going to put me up until I can find somewhere of my own and I’m going to get my life back on track.’

‘We’re both in need of a Kelly detox,’ added Connor.

‘When do you move out?’ asked Maxie.

‘I’m storing most of my stuff at my parents. I’ll spend Christmas with them and then I’ll move to Connor’s before the new year starts.’

‘I’m going to need addresses and numbers,’ said Andrew. ‘As well as an assurance that you’ll both be exactly where you say you are for the duration of this investigation. I don’t have to remind you that we still haven’t actually found your friend.’

‘Here’s hoping we do soon,’ said Maxie, ‘to give you the chance to say goodbye.’

‘Quite frankly,’ said Rowan, ‘I’ve said my goodbyes even if she’s not here to hear them. She left both of us – remember?’

Andrew signalled Maxie to leave. Connor and Rowan followed them to the door and stood silhouetted against the light of the hallway as she got into Andrew’s car for the short trip up to the Hendrys’. Maxie watched them as they closed the door and wondered if they’d finally get together.

They were bound together right now but as soon as the drama was resolved, they might no longer need the security and protection of each other.

Andrew and Maxie wanted to let George and Patricia Hendry know that they were still looking for Kelly. When the old couple opened the door, they both looked as if they'd aged even more with worry and were devastated to hear that there was still no news.

'Would it help if we gave some money to that fund on the telly?' asked Patricia. 'We have savings.'

Both Maxie and Andrew blurted out a loud, 'No!' startling the old lady.

'No,' said Andrew more calmly. 'The police are looking into this thoroughly and you've already funded us with your taxes over the years. Please save your money for a celebration when Kelly gets home.'

Patricia looked pleased with that and the elderly couple stood in the doorway, waving at them as they drove away.

The sleet started to fall yet again as they made their way back to the university to pick up Maxie's car. The professor watched Andrew blow out his cheeks in despair as he flicked on the headlights and the windscreen demister. Winter wasn't helping things at all. The blackness that arrived so early in the afternoon seemed to reflect his mood. Maxie knew he'd come with her hoping for a lead.

'New job, new man and new house. Rowan's done all right out of this hasn't she?' he said eventually. His foot slipped on the clutch which screeched, mirroring his frustration.

'Yep,' said Maxie thinking back to her conversation with Harry. 'Almost as if someone has conspired to give her the life he thinks she deserves.'

Chapter Eighteen

"GONE TO PARTY – STAYING OVER – K"

Maxie picked up the post-it note that her son had attached to a bottle of wine and looked at it. The note could have been written by Kelly, after all that's what should have happened with her. From his accounts, Luis had every reason to expect his party-loving girlfriend to walk through the door after sleeping it off at a friend's house. Maxie had no reason to think that Karl was in danger tonight and no reason to assume that he wouldn't be back in the morning but what if he wasn't? If he never came back and she couldn't get hold of him? What would she do? What would any parent or spouse do in the same situation? How long would she leave it before reporting it or investigating it? Too soon and she'd just look like the over-protective mother but too late and it might be … well, too late. What would she do if Karl asked her to stay away from him? What if she never heard from him again?

'Enough,' she said out loud, tapping the side of her skull to drive these thoughts out of her head. 'He *will* be back tomorrow and he wouldn't just vanish – I'm sure he wouldn't.'

It was late and Maxie hadn't realised how utterly exhausted she was until after she'd showered and got into her evening slouchies. Kelly's case was keeping her awake at night and she was sure that's why she wasn't thinking straight. Andrew had been right to reprimand her about discussing dissociative amnesia with Luis. She shouldn't have done that. Maxie had to clear her mind and for that she needed to relax completely. The only good thing about Karl not being here was that she could watch whatever she wanted. Even before the divorce, he used to stay in his room most of the night but very occasionally he'd pop his head round the door to see what she was watching. Any hint of a romcom and he'd be gone with a contemptuous groan so throughout his late-teens Maxie had taken to watching heists and car chases in an attempt to lure him onto the sofa with her. It used to work.

Cleansed and restored by the shower, Maxie strolled back into the kitchen and opened the fridge door. It didn't contain much but at least there was cheese. She poured herself a glass of red wine, grabbed a handful of oat biscuits from the cupboard and put them all on a tray to take into the living room.

'Not bothering to cook – just booze in front of the TV. I am such a divorcee cliché. Now what have we got on tonight?' she said to herself picking up the remote control. 'Ha! *The First Wives Club*, that sounds about right.'

Maxie watched Goldie Hawn and Bette Midler get revenge on their ex-husbands until the cheese and biscuits were gone and the wine glass empty. She cleared up and then returned to the sofa telling herself she'd go to bed after she'd seen the final song. She'd watched this ancient film too many times and always felt cheered by the musical finale – however schmaltzy it might be. She plumped up the cushions, relaxed along the length of the sofa and started singing along.

"Don't tell me what to do ..." were her favourite words from the song. It could have been her anthem on splitting up from her husband. As she belted out the words, she began to imagine Kelly having it as her anthem too. Where on earth was that young woman? Maxie thought that having a night off the case would help her think more clearly but she'd now had a couple of hours to relax and felt revitalised. She roused herself, flicked off the TV, collected her briefcase from where she'd dumped it earlier this evening and started looking through her notes and listening to her voice recordings.

Maxie was known at the university for asking her criminal psychology students to try walking a mile in a suspect's shoes. She tried to get them to imagine what it felt like to be that person and in doing so to understand why they might have committed the crime. The students really came to life during these sessions and it seemed like the right thing to do now. It would probably help her understand all the players in Kelly's life a little better. She started with Rowan as she'd seen her most recently. What did it feel like to be Rowan?

Maxie got up and walked around the room directing her imaginary supermarket employees, feeling good when shelves were full or tills were ringing. She went to the staff room and enjoyed the respect of her assistants, the praise of her regional director. At work Rowan floated in her shoes, life was good. Still as Rowan, Maxie opened the young woman's imaginary front door. Her legs were heavy now. She pictured seeing the mess left behind by Kelly, hearing the noise of her having sex. Rowan's legs were still heavy when she followed Kelly on a night out. Maxie imagined what it was like for Rowan as she watched Kelly having the time of her life, not noticing that her best friend was sitting propped on a stool, desperate to get home after a day spent lugging heavy deliveries around a huge supermarket. As Maxie stood in Rowan's shoes, she noticed her mood had changed and Rowan wasn't just weary, she was angry. Her legs weren't just heavy it was as if her blood were replaced with liquid vitriol. Her veins itched so badly, she clawed at her skin. Her feet wanted to kick out. To kick and stamp until the source of her anger was no longer there. Then she wanted to run.

'Is this how you felt Rowan?' Maxie said to her reflection in the mirror. 'Did you want to end her manipulation of you once and for all?'

Maxie shook herself into her own body and took a glug of wine just to be sure she was back. It was obviously all conjecture but she needed to imagine why even the most unlikely person might be holding something back. Rowan had freely said she'd be glad to wave goodbye to Kelly once and for all but would she really hurt the person she'd spent so much of life trying to keep out of trouble? And if she would, how would she do it? She might feel like kicking out but she wouldn't do that. Would she turn a blind eye if Kelly was out of her depth? Perhaps. Maxie could imagine Rowan becoming so frustrated that she'd let Kelly "make her bed and lie in it". Perhaps she came out of the toilets a moment earlier than she'd said, perhaps she saw her friend merrily going off with that hooded figure. Harry had originally intended Luis to fall for Rowan, perhaps that night she saw her chance. But even with Kelly out of the picture, would Luis fall for the quiet one in the end? This wasn't a movie script.

What did Luis's shoes feel like? As ludicrous as this process seemed to many people, Maxie was finding it giving her fresh perspective. In stepping into Luis's imaginary boots, she instantly stood taller. No longer the overlooked friend, she was now tall, handsome and strong. She gripped her hands into fists just to get a sense of that strength she now possessed. With that strength came a bloody bad temper and she found her breathing deepening, her nostrils flaring and her brow scowling as she got into character. Now these were the shoes of a person who could make a rash move. Just like the hulk, he'd turn green, rip off his shirt and do untold damage before sinking back into his rational self. Did he go to meet Kelly rather than going straight home as he'd said? Did he see her with another man? Did he chase him off and shake Kelly so badly that he hurt her? Has she bolted or is she hiding because she doesn't feel safe? When Maxie did the imaginary walk home in Luis's shoes, the weight of them made her sink into the sofa. She now felt the loneliness and sadness she'd seen in his eyes during their road trip. She threw off Luis's shoes. The problem with both Rowan and Luis being that neither of them could bear the guilt if they'd caused any harm to Kelly. Perhaps that's why they hadn't been able to share the same space for any length of time since the disappearance. They imagined the guilt showing in their eyes.

Maxie wished she could put on Kelly's shoes but she hadn't met her and the second-hand reports just weren't enough. She hadn't been lying to Andrew though. Twenty years ago that could have been her up on the dance floor. She remembered what it felt like to be centre of attention, to be the one always chatted up. Maxie raised her hands in the air and started dancing as she'd seen Kelly do in the video. It wasn't how she used to dance but without a doubt, it made her feel a little happier, a little younger and certainly more carefree. Maxie picked up the remote control and switched on a channel with party music. It wasn't to her taste but she could imagine a twenty-something enjoying it. She turned the volume up and turned towards the sofa, dancing for the imaginary audience that sat there. An R & B track started and the women in the video left little to the imagination. Maxie sexed up her moves and beckoned to the cushion eyeing her up. She picked it up and gyrated with it till the end of the song then exhausted she collapsed onto the sofa and threw her dance partner into the corner. She needed another drink. She pictured the video, Kelly dancing and downing shots. However – Kelly hadn't been snogging anyone despite the indignation of the general public.

'Do people even say snogging anymore?' Maxie asked the cushion.

Whatever the new word was for the age-old activity, Kelly hadn't been doing it. She was a girl out for a good time. A good time without being encumbered by her bodyguard of a boyfriend.

'So where did you go then Kelly? When Rowan was in the loo and you thought she'd left without you?'

In Maxie's heyday, she'd loved the chase too. Just to know that she could have almost any guy in the room even when she didn't actually want any of them. She wanted an escorted passage home and a cosy bed. She hated even staying over at friends because that would mean she couldn't lie in for the whole of the next day. Kelly had a gorgeous man waiting for her at home so what if Kelly just wanted to get back to him? With no Rowan to escort her, she'd have latched on instantly to the mysterious person she seemed to know – even if she hadn't known them that well. Maybe they were just a colleague rather than a friend; she'd ask Orlando, although none of his team claimed to be out at the club with Kelly, they might be lying and he might know which of the team would be most likely to stay out all night or perhaps had a crush on Kelly. She could ask him when they went round to hear his ideas for helping find Kelly and if Andrew were with her, well there'd be less chance of her making a complete fool of herself again.

Happy with a plan of action, Maxie relaxed again. The music show had moved on to love songs and she lay down on the sofa to watch Sinead O'Connor shed a single tear on screen. It never failed to move her – that genuine-looking heartbreak. She sobbed and it was no longer about the song or about Kelly but about her own loneliness, her hope that one day life might not feel this empty and the fear that it always would. Maxie cried herself to sleep.

The sound of people laughing outside as they walked home from the pub woke Maxie up. The music was long finished and some ancient detective series seemed to be filling the screen now. Maxie switched it off instantly, it being the last thing she needed before going to bed. She dragged herself off the sofa and stretched. She looked at her red-rimmed eyes in her phone but smiled at herself – she'd needed that. Maxie peered through the blinds to see the group that had woken her saying their goodbyes and heading off in different directions. She remembered Karl wouldn't be home tonight but decided against putting on the security chain in case he changed his mind. She thought about sending a message just to check he was okay then decided against it. "Paranoid mother syndrome" Karl would call it. What the heck, she'd rather be a paranoid mother than the mother of a missing son; she sent a text.

Got your note – have a good time.

Getting nothing back, Maxie went to bed and lay in the dark room listening to the silence. She thought through her conversation with Luis and the weight of emptiness they shared. If Karl didn't come back, she'd be totally and utterly alone. The past twenty years of her life had seen her juggling her career, her home and her family. She'd been happy enough with that, any spare time or a quiet moment she had would be spent soaking in the bath or in front of the TV with her husband, not nurturing the female friendships she might wish she had now. How quickly the noise and turmoil of family turns quiet.

She picked up her phone and opened the dating app. Karl wouldn't be around forever. He had a life to live. Unless she wanted to be talking to herself and watching crap movies every night, she had to get back out there. She swiped through the supposed matches to her profile but none of them seemed worth the effort. Perhaps she should start with something else, maybe try and make some friends first. Where do you get friends?

She searched for social groups in the area: book club – too dull; film club – not likely to be watching chick flicks; running club – you've got to be joking. Maybe this one, social outings for women over forty. Outings? It sounded more like the old people's home they'd gone to for Mrs Claus. She could imagine Karl's scorn when she told him she was going to an over-40s social club in the new year. Her phone buzzed with a message.

CU tmrw – will need bacon ☺

Maxie breathed a sigh of relief. Her son was coming back for breakfast at least.

Chapter Nineteen

Wednesday, 21 December

As Maxie made her way through the police station to Andrew's desk, she could see he'd a rough day already. He stood up before she reached him and beckoned a finger at her. She followed and from his direction of travel Maxie could tell they were going to see the new DI.

'So where are we on this missing girl?' asked the inspector from behind his desk. He didn't invite either Maxie or Andrew to sit down but Maxie did anyway, leaving Andrew looking like a naughty schoolboy. The DI glared at Maxie then signalled for Andrew to sit too. Andrew updated him on the case.

'So we're nowhere,' the DI said. 'And has the furore from that ridiculous appeal died down yet?'

'It's starting to, boss,' replied Andrew.

The DI looked across at Maxie. 'I know the ACU have permission to look into a missing person case but I don't think you're going to get much out of this one or be much help to me,' he said.

'I don't know,' said Maxie. 'We're already seeing how unconscious bias hinders the investigation. Previous research has focussed on the court system but it evidently begins much earlier.'

'As I said, not much help to me,' he said. Then looking directly at Andrew he asked, 'Do you suspect the boyfriend of having anything to do with her disappearance?'

'There's no evidence to that effect,' Andrew said.

'But something is keeping her from coming home,' added Maxie. 'I'm pretty sure of that.'

'Here's what I think,' said the DI getting up from his desk and walking around the office. 'We have a functioning adult who decided not to come home. No body, no leads and a history of similar behaviour. She's been gone five days and that's long enough for something to have been found. It's long enough to have gone anywhere in the world.'

'But we know she hasn't used her passport even if we can't find it,' said Maxie. Her phone beeped with a message and on automatic pilot she took it out and looked at it.

'Professor but she could be anywhere in the UK, you know as well as I do if you want to truly vanish off the face of the earth you lie low first of all until all the interest is over – if you're not too busy with other business obviously.'

There was an awkward silence as he turned his back on Maxie and Andrew and gazed out of the window.

'What's your next step?' he asked without turning round.

'DS Dawson has a follow-up meeting with Kelly's employer later this morning,' said Maxie holding up her phone. 'That was a message from him.'

'Okay, I know Orlando. Let's hear what he has to say. You have until Friday to make some progress. I want a narrative to explain our thinking on Kelly and then I want you to move on and leave it with Missing Persons. Focus on the boyfriend and friends – if there is foul play at hand here, then nine times out of ten, it's personal. I don't want this case devouring our scant resources past Christmas Eve.'

The DI turned to face them and with a look, they were dismissed.

Andrew punched the wall as they walked down the corridor. 'We've got to find something and soon,' he said. 'Or Kelly will join the purgatory of the missing, just a face on a database. The case won't be closed but it won't be active either. I feel as if we're letting everyone down – especially the Hendrys. I'm not sure I could sit down to turkey and roasties not knowing where she is.'

'Then let's get moving,' said Maxie.

'Where to?'

'That PR company of hers,' Maxie said. 'I wasn't lying in there. They said they've come up with an idea to find her.'

'Like what?' said Andrew. 'Not another appeal to backfire? The DI will have my guts for that.'

'I have no idea but there isn't much time so let's move. Give me one minute and then I'll drive.'

Maxie wafted into the ladies' toilets. When she emerged, her hair was brushed, the mascara reapplied, and her lips were a glossy red.

'You ready for action?' she asked Andrew as he stared, jaw dropped at his battle-ready companion. Maxie nodded meekly hoping she hadn't overdone it.

'Not as ready as you look but as much as I'll ever be.' Andrew smiled at her.

As they marched through each set of double doors, side by side, they could have been the odd couple from any TV cop show.

‘So turkey and roasties?’ asked Maxie as they got into her car. ‘You have a traditional Christmas then?’

‘Oh yeah,’ Andrew said. ‘I love it, what about you?’

‘I’ve always preferred the Boxing Day curry,’ replied Maxie. ‘Give me spices over sprouts any day of the week.’

They pulled up outside Orlando’s office building and Maxie purposefully parked in one of the electric vehicle bays. Andrew looked at her, raising his eyebrows in disapproval.

‘Don’t you just hate it when someone tells you not to do something?’ She smiled.

The receptionist had only just put down the phone after informing Orlando of their arrival when he rushed up to greet them.

‘Fabulous, you’re here! I have so much to show you,’ he gushed.

Maxie and Andrew followed him as he hurried down the familiar corridors but this time he didn’t bother with the history lesson. He lead them past his office to a door which had a big thought bubble declaring *“Thinking Space – Leave Negativity Here ☺”* on the outside. Maxie resisted rolling her eyes.

Orlando opened the door with a flourish. ‘Welcome to the War Room.’

Inside, the room looked like something from a TV charity event. The walls were festooned with huge pictures of Kelly at her party-loving best: tongue out, cleavage flashing, a drink in each hand. A graffiti-style banner read “Kelly’s Army”, loud music played and young interns manned laptops and mobiles. The noise was intoxicating. Luis was already there standing at the centre as if conducting an orchestra. He turned to face Maxie, his face more alive than she’d ever seen it.

‘Isn’t this amazing?’ He beamed. ‘They’re going to get every young person in this town looking for her.’

Orlando took over. ‘The problem with the last appeal was that her parents tried to portray Kelly as something she wasn’t. The public felt cheated when they saw the real girl,’ he explained.

‘That’s true,’ said Maxie listening to her words reworked.

‘After what you said about unconscious bias’—Orlando’s cheeks were rosy with excitement—‘I had this idea – let’s get people to confront their own bias. This time we’re going to celebrate everything that Kelly is. To tell the holier-than-thou that they have no place here, we’re all valuable citizens no matter how we like to relax.’

'And what about the clients you were worried about? Don't they mind you being on this side of the fence?' asked Maxie.

Orlando shook his head. 'They've been great actually. I spoke to them after you left and explained what had happened,' he said. 'Lots of them have teenage daughters, know what it's like and they'd want people to look out for them. We've even managed to get the campaign sponsored so we can host another appeal across all media, put up a reward and give these interns a little Christmas bonus.'

Orlando flashed his several thousand pound smile and Maxie couldn't stop the stirring in that long forgotten hollow. Damn it, she shouldn't be finding this guy attractive at all. He was one of life's winners, the type who always landed butter-side up and she knew they didn't go for people like her. Or at least they never used to; Orlando winked at her before turning his attention to Andrew who was looking about the room as if Christmas had come early.

'My boss will probably even go for this,' he said. 'It'll help with his inclusivity commitments.'

Maxie could see that this could well be the narrative the DI was looking for and best of all, someone else would be paying for it. It would look good for the force as a whole and by engaging a local business he would be able to demonstrate that he could reach out to all communities. It would show that the force was doing everything possible and even if Kelly weren't found this campaign was innovative, inclusive and high profile. Who knows, it might even work.

'I know,' Orlando said. 'I called him just before you got here and he loves it.'

It was no surprise to Maxie that he'd already spoken to the DI and could imagine them attending the same charity balls or being members of the same gym. At the mention of the word gym, Maxie suddenly had an image of Orlando in the sauna dressed only in a towel. She pushed it to the back of her mind as quickly as she could.

'So Luis is going to front the appeal,' continued Orlando. 'He's already known to the media – maybe for the wrong reasons at the moment but we can change that. The DI also wants to appear emphasising the commitment and resource going into this search but we have time for someone else if you want to say a few words too?'

Andrew shook his head and said he had no desire to say anything. 'But what about George and Patricia?' he suggested. 'They can challenge people's perceptions about Kelly – show that she's not some two dimensional character.'

'Good idea,' said Maxie. 'And I can get my students to help spread the word and I know Craig Johnston will host a podcast special featuring this – it's quite a broad audience.'

Orlando rubbed his hands together with glee. 'Brilliant,' he said. 'We've got a live broadcast this morning on Facebook and then we'll be seeding the story everywhere on the internet to carry it through the day and evening. This team are going to pull a twenty-four hour shift sifting through the information we get. I imagine that you'll want to be here with them deciding what's worth pursuing and what isn't? The DI was okay with that if you are.'

'Which means it's not actually an option,' replied Andrew. 'Maxie – what about you, will you stay?'

As if reading her thoughts, Orlando added, 'We could do with all that brainpower here if you can make it. I'm staying all night.'

'I'll pack my jimjams.' Maxie smiled.

Orlando and Andrew were called away by one of the PR team so left Maxie to look around on her own. It was impressive and if energy alone could find Kelly, then they had every chance of success.

'It's good of you to get involved,' she said to one girl scouring the internet.

'I had to. When I saw what they were saying about her just coz she likes a drink? Hell, I get plastered with my mates all the time so they're like basically saying that if I were murdered or something, it would be like, totally okay. That I deserved it.'

Maxie nodded, exactly her sentiments. Maybe this little army would get the victory she felt Kelly deserved. Maxie wasn't exactly sure what role she'd be playing but she knew she'd need an overnight bag. There was no telling what the appeal would throw up. She might have to sit here all night, visit homes, appear on TV or scour the streets. She was still the public face of the Criminology department, a local university professor and she needed a few things to cover all possibilities. Not wanting to leave the war room so close to the broadcast, she called Karl.

'Hi, did I get you up? Look I'm really sorry but there's going to be a twenty-four hour vigil to try and find Kelly and I wondered if you'd mind packing me some things?'

Maxie's face lit up with surprise as she listened to the response. 'Brilliant, see you soon.'

‘Who was that?’ asked Orlando coming back to stand at her side.

‘My son, Karl,’ she replied. ‘Who has not only already heard about this operation through social media but also wants to be part of it. He’s even bringing his girlfriend over to help.’

Orlando nodded approvingly.

‘I can’t remember a time when any man has actually asked to spend a whole night with me, let alone a whole room full of men,’ added Maxie as she looked around the room.

‘I can’t imagine that for one minute.’

Maxie raised her palm for him to stop right there. ‘Let’s just focus shall we.’

At 11a.m. the launch of Kelly’s Army was about to broadcast live. The DI had arrived and looked the ultimate professional. A wardrobe assistant was helping Luis to pick something suitable. They went for a Christmassy red sweater with the sleeves rolled up to reveal his tattoos. The make-up woman ruffled his wavy hair a little and applied a little powder to take the shine off both Luis and the detective inspector. They were ready.

As the cameras rolled, they both sat on the edge of a desk with the war room in the background. The banner and the sponsor’s name dominated the back wall. It was so unlike the appeal Kelly’s parents had done. Maxie panicked for a split second, not knowing whether anyone had asked their permission to do this. She looked round for Andrew and then calmed as she saw Mrs Ingles being led into the back of the room. Karl and his girlfriend were not far behind and he waved at his mum as he wove through the crowded room to hand her the overnight bag.

‘There’s a queue of people trying to help,’ he whispered, wary of the lights and cameras now springing into action. ‘If we hadn’t have been with you, they would have turned us away.’

‘It’s like you’re a celebrity – can you get us into gigs too?’ Olivia laughed, getting an affectionate nudge in return.

Maxie laughed with Olivia and her heart had skipped a little because her son seemed pleased to be with her again – at last.

The production team called for quiet and as a determined silence fell over the room, the countdown to the broadcast began,

‘Three, two, one and we’re … live.’

Luis spoke. ‘We are all here because five days ago, my girlfriend Kelly went missing.’

He held up a picture of them both.

'Her mother made an appeal to find her but it didn't work, in fact it was a disaster. It didn't because Kelly isn't perfect and some people out there think you should only care about perfect people. The rest of us you can just ignore.'

Luis swept his arm to one side in a throwaway gesture and his eyes blazed. He was the perfect TV hero. Maxie watched through the monitor as the cameraman closed in on Luis's intense face – Helmsforth's answer to Antonio Banderas.

'My girlfriend drinks – a lot. She parties like there is no tomorrow and she flirts so much it drives me crazy. She has a lot of piercings, and I mean *everywhere.* Some would say she's the wrong sort of girl to care about – the kind your mother warns you about.'

He laughed and the whole room laughed with him. He was mesmerising.

'But you know mothers aren't always right.'

Maxie glanced at Karl who was nodding along smiling.

'So tonight I want to appeal to everyone who isn't perfect, who has a son or daughter who isn't perfect. Would they be worth finding? Then so is Kelly.

'And I don't mean for you to just share her picture on social media – that's no good to me. I want you to get off your asses and look. Look in your street, in your bar, your shop, your school, your hotel – has she been there? The police cannot cover every inch of this county, but together we can cover the whole country if we choose. And if anything ever happens to you, I promise I will return this favour. I will look for you personally.'

Luis finished off pointing directly at the camera and the room erupted into applause. The camera panned across to the DI who formalised the search saying that the force cared about everyone in the county and that they'd take any leads seriously. He announced the reward being offered by the sponsor, repeated the description of Kelly, showed a photograph of her very distinctive shooting-star tattoo and relayed the contact details for anyone with news or thoughts.

'None of us are perfect but all of us *are* important.' The DI ended with the catchphrase he'd probably been practising.

His section went well and he managed to look both authoritative and caring. After him, George and Patricia were interviewed by Orlando; they explained how Kelly visited them every week and how they loved to hear about her shenanigans.

'She makes us feel young again,' said Patricia, snuggling into George.

As soon as the recording went live the room started buzzing with requests for interviews, with information and with contributions to the reward pot. Maxie breathed a sigh of relief – this type of appeal had truly resonated and people were finally looking for Kelly.

Chapter Twenty

As she looked around the room of strangers who had come together to find Kelly, Maxie noted both Rowan and Harry were absent. Maxie could imagine that Rowan would be elbow deep in parsnips or Brussel sprouts but she wondered why Harry hadn't come to support his friends. Maxie decided to leave Kelly's Army for a couple of hours and go speak to him again. She found Andrew who was trying to get the whole platoon organised. While Orlando and the DI patted each other on the back for having launched this initiative, they'd glossed over the details on how it would actually work. Maxie knew that for Andrew, too much information would be almost as useless as too little. Without a leader or directions, it wasn't an army, it was a mob. She had to give him a hand before she went anywhere.

'What can I do?' she asked him.

Andrew was setting up a timeline focussing on sightings of Kelly since her disappearance. It was similar to the one they had at the station and seeing it, Maxie shook her head.

'You need to focus on the week or weeks beforehand now,' she told him. 'If she planned to run away or vanish from her family as you suspect, the chances are she made some arrangements way before any of this actually began.'

Maxie took over the organisation and helped to clear the walls on every side of the room to create huge spaces for each day of the week that volunteers could fill as the information flowed in. The hour by hour account was important so the spaces were divided into morning, afternoon and evening slots. She gave them a colour coding so that information which was confirmed was posted on the wall using a green post-it note and if it were speculative, they had to use orange.

'Okay, I think they know what to do,' she told Andrew when she'd finished. 'I'm going to head out for a couple of hours if that's okay with you. I'll be on the mobile if you need me.'

Maxie left Andrew and got into her car, turning it towards Harry's warehouse. It was bitterly cold and dark clouds hovered over the town like enemy spacecraft ready to spill forth more torrents at an hour of their choosing. The sleet had stopped and there was no wind. The air was still and a sense of anticipation hung as if the elements were joining in the twenty-four hour search. They were giving the population a chance to look for Kelly without the hoods or umbrellas that kept everyone blinkered. Maxie drove past a tattoo parlour and saw a young woman posting a picture of Kelly in the window. Then she saw a hairdresser with blue spiky hair who was handing out the picture to people passing in the street. It was happening.

Maxie continued her journey back to Harry's warehouse building. It was easy to see why he'd want to work here. The redeveloped riverside was now home to the bright shiny offices of the internet companies and marketing agencies who would probably commission his work. Maxie marvelled at how the old Victorian mills sat comfortably alongside newly built buildings with shiny glass facades which caught and reflected the ominously clouded skies. The whole place held a mystique for Maxie. Everything inside these buildings was fake, just an image to be shared. The area kind of reminded her of those Hollywood films she used to watch where the producers would drive around the studios in those little golf carts. Every warehouse they visited would house something completely different. Inside one would be the pyramids of ancient Egypt while another might house a lunar landing. Maxie mused that it must be nice to work with make-believe rather than have to justify every element of your work with statistics and robust methodology just for once. Maxie reached Harry's building and turned onto the rugged tarmac outside that served as the car park.

She guessed she'd find Harry still here and she was right. She walked freely around the inside of the building marvelling again at the lush green grass and bright sunshine that still filled the space. They'd evidently finished their Easter egg shoot and had moved on to another of Maxie's favourites. She found Harry just outside the poky little room they'd spoken in instructing his team on the new shoot. He looked up and saw her but continued talking.

'You've moved from chocolate to wine,' said Maxie looking around. 'I approve.'

Harry finished giving his instructions before dismissing the team and turning his attention to the unwelcome visitor.

'Well we had the whole thing set up so with just a few changes, spring became summer and it was perfect for chilled summer wine shots. Our clients get a lower cost because we're set up anyway and they're ahead of their advertising schedules which is always a good thing in this business.'

Maxie looked at the set and it clicked, the trees were now simply lush green leaves having been stripped of their blossom and instead of daffodils around the fake lawns, there were roses.

'I still think what you do here is totally amazing,' she said trying to engage Harry who was keeping this meeting very business-like. 'I'll never look at anything in magazines in quite the same way.'

'Nothing is ever as it seems,' stated Harry making him the second person to have said that to her over the past few days. Karl had said it too.

Harry turned and walked into the room, busying himself with tidying up that Maxie suspected wouldn't have been sorted out if he weren't trying to avoid a conversation with her. It wouldn't work.

'Have you seen the initiative your boss is putting together?'

'Orlando isn't my boss, he's a client,' bristled Harry. 'I am my own boss.'

'Sorry.'

Silence again until Maxie started picking up some photographs. Harry took them from her abruptly.

'Yes, I have heard about it. It seems like a good idea and I'm sure he'll do very well from it,' he said.

'Hundreds of people out there hunting for a girl they don't even know, incredible really,' said Maxie.

'If they find her they're pretty much guaranteed their fifteen minutes. It's not that incredible or altruistic in this day and age.'

'You're even more cynical than I am.' Maxie smiled. 'I didn't think that was possible.'

The ice was broken and Harry offered to make Maxie a coffee which she didn't really want but accepted all the same.

'Did you not feel like being down there? Giving Luis some moral support?'

Harry handed her the cup, shaking his head. 'Do you have any children Professor Reddick?'

'A twenty-year-old son.'

'And would you want him going out with Kelly?'

'I don't want him going out with anyone at all really. He has to stay with his mum all his life.'

Harry sat down and Maxie followed suit. 'What was that expression that other copper used on TV – "none perfect, all important"?'

The PR team really got that slogan spot on.

'Well I totally agree with that. It wasn't so long ago that people would have said I deserved everything I got being openly gay. You must remember all the HIV hysteria and people saying that if we died then it was our own fault? We should all be able to be true to ourselves and not be at risk of harm.'

'I'm sensing a "but" coming.'

'*But* ... you also have to respect other people's feelings and not treat them like shit. Luis adores that woman and yet there she was all over the internet, draped over some no-hoper. Rowan also adores her friend but time and time again, Ro is left to get her out of trouble. I have to listen to them both telling me how hilarious she is, how the good times more than make up for the bad. Let me tell you, no one is that hilarious. I'm glad she's decided to go. I'm delighted to see the back of her.'

Maxie raised her eyebrows at the outflow of honesty. If Karl brought home someone who kept breaking his heart, she'd probably feel the same. Maxie stayed calm in her questioning.

'So you think she's gone of her own accord?'

Harry nodded. 'I do and really it's the best thing for everyone around her especially Rowan but Luis too. He might find someone worthwhile now.'

Harry then looked directly into Maxie's eyes. 'I hope this disappearance makes him think again about the proposal and if she does turn up again, he decides not to go through with it. It would have been good of her to say goodbye but she is probably doing just fine somewhere and trust me we're all better off without her. Now I'm sure you've got much better things to do. I know I do.'

There was something very deliberate and finite in Harry's words. 'Do you know where she is?' asked Maxie.

Harry raised his eyebrows. 'What a stupid question.'

One that he hadn't answered. Somehow Maxie suspected that if he did, he wouldn't volunteer the information if it meant Kelly coming home too soon. One of Harry's assistants knocked on the door and popped her head round to ask for his sign off. He told her he'd be there in a few seconds.

'I have to get back to work.' He held the door open for her.

'Would you mind me staying for a while and having a little look around? I do love this place,' said Maxie.

'You won't find anything incriminating if that's what you're thinking,' replied Harry. 'But if I say no you'll call that detective and you'll both come back with a warrant won't you? So go on, fill your boots. The set is on lockdown so stay away from the tech stuff but knock yourself out with the rest of the place; you can rummage anywhere else that takes your fancy.'

He left her to it and as soon as he was out of sight, Maxie started looking in boxes, opening cupboards, drawers and doors. She wasn't sure what she was looking for but Harry seemed like the kind of guy who would have helped Kelly disappear if she'd asked him. He obviously wanted her out of his friends' lives.

The warehouse looked grungy but it was extremely well organised, like a car mechanics workshop. To an outsider it looked like chaos but she imagined Harry and his team were within arm's reach of whatever tool they needed for the job. There was nothing that raised her suspicions, nothing that looked out of place, or as if it had been moved recently. She stepped outside to look at the rubbish crates and saw rows of coloured skips to indicate the recycling that they should contain. Maxie wished she had some of Andrew's junior officers with her so he could instruct them to do this dirty part but she didn't so she held her breath and opened the first one. It was labelled "paper & card" so she reckoned on it being the least vile. It was empty. Maxie was both relieved to have been spared the job of going through it and disappointed that she'd found nothing. The other skips were empty too. If there had been any evidence disposed of here, the extremely efficient borough council had now made sure it was long gone.

Maxie stood outside the warehouse trying to collect her thoughts. Today she felt torn apart by the weight of opinion about Kelly. As if she were the flag in the middle of a tug-of-war rope. One side pulled hard to say find her at all cost, the other tugged equally hard to say let her go, she's just not worth it. Both sides would do everything they could to convince Maxie they were right. She'd let everyone get to her and had lost her objectivity.

It didn't matter what anyone thought of Kelly, Andrew had until Christmas Eve to find out where she'd gone and then the case would be allowed to go cold and she couldn't bear the thought of a mother, even a bad one, waking up on Christmas Day not knowing where her child was. Maxie checked her watch. She still had eleven hours of this day to get some answers; Harry had cleverly directed her search ensuring she stayed away from the set and any technology, so she needed the police to go back and look at the places he didn't want them to see.

‘Andrew?’ she called down the phone. ‘I’m down at Looking Glass Productions. It’s Harry’s company and I’ve got a real sense that he’s not telling you everything he knows. I think you need to look at his computers to see if he’s booked any travel for Kelly.’

Andrew told her he’d send someone over but that she should probably call back into the war room while it happened. Maxie didn’t want to leave yet. She still felt that this place held some clues so she decided to stay and have a sugar boost instead. That would put her back on track and help her think things through. There had to be a place for cake around here. Maxie walked away from the warehouse and after only a couple of minutes, she realised she was near the Christmas market Mrs Claus had visited. If you turned one way out of the warehouse you were among other similar buildings but turn the other way and you found trendy streets with bars and cafés – exactly what she needed right now. Maxie settled into a quiet coffee shop and ordered a slice of chocolate cake. “Thinking food” she liked to call it. When it arrived, the slice was enormous and piled high with chocolate sauce and cream.

‘Oh my goodness, how on earth am I going to manage all of this,’ she lied to the waitress.

Maxie dug her spoon into the plate of pure pleasure and slowly let the chocolate work its magic. She always told people that not only would the endorphins in the sugar lift her mood but the caffeine in the chocolate would ping around her head and revitalise her brain cells. Despite his brusqueness with her, Maxie quite liked Harry although she now wondered just how far Harry would go to get Kelly out of his friends’ lives for good. He appeared to have his own moral code and if lying during a police investigation was the price of achieving his goal then she could imagine him doing that. He’d see it as “the greater good”. Maxie was convinced he knew more than he was saying but would have to wait until there was some evidence to go on. There was nothing she could do right now so she finished her cake, left a healthy tip and walked back out into the market. A truck with Christmas trees trussed up in netting went past and she saw that someone had plonked a ballerina Barbie on top of one of them. Maxie smiled. The angel looked far from comfortable with a tree up her backside.

Her mind clicked back to a jewellery box her older sister had. Every time she opened the lid, it played a tune and released a twirling ballerina. Her sister was much trendier than she was so Maxie was usually trying to borrow a necklace or earrings for going out and her sister would hear that tune and call for her to put whatever she'd taken back. Eventually Maxie realised that if she held the ballerina still then the music didn't play and she could select what she wanted without anyone knowing. One night she'd taken one of her sister's favourite chokers and worn it to a festival. She partied all night and woke up in a stranger's bed with a raging hangover but no choker. Her sister looked everywhere for it, very distressed that she'd lost a piece of jewellery she'd had since she was a girl. Maxie lied and said she had no idea where it was and she even helped to search for it. After her sister was killed she left the box and all of her jewellery to Maxie. It wasn't valuable but Maxie couldn't even look at it. To her the absence of that one piece embodied every petty row she'd had with her sister. And the ballerina hadn't twirled for some time now.

Chapter Twenty-One

'Did you know there were this many army themed songs?' asked Andrew greeting Maxie as she returned to the war room. He held out his phone to show her the "Kelly's Army" soundtrack set up on Spotify.

Maxie mused that she could probably only have thought of "Oliver's Army" but it had been very many years since she even listened to the chart show – if such a thing still existed. She stored that thought away as something to ask Karl later on. Now that he was back in her home, she liked to have a range of topics ready so the conversation never got dull. He enjoyed mocking her reminisces of "the good old days" which Maxie still found a rather bizarre term to use for the 1990s.

'You're hearing these tunes everywhere now. It was a really good idea,' continued Andrew. 'One of the volunteers came up with it.'

Maxie nodded and said it had indeed been an inspired idea as she'd heard one of the tracks playing on her drive back. Now, even without the news footage and appeal, shops and cafés could remind people about the search and get them talking. In the few hours since Luis's broadcast, at least thirty people had come forward with useful snippets of information about Kelly. The team were like puppies, anxious to please and hoping that their caller would be the one to deliver the breakthrough. Maxie watched affectionately as each of them came up to Andrew with that pleading look in their eyes, holding up the piece of paper they'd used to scribble down the details.

'I really think this one could lead somewhere,' they each told him.

So far the calls had revealed a great deal about Kelly's party preparations: she'd had her hair done, a manicure and pedicure, she'd bought several cans of red bull from the corner shop and had taken delivery of a parcel at around noon on the day of her disappearance – the delivery driver remembered her being all dressed up and having a drink in her hand and thought it a bit early for that. As Maxie reviewed these finer details, they still simply told the story of a young woman ready to party and having a little livener before going out. The timelines for the days after the party were a blaze of unconfirmed orange. These were the details that had to be checked out although those from people who still felt that the devil had taken her to punish her for her evil ways could be eliminated. Not for the first time, Maxie wondered why people bothered contacting them with such rubbish and pondered whether the psychology of fake callers might not be a useful research area for one of her students.

'Excuse me.' A gentle voice interrupted Maxie's thought flow.

She turned to Olivia holding out a sheet of paper. Her son Karl appeared behind her, arms folded like a bodyguard. The protective, proud stance told Maxie just how much her son cared about this girl.

'This call is slightly outside the priority timescales but Olivia thinks it might be important and I agree with her,' Karl said.

Maxie nodded and took the piece of paper. It noted the contact details of a clothing store. Karl took his mother by the arm into the corridor and Olivia followed them.

'Tell Mum what she said,' Karl prompted.

Olivia spoke and Maxie nodded with an overt display of authority. This person meant a lot to her son and she had to take the lead seriously. If she dismissed it, she risked losing the ground she'd gained with him. Even if this were another alien abduction theory she'd have to promise to look into it but to her immense relief, it was new information and she suspected it really was worth following up.

'I'll go now, while they're still open,' she said. 'Thanks for this, it shows real insight.'

She nodded at Karl who shrugged but the pride and relief he really felt had already coloured his cheeks. Olivia was smiling too and Maxie left them to talk while she signalled Andrew to join her outside. He listened to what she'd just learned and grabbed his coat.

After the cloudy day and then the glaring lights of the war room, the beauty and serenity of the clear black sky and early moon calmed them both as they headed to the car. A thick frost was threatening and it would no doubt lead to speculations and hope of a white Christmas. Maxie took a deep breath, tasting the freshness of air that hadn't been already exhaled by a roomful of anxious hopefuls. This was the longest night of the year, the winter equinox. Tomorrow they'd start to get more daylight hours and if Maxie remembered her pagan folklore correctly, the earth would be reborn, hope would abound and darkness, in all senses of the word, would be banished.

'If you could send us a bit of light tonight, I'll be eternally grateful,' she called to the heavens.

'I wouldn't have put you down as a Believer,' said Andrew.

'I'll believe in anyone or anything right now. Isn't there a god for lost things in some religion?'

‘I think he finds keys not people – I’ll drive.’

Maxie smiled then got into Andrew’s car as he entered the address of the dress shop they were about to visit into the satnav.

‘Have you heard of this place?’ asked Maxie.

Andrew nodded. ‘I have three sisters and they all want dresses from here. It’s very exclusive.’

‘Then they probably don’t do anything in a size sixteen do they?’

‘I think they stop at size six.’ Andrew smiled.

Maxie could picture Andrew as the harassed brother in a chaotic house of young women and wondered whether work was his sanctuary as it frequently had been for her.

‘What do your sisters think about this case?’

‘You don’t want to know.’

Maxie peered over those non-existent spectacles in her “tell me” gesture. Andrew sighed then shook his head before saying, ‘The eldest hopes Kelly isn’t found so that Luis needs comforting.’

Maxie nodded. She imagined a few women who’d watched that appeal were thinking that.

He continued, ‘My mother thinks Kelly’s mother is a disgrace to let her daughter go out like that.’

Another nod, again many mothers would be thinking that.

‘And the youngest two are protesting solidarity with the search just to try and get a tattoo.’

Maxie snorted. The shooting-star tattoo had emerged as a symbol of unity amongst young people concerned about Kelly. Luis’s dismay over symbolic gestures of support ran through her mind. Not only were people sharing her image on social media but they were also downloading her playlist and getting identical body markings. At least they were also out looking for her. Strange how there needed to be a package of activity to get people interested. Solving crime had to have the right marketing for the public to be interested. This could be another very rich vein of research and maybe it could be something Orlando would be interested in funding. He’d surprised her in the end as he hadn’t been all talk after all. He’d known they’d need more than an appeal and he’d captured the imagination of all these new foot soldiers. Maxie made a mental note to thank him as soon as Kelly was found. Just the thought of finding a way to do that warmed her through and through.

They were now leaving Helmsforth and heading towards a far wealthier suburb that was home to dress shops and beauticians of a more celebrity style of social standing.

'One of those reality stars has a boutique here,' said Andrew. 'She's always plugging it on the show.'

Maxie guessed he'd gathered this fact while watching one of his sister's choices but who knows? Maybe this quiet DS was also secretly enthralled by the cult of celebrity.

Christmas buying was in full flow as they arrived in the exclusive shopping area. They queued alongside the sports cars and Range Rovers to crawl through the speed-restricted high street. It wouldn't come as a surprise to Maxie if the speed restriction was nothing to do with safety and was in fact a measure put in place to encourage gawping. This seemed to be a place that liked being looked at. Expensive and tasteful looking Christmas decorations twinkled from shop windows. No major retail brands were housed here, probably because they would have looked very brash against the gentile facades of the upmarket boutiques.

'One day I'll get paid enough to shop here,' said Andrew.

'Somehow I doubt that either of us ever will.'

They reached the shop they were looking for and parked outside on the double yellow lines.

'We might not be able to afford to live here but we cops can still do a few things that they can't,' Andrew told Maxie, looking ridiculously pleased with this small victory.

The scene as they walked through the door was more like a cocktail party than a clothing store. Initially it was hard to tell the shoppers from the staff as they were all stunningly glamorous. Maxie noticed that two-thirds of the people in the room held flutes of champagne and guessed they were the shoppers. The man in the chain-store suit and his large companion in the thick black woollen poncho stood out enough to quickly attract the attention of the store owner. Rather than being rushed to the back of the store out of sight of the customers as Maxie had expected, the owner greeted them with a flourish.

'Oh thank you for coming. We want so much to help dear Kelly.'

The room stopped chatting and tilted its head in empathy towards them both.

'And when I heard what Louisa here had to say, then I knew we had to call you. Is the young man who made the appeal with you?' The owner looked over Andrew's shoulder, hopefully at first and then disappointed when she noted only Maxie.

A beautiful young woman was thrust in their direction. 'Let these lovely people know what happened Louisa.' She opened her mouth to start talking and the room seemed to collectively lean in.

'Do you have somewhere private we could all talk?' Andrew asked the owner although Maxie very much doubted that the story hadn't been repeated several times over already.

The owner led them through to her office where Andrew asked everyone to sit down.

'Take me through everything that you remember Louisa. We're running out of time now so even the smallest detail might be relevant.'

Louisa nodded, took a deep breath and began. 'I saw that really good-looking guy talking about his girlfriend on the news and I thought that I'd seen her before. I wasn't sure at first because we get so many people in the shop especially before Christmas and New Year. Anyone who wants something that isn't chain store comes here.'

'As you can understand, our clientele don't want to turn up at a party and find someone else in the same dress,' chipped in the owner.

Maxie nodded but really didn't understand the problem. No one ever dressed like her. She nodded at Louisa to continue.

'She was lovely and slim so I knew she'd be perfect for our range.'

'Though we are both very surprised to find out that one of our outfits had been worn to that Printworks place,' the owner interjected again getting a scowl from Andrew for the interruption.

'I listened to what she was looking for and brought out a few dresses for her. She was looking for sexy but professional – she said she had an important work party to attend. We always ask customers what they feel is their best feature – it could be their legs, their décolletage even their hair can be enhanced by the right dress – and then we find something to make them stand out from the crowd.'

'So what did Kelly say was her best feature?' asked Maxie.

'Well this is why I'm explaining it all,' replied Louisa. 'It may sound silly but we really do try and find a dress that you may not pick out for yourself. I noticed that Kelly had a beautiful shapely back and I just knew that she'd be one of the few people who could ever carry off one of our backless range. I even thought of asking her to model it for a publicity shot. She really didn't want to but I went off to look for her size anyway while she was trying on other things. I came back and thought she'd heard me approaching so I didn't knock, I just walked right in. She was in her underwear and I know it was definitely her, she had that shooting-star tattoo that's been mentioned.'

'And what happened?' asked Maxie.

'She grabbed her clothes really quickly to hide them but I saw anyway. She couldn't wear anything backless because she was really badly bruised, and I mean really badly, all down one side and along her ribs. It was awful.'

'Did she say what had happened?'

'No and I didn't like to ask. I pretended I hadn't seen them. We're trained to respect our customers' privacy.'

'And what did you do next?'

'I found her a dress which was sexy and short but covered her body.'

The owner handed Maxie a catalogue photograph of the dress she knew Kelly had worn to the party and it would certainly have covered the injuries described.

'You don't think her boyfriend did it, do you?' asked Louisa.

'I can't speculate right now,' Andrew responded. 'And I must stress that you shouldn't either.'

'Of course not,' said the owner. 'Because we also have an exclusive men's range and if he's innocent we'd be delighted to offer him a discount.'

Maxie stifled a laugh of dismay but Andrew scowled.

'I hope you're telling me the truth,' he said. 'Did everything happen exactly as you've described?'

Louisa protested that it had and that she was so sorry she hadn't thought about it earlier. Andrew got up and started walking out of the shop. Maxie thanked Louisa and quickly followed the DS. As they walked out onto the shop floor, the waiting crowd started chatting instantly, pretending that they hadn't just eavesdropped on every single word.

'I would prefer it if you didn't discuss this with the media until we're further into the investigation,' said Andrew, knowing full well that the man with a camera lurking by the doorway was from the local press.

'What did you make of all that?' Andrew asked Maxie when they'd returned to the car.

'It seems everyone has their price for helping us don't they?' replied Maxie. 'They want Luis as a bloody model for God's sake.'

'What did you think of the bruise story? Do you think she was telling the truth?' he asked.

Maxie considered before replying. 'Yes, the young girl seemed genuine. If people are making things up they generally keep their gaze upwards and left but she looked directly at us throughout. She displayed none of the signs of lying to us.'

'It didn't seem to enter their heads that Luis might be the cause of the bruises, did it? I imagine they can't have him branded as a thug if he's to front their "exclusive men's range",' said Andrew. He then added, 'And they didn't offer me that discount, did they?'

'That's their loss,' Maxie said. 'So these bruises – they could be innocent I suppose. Kelly might just have fallen somewhere. People are always falling when they're plastered and she seems to do that a lot. But we have to speak to Luis. He must have known about them.'

Maxie opened the window and sat quietly exhaling a few frosty breaths into the darkness and watching the air dance then disappear. She hoped Luis had nothing to do with them but couldn't help thinking that Kelly would probably laugh the bruises off in the shop if they'd been innocent.

'Shall we go and find Luis?' she said eventually. 'I think this longest night might just have got a little bit longer.'

Chapter Twenty-Two

Rowan sat in the dark scrolling through the posts on social media. Orlando had developed a way for people to change their profile pictures so that they said *"I'm with Kelly's Army"* and so many people who never even knew her were using it. The campaign also encouraged people to post the worst picture of themselves possible with the slogan *"Not perfect, Still Important"* scrawled across it. It was promoted as being the exact opposite of the pouting selfies normally adorning the website.

Rowan imagined most of those posting would take the pictures down as soon as they could – some of them were truly awful. Although Rowan hadn't posted anything, it didn't stop her name appearing online. Mutual friends kept tagging her and Kelly in photographs and most of them were not flattering. The only thing she could do to stop this happening was to delete her account so that's what she was doing right now. It felt good to be out of the clutches of the online frenzy and almost immediately after her profile vanished, she felt her shoulders relax a little. A social media detox was probably healthier for body and soul than giving up alcohol for the whole year.

Next, using Kelly's well-known password, she went through her friend's profile, taking down any pictures Kelly had ever posted of their history together. Rowan wanted a fresh start, she wanted invisibility. After all she'd been through in these past few days, she simply couldn't understand why anyone craved fame. How did they cope with complete strangers commenting on their appearance, damning their actions and in extreme cases, threatening to kill them?

As Rowan went through Kelly's posts, it was like reading her friend's personal diary. It was strange to think that when she'd been a little girl she'd had a diary that she'd locked up each night with a little key to keep things secret. Nothing was secret now. Strangers shared everything with each other, not that the daily lives recorded online were necessarily true. The photographs Kelly posted never told the whole story and for every image, Rowan's memory filled in the backstory.

There were pictures from their graduation where the two girls stood in their mortar boards and gowns, flanked by their proud parents. Even Mrs Ingles came to that event although when they went out for a meal together, Kelly spent the whole evening moving the bottles of wine along the table so her mum couldn't get hold of any. Rowan's mum used to feel so sorry for Kelly and tried to compensate by always inviting Kelly to family parties. Kelly repaid that kindness when she got her job in PR; there she had access to audience tickets for TV shows and every now and then would bring Rowan's mum an autograph from some ancient celebrity who still preferred to sign pieces of paper rather than pose for a picture. Rowan smiled as she remembered her mother's absolute joy in meeting a quiz show host who'd been a radio DJ in her youth. Fortunately he was one of the few who hadn't been arrested in his dotage.

As Rowan deleted photographs taken over the years, she noticed for the first time how much they'd both changed since their university days. They seemed to have morphed into the jobs they'd taken, almost as if that old saying were wrong and "what you do" really is "who you are". Rowan shook her head at the image of her as a naïve girl clutching a bottle of WKD at the Fresher's Ball. She could remember that evening very clearly, everyone seemed to know what they wanted to drink but she had no idea so picked the thing that looked least like alcohol. It had tasted okay. Kelly was there with her usual voddie and tonic – the drink they'd both later adopt. She couldn't recall Kelly ever looking the fish out of water. She always owned the space she was in. The photographs chronicled the lives of the student friends as each grew into their own personalities, one sensibly managing the nation's food supply, the other glamorously keeping the leaders of industry successful and entertained.

The phone rang and Rowan knew who it would be. Her mum was very concerned about Kelly's disappearance and simply couldn't believe all the terrible things being said in the papers. Throughout the years, Rowan had sheltered her mum from the worst excesses of her friend's behaviour. Fortunately, she didn't have a social media account so now called her every day for an update on Kelly's disappearance and at the same time, relayed the speculations from the neighbours. Rowan could imagine they thoroughly enjoyed being at the epicentre of the rural Lancashire branch of Kelly's Army. Her mum simply couldn't understand why her daughter wanted to leave the glow of Kelly's halo, especially while no one knew where she was.

'But you two girls were always the best of friends,' she said as Rowan confirmed she was definitely still taking the transfer.

'We *were,'* murmured Rowan as she said goodbye and scrolled through the more up-to-date images, studying then deleting each one.

She didn't know where Kelly was but had come to the conclusion that Kelly didn't want to be found for some reason. That she'd moved on again. It hurt to think that she'd left without saying goodbye and Rowan wondered if Kelly was watching the whole debacle from a distance. If she was, she'd probably be quite flattered by all the fuss.

Rowan felt annoyed by all that was going on but not concerned; she truly couldn't imagine any scenario in which harm had come to Kelly. Rowan truly believed that at a time of her choosing, her friend would turn up and bask in the glare of the spotlight. At one stage Rowan had thought all of this vanishing into thin air might be a publicity stunt in aid of one of Kelly's clients. She thought about suggesting that to the police officer but every time she rehearsed the words she knew she just sounded like the bitter friend left behind. Which in effect, is exactly what she was.

Rowan played that night in the bar over and over again in her head. She knew that some people blamed her for Kelly's disappearance and no matter how many times she said it they didn't want to hear the truth. Kelly had walked out on *her* and left her alone. The police said she'd waved at someone and left with them. How could she do that? Kelly hadn't thought about her for one moment. People were saying that it was awful she'd gone missing at Christmas but there was something about this time of the year – old acquaintances could be forgotten and all that. That professor had been right and fresh starts with clean slates were just around the corner. However wounded Rowan felt now, she was determined not to carry this feeling into the new year. It was time to put all this behind her and live her own life.

'Adios my friend,' she said as she deleted yet another unflattering image of the two of them together.

Suddenly her laptop burst into life, pinging with notifications. This meant someone, somewhere had news. There was a hammering on the door at the exact moment and an avalanche of words rolled onto her social media feed. She was speed-reading and simply couldn't believe what was being said. The hammering got louder and more desperate, echoing through the packed-up empty house.

'You have to hide me.' Luis smashed into her hall as she opened the door. 'They're saying that I used to beat her.'

Rowan couldn't listen to the rest of his expletives but in the midst of them she gathered that the clothing store where Kelly had bought her dress had noticed bruises on the young woman. They'd posted this on their social media account and now everyone had something to say about it. They ranged from "it's always the boyfriend" and "He's killed her for sure" to "wouldn't mind being locked up with him".

'Ro? Are you listening?'

She wasn't. She'd gone back to the laptop. Her brain felt as if it would explode. She dropped her head into her hands and tightened her grip, digging her fingernails through her hair into her skull as hard as she could, willing the sharp pain to take this nightmare away.

'How could anyone even suggest that she's dead?' she sobbed. 'Have they forgotten she has friends and family? That she's a real person?'

'She's not to them, nor am I. This morning we were heroes and now we're the villains. We're today's entertainment in the cyber-coliseum that is social media.'

'For God's sake, Luis, this is not a fucking crusade – what's happened to Kelly? Did you do something? You have to tell me.'

He grabbed the laptop from Rowan and threw it against the wall. It didn't give him the satisfaction of smashing into tiny pieces but rather defiantly thudded to the ground, leaving a big dent in the plaster.

Rowan stood up and started backing out of the room.

'Where are you going?' asked Luis.

'I want you to leave,' Rowan said.

Luis punched the wall and edged closer to her. 'You have got to be joking.'

Rowan fought to steady her breathing and weigh up the options. Her phone was in the kitchen, equidistant to the front door. She had to call someone or get out. Either direction required another step back before it was safe to make a move. She slid her foot along the floor, keeping her upper body as still as she could.

'Oh no you don't.'

Luis thrust his leg against hers so she was pinned to the wall. He leant over her, his arms imprisoning her. 'You're the one who left her on her own in a bar or have you forgotten that?'

'I told you, she wouldn't come with me, I tried.'

'I didn't do anything, you hear me? Promise me that you'll tell the police that.'

Rowan hesitated and Luis slammed his fist to the wall beside her head. 'Say it!' he yelled.

'I promise. I'm sure you didn't do anything. I'm *sure* you didn't!' she shrieked only half believing her own words.

'What will you say to the police about these bruises then?' he asked, keeping her caged with his body. 'Was she seeing someone else? She would have told you. You must have known.'

Rowan would tell him anything he wanted to hear just to get out. This wasn't the Luis she knew. 'She hasn't said anything to me, really she hasn't.'

Luis took her by the arm and pushed her into the living room to sit on the sofa. 'Did she show you the bruises they're talking about?'

She shook her head frenzied.

'But you probably wouldn't tell me if she had.'

Rowan gulped her tears and frantically tried to work out what was coming next.

'What about Connor?' he asked. 'He's still around isn't he?'

'H-he is,' stuttered Rowan. 'What does that have to do with anything?'

'What if *he* hurt Kelly just to get revenge or to pin the blame on me!' yelled Luis grabbing both of her arms and shaking her. 'You can say that to the police can't you?'

'Leave me alone!' screamed Rowan. 'Get off me.'

Harnessing all her strength, she pulled herself loose and ran out of the door. A hundred cameras flashed as Luis barged through the journalists and social media followers who'd tracked him down to Rowan's house. Luis reached out frantically, grabbed some of the mobile phones pointing at him and smashed them to the ground. Those outside his grasp continued recording everything that happened.

'You're so fucked,' said one anonymous voice, clear and loud.

Andrew's car pulled up just in time to see Luis thumping the speaker. The young man spotted Maxie and the detective in the car so pushed through the throng, running as fast as he could up the street. Andrew made chase but Luis was too fast so he went back to the car to try and catch him. Maxie turned her attention to the sobbing Rowan who had her arms wrapped tightly around herself, hunched down on her doorstep in a foetal position.

'Sorry we got here too late,' said Maxie. 'We thought Luis would still be at Kelly's office and when we got there we heard he was on his way here. The shop wasn't supposed to release that information about the bruises.'

'I don't care – just make this stop,' pleaded Rowan. 'I want my life to go back to normal. Please make this stop.'

Chapter Twenty-Three

Having waited with Rowan until the crowds outside her house got bored and dispersed, Maxie called herself a cab to get back to the war room but first of all dropped the young woman off with Patricia and George who promised to take very good care of her. As she was leaving, Maxie saw the elderly lady cut a huge slice of fruit cake for Rowan. She smiled to herself, picturing Rowan relaxed but at least a stone heavier by the time she left this house.

'A weight off her shoulders but not off her belly,' Maxie said to herself as she got back into the waiting taxi.

The building housing OrlandoPR was exceptionally busy with people rapidly criss-crossing the reception, all looking as if they had something urgent to do or convey. It felt good to be back in a place with a real sense of purpose. Maxie walked towards the war room and caught a savoury aroma in the air as she approached it. The smell which had been quite tempting while mixed with fresh air in the corridor was suddenly nauseating as she opened the door and mozzarella, chorizo and onions mixed with the sweat of thirty people. Maxie looked around the room for Karl and nodded at him when she saw him on one of the phone lines then grimaced as someone held out an open pizza box offering her a gooey slice.

'An army marches on its stomach,' said Orlando, bouncing up to her. 'The local pizza company have sent these in for free and have also said their drivers will hand out Kelly flyers with every delivery they make – great news eh?'

Maxie nodded while watching a guy she presumed was the boss of the delivery company being interviewed for the latest broadcast. He was wearing a shirt bearing the company logo so it was a reasonable guess. These videos were being downloaded by tens of thousands of people across the town so she couldn't blame him for getting something out of it for himself.

'Although obviously the police may have their man now,' continued Orlando. 'Or at least they will do when they catch him.'

'Well they seem to think so,' said Maxie. 'I'm still not so sure. Are there any other leads?'

She glanced over at the wall and saw a clutter of orange post-it notes, including many for the days after Kelly's disappearance.

'The police have already taken the ones they thought most relevant,' Orlando said. 'But the rest are still up there.'

Together they glanced over those still on the wall. There had been sightings of Kelly everywhere from a curry house in Solihull to a rooftop cocktail bar in Sydney.

'I hope for her sake she's in the latter,' said Maxie pointing at it. 'I don't mind going out there to bring her home.'

Maxie looked around the room, if anything it was buzzing even more than it had at the launch. 'Why did Luis leave anyway?'

'That was my fault. I suggested he go home and rest. I didn't know that boutique story was going to break,' replied Orlando. 'We wanted to record another message which we'll put out at 2.30 a.m. to mark the moment she disappeared. He needed to look as dynamic as he was in the first film to keep everyone's energy up. The DI was going to make another statement too but I guess that's out of the question until they've ruled out the boyfriend.'

Maxie blew out her cheeks exasperated. An intern approached them and handed over a post-it.

'We've got a report from a guy who says Luis threatened him in the street,' Orlando said, reading the note. 'Grabbed him by the throat apparently.'

'Is that recent?' he asked the intern.

'No – this was a couple of weeks ago. The guy says he was just having a laugh with Kelly as they left the pub. You know, holding up some mistletoe and trying to give her a kiss. He says he didn't mean anything by it and she was laughing it off but when Luis came out he went straight for the guy. Kelly had to pull him off.'

'He didn't report it at the time?' asked Maxie.

'No, he says it wasn't worth it but now he's seen the appeal, he thought he should mention it.'

Maxie didn't know what to think. There were so many opportunists surrounding this case. How were the police going to separate the real incidents from the fake?

'If Luis was angry with Kelly over that, he may have lashed out at her. It would explain the bruises and if it was a couple of weeks ago, the timescales fit,' Orlando said. 'I'll get this information sent over to your man Andrew.'

Maxie rolled her eyes skywards.

'What's the matter?' Orlando asked.

‘I just can’t see Luis harming Kelly but I think his trial by popular opinion is about to begin. I’m sorry but I have to get out of here. Will you call me if anything else happens? I’ll be up all night.’

Orlando promised he would, then squeezed her hand as she left. ‘Take care of yourself and try to get some sleep,’ he called after her.

As she drove through the unusually quiet streets, Maxie mentally sifted through her reasons for thinking Luis innocent but knew each of them could be knocked down.

He searched the streets for her in the middle of the night, she thought to herself.

‘Proving he could get to that bar after leaving the pub,’ replied the devil on her shoulder.

He drove out to every church in town to look for that stag party.

‘Classic misdirection.’

He put himself in the public eye with this appeal.

‘How many times have you seen a guilty party do that? Borderline narcissist behaviour.’

But I honestly believe he loves her. He couldn’t live with himself if he’d hurt her.

‘Dissociative amnesia – as you’ve already educated him about.’

No matter how she argued his case, she could always find an equal and opposite response. If there was even one more call questioning Luis’s character, the police would have no choice but to charge him with something when they found him and they could always make either wasting police time or perverting the course of justice stick for a few days. Her phone buzzed and Maxie opened the text with a video attached. Orlando had sent her the footage from outside Rowan’s house showing Luis like a raging bull.

‘There’s the final nail in that coffin,’ she murmured as she arrived at her house.

Maxie opened her own door and made straight for the kitchen, throwing her poncho and bag onto the bench. She poured herself a glass of wine and flicked on the local news. A “breakthrough” in Kelly’s case was being reported and the mobile footage from Rowan’s house was played over and over again. The report then switched to a presenter outside the police station just as Luis was being brought in earlier. They’d found him.

‘This is a waste of precious time,’ he was shouting.

Maxie's heart sunk as she watched Luis, who was certainly not co-operating. He thrashed out as the officers tried to get him into the station as quickly as possible. Cameras flashed and phones recorded every movement and voices yelled questions at the poor guy.

'Luis what do you have to say about the bruises?'

'Did you hit her Luis?'

'Is the boyfriend under arrest?'

Andrew, sensibly in Maxie's opinion, avoided all the questions but then was joined at the doorway by his DI.

'Mr Caballero is helping us with recent developments,' he told the press. 'We'll let you know his status as soon as we can.'

Maxie could see that this new DI certainly liked the cameras and while it had been positioned as a neutral sounding statement, in her mind it raised expectations of an announcement. It was no use. Maxie couldn't simply sit here and watch it unfold on TV. She had to get down there. She left the wine glass untouched and called a taxi – she really didn't feel like driving any more this evening.

By the time Maxie had arrived at the station, the crowd of journalists had grown and there was an air of excitement about them. Cold clouds of air hung in the glare of lights adding to the sense of anticipation. Everyone was expecting news. Maxie knew her way around the station but at this stage in the investigation, she knew she wouldn't be allowed anywhere near Luis. She took a file out of her bag and as soon as she spotted one of Andrew's team, she waved it at him. As she'd hoped, he came over and asked if she had something for the DS. Maxie feigned innocence and apologised over-profusely for making him think that. She then asked to sit by Andrew's desk and wait for him. The poor rookie didn't seem to know how to say no to her. Maxie took up a seat and waited.

Half an hour lapsed before Andrew appeared. He looked drained and also very surprised to see Maxie.

'Who let you in?' he asked. 'The DI won't be happy.'

'I don't care,' she replied. 'You look like you need a break.'

Andrew allowed himself to be led to the vending machine and accepted the bitter tasting espresso. Maxie waited for the drink to take effect then asked how the interview had gone.

'He just keeps saying he hasn't done anything,' said Andrew.

'Have you asked him about the bruises?' asked Maxie.

Andrew nodded wearily and Maxie asked if he'd do it again while she watched Luis's responses. Andrew agreed and led her into the observation room where she watched the interview taking place.

'Tell me again about the bruises,' said Andrew.

'You haven't told me where these bruises were, I mean where on her body?' Luis replied.

'I still think you know the answer to that question,' said Andrew. 'The shop assistant said they were down Kelly's side along her rib cage. Does that ring a bell?'

Luis shook his head. 'I knew nothing about them but as I said, Kelly has slept in the spare room recently.'

'And that must have angered you when she decided to do that. I can imagine you getting very frustrated at that,' said Andrew. 'I mean what's the point in having a gorgeous girlfriend like that if you're not getting any action.'

Maxie had wanted Andrew to provoke Luis with this comment but when it was made the boyfriend simply looked deflated.

'I didn't really know her did I?' he said before dropping his head into his hands and swallowing back the tears fighting to form. 'If someone had hurt her why would she hide it?'

Andrew's phone beeped so he ended the interview and instructed a colleague to get Luis a drink.

Maxie waited for Andrew to call in and collect her. When he didn't she excused herself and made her way back to his desk. The look on his face told her he'd forgotten she was there.

'Has something happened?' asked Maxie

'We've found a flight booked in Kelly's name,' replied Andrew.

'Really?' asked Maxie. 'Has she left the country? And how come we didn't find it earlier?'

'It wasn't booked by her and we were looking at December,' said Andrew getting quite animated. 'It's for late January – to New York. The DI was right, Maxie. Either he was beating her up or they were having so-called friendly arguments but Kelly was planning to get away from him and she wanted to do it cleanly. She left without telling anyone and she's hiding until it's time for the flight. She has some clothes and her passport already with her.'

Maxie followed Andrew into a briefing room and sat at the back as he went through his theory with the investigation team.

'Luis does love Kelly but it's the kind of love we see too often in this station – possessive love,' said Andrew. 'He cannot stand to watch her flirting and gets bloody angry when she does. Who knows she might even do it on purpose to provoke him. He told us they have great make-up sex.'

'It might only be great for him,' added a young police woman. Everyone in the room nodded at this.

'He doesn't know his own strength and he flips pretty easily,' continued Andrew. 'We now know of several incidents when he's threatened someone for saying something about Kelly or chatting her up. We also know that Kelly was badly bruised. He claims to know nothing about it but what if he did it? What if Kelly lived in fear after that day? She didn't want to rouse his suspicions so she carried on as normal but was making plans to leave him. She took her passport so she could get away. She went to the works party to say goodbye to all her friends because she knew she wouldn't be seeing them again and was planning to leave immediately afterwards.'

'So someone came to fetch her from the party?' asked one of the officers. 'To help her get away?'

'We don't know,' replied Andrew. 'It could just have been a wave to a cab or a group of blokes but she knew that leaving in the way she did gave her a good twenty-four hours before anyone started looking for her. We've got bruises, a passport and a ticket out of here. She's run away, it all adds up.'

There were a few nods acknowledging the plausibility of the theory particularly from Andrew's boss who'd walked in on the briefing very quietly.

'Good work DS Andrew,' he said giving Andrew a pat on the back and instructing the team to find evidence supporting this theory. 'Now let's find the evidence, give the public some news and then put this case to bed.'

'And if we could find Kelly too,' said Andrew. 'Encourage her to get in touch now she's safe.'

'That would certainly be the icing on the Christmas cake,' added the DI.

Maxie said nothing but her mind whirred as she walked out with Andrew to his car.

'It all fits doesn't it?' he said and then taking note of the doubtful expression on Maxie's face added, 'What's the matter?'

‘There are things that don’t add up. Yes he has a temper but that isn’t enough to trigger a violent attack on a person you love. He isn’t displaying the classic mind-set of someone guilty of domestic abuse or familial violence. There is definitely something up and there’s no doubt he’s frustrated by the case but he hasn’t shown any signs of being controlling of Kelly. She’s gone out with her friends to get drunk time after time and he just waits at home for her. He’s not trying to isolate her from people and he seems quite proud of her career. These are not the behaviours of a violent partner no matter how angry he gets with journalists. He doesn’t try to hide who he is and that’s inconsistent too. If he were guilty we’d be seeing Jekyll and Hyde type behaviour – being charming with us and doing everything he could to hide his true nature. He’s not doing that either. I think you might be wrong on this.’

‘Real life is different to text books, to quote my boss.’

Maxie sighed. She and Andrew were wanted back at the PR offices for the next recording so they left together silently. Craig Johnston was going to host this one but Maxie would play no role in it and was only present for a show of solidarity which unfortunately she didn’t feel. At twelve on the dot, the recording began. Craig walked up to Orlando who was standing with Andrew in front of the army of volunteers. The smiles on people’s faces sent a sickening feeling of *fait accompli* through Maxie. She hid as far back as she could and watched the charade.

‘It is exactly five days since Kelly Ingles vanished and just under twenty-four hours since Kelly’s Army was mobilised here at OrlandoPR,’ said Craig getting a cheer from the room. ‘The team led by Orlando himself asked everyone to get out there and look for Kelly and to contact them with any information whatsoever. Orlando, can you tell us how it went?’

‘It’s been hugely successful,’ replied Orlando. ‘Thanks to the Army, the police now have several vital clues, things they wouldn’t have known about without everyone out there.’

He held out his arms as the camera panned across to the wall of post-its now reconstructed for the cameras.

There was a huge cheer and some high-fiving across the room.

‘And has any of this information led to a breakthrough in the case DS Dawson?’ Craig turned and asked Andrew.

‘All I can say is that we now have a lead that we’re actively investigating,’ said Andrew, ‘and that we are immensely grateful for the support this community has provided. It has been invaluable.’

Orlando turned to face the Army and started another round of applause which the room joined in with. The camera then went to the sponsor who reiterated their delight at being able to help and bring about such rapid results.

Maxie snuck out of the room as the transmission ended and waited for Andrew to join her in the corridor. As she waited, Karl hurried towards her.

'Mum,' he said, holding out a piece of paper. 'You need to see this.'

'What is it?' asked Maxie, taking the note and unfolding it.

'I brought it straight to you,' he said. 'It may be too late but it's from a guy who said he was her martial arts instructor.'

'Her what?'

'She's learning kick-boxing. She started about three weeks ago,' replied Karl.

'So the bruises …'

'He said she was messing about and not paying attention,' continued Karl. 'Apparently they could be the classic marking from a side kick not blocked well enough.'

Maxie grabbed her son in the tightest bear hug she could muster then released him to let the poor guy breathe. She marched back into the room, pulled Andrew to one side and relayed what she'd just been told.

'So the bruising may have nothing to do with Luis,' she said.

Andrew blew out his cheeks. 'It still doesn't explain why she needed to learn kick-boxing in the first place,' he said. 'I don't want any of this news getting out and I certainly don't want my boss to think we're opening up new avenues and not closing them down.'

Chapter Twenty-Four

Thursday, 22 December

In the small hours, just after the broadcast, Orlando told the team who'd been working for much of the day to hand over to the new volunteers. With the students Maxie had recruited and the young people who just wanted to help, they really did have a Kelly's Army and there were enough of them to march on all night. Not that it seemed there'd be much for them to do. There'd been a flurry of calls immediately after the transmission, most of them still supporting the idea that "the boyfriend knows more than he's saying", but for the past hour since the police announcement that they had someone helping with their enquiries, the lines had been very quiet.

'Even the general public think we've got the right man,' Andrew said to Maxie as they sat yawning on the sofa.

'They probably wouldn't care if you arrested Prince William just as long as it meant they could say they helped and could now go back to enjoying their Christmas pudding without feeling guilty.'

'I'm taking the guys for some "thank you" drinks and food,' announced Orlando, suddenly appearing to stand over them. 'I hope you'll come with us.'

'It's too late for me, thanks all the same,' Andrew said, shaking his head at Maxie.

'What have you done to annoy your best buddie?' asked Orlando as Andrew strode from the room.

'Suggested it may not be as straightforward as he thinks.' Maxie dragged herself to her feet. 'Anyway, I should get home too. This is way past my normal bedtime and I know we can't do much more tonight but people seem to have forgotten that we haven't found Kelly yet. I should probably read through my notes again and then eventually I have to get back to my real job before the break. I've a ton of work to get through at the university tomorrow – or rather later today.'

'Me too, but it isn't late for this lot and I don't want to look like an old fogey. Come for one hour.' Orlando pressed his palms together pleading. 'I genuinely don't believe that reading notes at this hour of the day will help anyone and you being there would mean a lot to the Army. I think Karl and Olivia are coming.'

She knew she was being manipulated but she glanced over Orlando's shoulder and saw her son helping the love of his life with her coat. Karl caught Maxie's eye and gave her the slightest of nods. It couldn't do any harm to ride this temporary wave of coolness and spend another hour in his company.

'An hour,' Maxie said. 'Then I really need some sleep.'

Orlando piled the Army onto a minibus that waited for them all in the parking lot and then took them to an all-night diner designed to look exactly like the 1950s ideal. Everyone piled into red vinyl booths and Maxie watched as Karl and Olivia huddled together opposite each other and seemed to have eyes for no one else.

'It's good to see him happy,' said Maxie, nodding over.

'Yes,' said Orlando. 'And she seems lovely from the few conversations I've had with her.'

Maxie dragged her eyes from her son to give him the privacy he deserved and allowed herself to be led into a booth designed to sit two people, the type where Harry would probably meet Sally if they were in a Hollywood movie. Burgers, fries and milkshakes were dished out to everyone and a hush fell over the diner as teeth sank into the salty, sugary food.

'You look as if you needed that,' Orlando said as Maxie drained a cup of milkshake.

'I didn't realise how much.' Maxie wiped her mouth with a paper napkin. 'It's been a long day for all of us.'

'But a good one. We got results.'

'The jury's still out on that one,' said Maxie. 'The police seem to have decided what's happened to Kelly but we still don't know where she is or why she hasn't at least been in touch with us. Although if they're right, she may appear now she thinks she's safe.'

'You don't wholeheartedly agree with the police theory then?' asked Orlando. 'That Luis holds the key to all this and that she's run away from him?'

Maxie shook her head and started picking at the scrappy little fries still at the bottom of the cardboard packet. Her own views were still based on her perceptions of a woman she'd never met. Orlando had far more insight into Kelly's character and he seemed to think the theory plausible.

'Let's just say I have some doubts, which I've expressed but which weren't exactly welcomed. But you know Kelly better than me – what do you think?'

‘Well first of all, the DI tells me that Andrew has a pretty good record,’ said Orlando. ‘He’s seen as one of their rising stars. And as for your question, I wouldn’t have put Kelly down for the running away type either but I do think she’d have the guts to do exactly what she needed to and that includes getting away. I also agree that if she now thinks she’ll be safe with him on everyone’s radar, she might reappear then again she might not.’

Maxie picked another paper napkin out of the dispenser and wiped her hands. She tidied their tray of food and edged herself out of the booth.

‘I think I’d better go and get some sleep,’ she said. ‘But thanks for persuading me to come out. I did need that.’

Maxie walked over to Karl’s booth and told him she was leaving – he didn’t ask to share a cab so Maxie didn’t suggest it. On hearing that Karl was staying, Orlando offered to take her home.

‘Don’t worry,’ she replied. ‘I’ll be perfectly safe. You stay with the Army.’

Orlando nodded and walked her to the door, then as they stood outside he gently kissed her cheek goodnight. When he’d gone back into the diner, Maxie called a cab and stood stroking the spot he’d kissed as she watched him through the window. He was walking around the booths, patting people on the back, taking photos for them and shaking hands. He wasn’t at all like the person she’d first met. Perhaps that was just her prejudice about people who work in PR but everyone has a profession they distrust and it was most commonly estate agents. People heard her title and immediately assumed she was a man or very stuffy or both. Orlando’s job was to make people look good and although that seemed a very shallow aim in life, Maxie couldn’t deny that he’d turned public opinion about Kelly and he’d achieved more in one day that the police had done all week. He suddenly looked up and caught her still staring at him. He smiled and waved. By God he was good-looking.

The cab arrived and Maxie slumped down into the back seat. Her phone pinged with a text from Karl asking if it was okay to bring Olivia home for the night. Her heart did a merry dance as she’d been more than a little anxious that her son would be staying somewhere else with his girlfriend. But more than that, her son had asked to bring Olivia *home*. He’d called it home and he felt comfortable bringing girlfriends back. Maxie leant her head against the window of the cab and smiled – she would roll out the red carpet for Olivia every time she visited if that’s what it took. She replied telling her son almost as much.

The cab was overly warm and the driver was tuned into a station playing late night rock classics. Maxie smiled to herself as it belted out anthems she recognised. "Don't Stop Believin'" was exactly what she needed to hear right now and she would have kept it on repeat if she could. By the time they reached her home, Maxie and the driver had sung along to "Bat out of Hell" and "Sweet Child O' Mine". Maxie had gone from barely awake to buzzing.

Once inside, she knew the sensible thing to do would be to have a cup of camomile tea and try to get some sleep but she could positively feel the neurons sparking in her brain and was absolutely sure a small nightcap would lead to some mind-blowing insight as to Kelly's whereabouts. She took her notes on the investigation out of her briefcase and tucked them under her arm, poured herself a small brandy and plonked down on the sofa.

Her legs pulled up and wrapped in a blanket, Maxie took out the photographs and forced herself to see them with fresh eyes. Everyone was naturally drawn to the central image in a picture but in this case Kelly was at the centre. Maxie tried to ignore her, examining the expressions of everyone else in each picture instead. It wasn't the first time she'd done this since the young woman's disappearance but it was always possible she'd spot something new.

Some of the faces were now more familiar. Kelly's Army had mobilised more of Kelly's colleagues at the PR firm and Maxie now recognised them. They'd been questioned as a matter of routine but like the door-to-door enquiries, they'd had very little to contribute apart from seeing Kelly as a rising star at work and a party animal outside of work. Maxie picked up a picture of an award ceremony Kelly had attended and mentally ticked off everyone she'd seen manning the phones tonight. She picked a pen from the table and circled the people she still didn't recognise. In the morning she'd visit Orlando and see if he knew who they were. Someone in this picture might be the mystery person Kelly had put her trust in.

The strain of studying each picture started to weigh on her and she finally found her eyelids starting to close. She thought about going upstairs and organising herself for the morning ahead but this spot on the sofa was now just too warm and cosy to leave. She looked at her phone; it was a near enough 4 a.m. so she only had a few hours before she'd have to get up anyway.

‘It won’t hurt for once,’ she muttered to herself as she snuggled down, fully dressed, into the curve of the sofa. It seemed to hug her and hold her until the morning, not even waking her to tell her when Karl arrived home with Olivia and not stirring her at all when they looked into the living room and giggled at the sight of the university professor, face flat down into the cushion, drooling and snoring away.

Chapter Twenty-Five

The sofa hugged Maxie tightly until the alarm on her phone told her it was 6.45 a.m. and time to get back to work. Despite the limited amount of sleep she'd had, Maxie woke up feeling remarkably invigorated and ready to tackle everything the day threw at her. She got out from under the snuggly blanket and noted the two coats hanging over a chair – Karl's and what must have been Olivia's. His bedroom door was closed and as she walked past it, Maxie gently placed her hand on it, leaning in for any sounds of wakefulness – there were none so she tiptoed away.

After showering, Maxie pulled open her wardrobe doors and looked for something that matched her mood. She chose a Christmas red dress and putting it on, felt pretty determined. She drove to the university via the coffee shop and this time chose a cranberry muffin and the largest cappuccino with nutmeg they had. Buzzing on adrenaline, sugar and caffeine, she cleared all the emails waiting for her, approved the appointment of a new lecturer and made amends to the proposed forensic science curriculum for the next academic year, all without skipping a beat. Maxie looked at the clock and noted she'd worked solidly and cheerfully for over two hours. It was nearly eleven o'clock – the hour when even PR offices were open. It was time to call Orlando.

'I'm sorry he's not in yet,' said the receptionist stifling a yawn. 'I think it was a really late one with the team. He's in later this afternoon. Shall I put you in his diary?'

Maxie made the appointment but having built up a head of steam couldn't wait until the afternoon to get some answers. She called Andrew who also wasn't in but his constable told her they were still questioning Luis but would probably have to release him later in the day as they'd concluded that they had no reason to hold him. She exhaled a little sigh of relief and hoped that Luis wouldn't ruin it for himself by hitting someone. Maxie looked at the photograph she'd been studying last night and knew it was a long shot but she still wanted to find out who everyone was. Who else could she call? She decided that Rowan and Harry might know some of these people so called Rowan and explained what she needed. A very weary sounding Rowan agreed to look at the picture so Maxie emailed it over immediately. Within ten minutes Rowan had called back.

'Her boss Orlando is in the centre as I'm sure you already know,' she said. 'I recognise some from her work but I don't know their names, just the faces. Sorry.'

Maxie asked for Harry's email address and with Rowan still on the line, wedged the phone between her chin and neck and sent him the picture too.

'What's happening to Luis? How is he?' asked Rowan. 'Is he under arrest? Should we be helping him to find a lawyer?'

'He's being questioned and may be released later today. I know you're not making any complaint but I'm guessing he could be charged with the assault on the photographer but there are such extenuating circumstances at play. They really think that Kelly has run away.'

'To get away from Luis?'

'Who knows?'

'To get away from all of us.' Rowan sighed. 'Why didn't she tell me if she wanted to disappear? If she was so unhappy or in trouble? I haven't been much of a friend have I?'

Maxie tried to comfort her but the phone went dead. Rowan had hung up. Maxie refreshed her screen but there was still nothing from Harry. She knew it was the digital equivalent of watching the kettle boil so stopped and tried to focus on her work. It didn't work and her mind was constantly being drawn to the research about missing persons. Over and over again she read that it was highly unusual for an adult woman to go missing, especially one with a home, a job and no history of mental illness. The police conclusion that she'd run off was a sensible one but it niggled Maxie.

Why wouldn't she tell Rowan or Harry or Orlando if she wanted to leave? Why wouldn't she at least say goodbye to George and Patricia? Maxie believed that if someone as distinctive-looking as Kelly had suffered an accident or worse, then an army of people would surely have found her by now. The facts were that she'd been missing since the early hours of Saturday morning. She hadn't contacted anyone and hadn't been found in a hospital, hostel or anywhere else. Andrew was also sure they weren't looking at a murder case as he felt that a body would have been found by now and Maxie really wanted to believe that.

It was the fact that Kelly hadn't said goodbye to George and Patricia that niggled Maxie most of all. It seemed to her that Kelly had adopted the elderly couple after the death of her grandfather and for that reason, Maxie couldn't imagine the young woman leaving them in any state of distress.

The possibility of this being an abduction case stirred in her mind. It was such a rare occurrence that the police would think her truly insane if she raised it with them but to bastardise the famous Conan Doyle quote, maybe all that remained now, "no matter how improbable, must be the truth".

Before she even ventured this idea, Maxie knew she had to exhaust the "ran away" theory. Kelly didn't take her suitcase to the nightclub so that had to be somewhere, maybe the girl did have help but whoever it was from, it wasn't from her best friend. Maxie looked again at the photograph. She wondered whether Orlando would help Kelly get away if he felt she were in danger? Whether Kelly would trust him to help? If he did know where she was, would he have set up the Army? He didn't seem like the type of person to waste police time – not when he was so friendly with the DI. Anyway, Maxie had another couple of hours before she could talk to Orlando and couldn't sit around doing nothing.

Was there anyone else Kelly might trust to tell? The light bulb flashed and Maxie leapt up full of purpose – the martial arts instructor. She'd probably have a locker at the centre and the centre was where Kelly's bruises actually originated.

'All I want to do is help find her,' Maxie said to the extremely defensive owner of the kick-boxing club when she'd eventually found the place and introduced herself.

'We all do but she doesn't have a locker here and I can't have this place labelled as somewhere that a woman might get beaten up,' he replied. 'These classes can be pretty hardcore but it's what people come for. We get lots of city types coming to let off steam.'

Maxie nodded her understanding and then asked whether he'd ever personally met Kelly.

'Yes,' he said. 'She's pretty good for a beginner and seems to enjoy it. She really goes for it.'

'Were you here when the bruising happened by any chance?' Maxie ventured cautiously.

'I don't know if it's exactly the same bruising but if it was, then it wasn't that big a deal really,' he emphasised. 'She was messing around instead of paying attention. Her sparring partner made contact with a kick when they shouldn't have. Kelly wasn't expecting it so wasn't defending herself but she knew it was her mistake.'

'Did the kicker apologise?'

‘Of course she did. She was mortified but like I said, it wasn’t her fault.’

‘Any idea why Kelly wanted to learn kick-boxing? Did you get the sense that she was in danger?’

‘Not particularly,’ replied the owner. ‘But she did say that she believed everyone needed to be able to take care of themselves.’

The day was dragging and Maxie still had an hour before she was due at OrlandoPR. She was wondering how on earth to progress this case when she got a call from Andrew – who sounded very weary.

‘We’ve released him.’ He sighed. ‘He might be a hothead but he doesn’t seem to know where his girlfriend is.’

‘So what happens now?’ Maxie asked.

‘Back to plan A. We’ll file it as a voluntary disappearance on Friday – tomorrow. Leave it open and let Kelly sit on the missing persons database. Is there nothing the ACU have that could help here? It doesn’t seem to have added anything to this case.’

‘We still have until tomorrow don’t we?’ Maxie asked ignoring the insinuation which sounded as if it had come directly from his DI.

Andrew said they did, not that they had any more leads to follow. Maxie told him about the photograph. ‘I’m not giving up,’ she said. Someone knows where she is. I’m off to find out who this lot are and see if they know anything or helped her.’

‘I guess we have nothing to lose,’ Andrew said. ‘I’ll meet you at Orlando’s building.’

The receptionist waved them through without any ceremony and as they walked towards the war room, some employees greeted them like old friends. Maxie noticed that Orlando looked like a man who’d been up all night partying with people twenty years younger than him. She was glad she’d gone home when she did. Unshaven and baggy-eyed, he was evidently struggling to focus.

‘What’s going on?’ asked Andrew.

‘I’ve asked the team to take down all of these post-it notes.’

‘The case isn’t over yet,’ said Maxie.

‘I thought it was.’ Orlando looked slightly shocked. ‘I’ll have it all reassembled if you like. I’d be more than happy for you both to base yourselves here. It’s been invigorating having you around – despite the circumstances.’

Maxie caught Orlando’s glance in her direction, then noticed Andrew staring at them both.

‘Thank you,’ said Andrew. ‘It would be good to keep things in place for a couple of days, if that’s not inconvenient.’

Orlando signalled his team to reassemble the wall and showed Maxie and Andrew to a corner of the room. Maxie handed him the photograph of the award ceremony.

‘I recognise most of these people but can you help us with the ones circled?’

Orlando looked at it and quickly nodded. He pointed to the different people as he spoke. ‘Employee – off sick right now, Ex-employee, client and head of the judging panel for the award we won.’

‘Is there anyone here you think it would be worth us talking to? Anyone that Kelly might really trust?’

He stroked his chin. ‘I don’t think Kelly really knew any of them that much but I can get you contact details if you want?’

‘That would be great,’ Andrew said. ‘They may not tell us anything new but it would be good to have them.’

Orlando asked for a little time to find them all and Andrew replied that they didn’t have much left so asked Orlando to email them as quickly as possible. He promised that he would.

‘It doesn’t look as if that’s going to lead anywhere does it?’ said Andrew as they headed back to their cars.

‘Not really.’ Maxie yawned, checking her watch. Six o’clock – almost twelve hours since she’d left that cosy sofa.

As they reached their vehicles, Maxie’s phone rang. ‘Stay there and don’t touch anything!’ yelled Maxie. ‘We’re on our way.’

‘What’s happened?’

‘That was Rowan. Something’s happened to Harry. Quick we need to get to his warehouse now.’

They both jumped into Andrew’s car, put the blue lights on and skidded out of the car park.

Chapter Twenty-Six

As Rowan gasped out some of the detail, Andrew called in the incident. Rowan hadn't reported it properly so they drove while Maxie kept the young woman on the line and tried to calm her down. She was hysterical but if what she were saying were true, they were about to face an awful situation which would be very tough on all the people they'd come to know over the past few days. Andrew turned off the siren as he swept the car into the warehouse car park. They were the first people there.

'This sounds like a crime scene. You shouldn't go inside,' Andrew said to Maxie as he reached out and tried to grab her arm.

'Rowan's in there and she called me for help.' Maxie ran away from him. 'I'm going in.'

Andrew ran after Maxie and forced gloves and protective shoes onto her. They pulled open the door to the vast empty space and walked slowly in. The aftermath of an office party lay everywhere but on top of that the studio lighting rigs were smashed, locker doors were forced open and wires hung where computers once sat. Maxie couldn't help thinking that if Harry had wanted to create a crime scene for a client he'd probably have gone for something like this. They heard crying.

'Rowan, it's me Professor Reddick.'

The crying turned to a gasping sob. 'Quickly, he's here. He needs help.' Rowan gulped. They walked towards her voice.

'Where is he?' asked Andrew when they reached her. She stood up and with a bloody hand pointed towards the spot that Maxie had last seen as a grassy knoll hosting a cheerful picnic. Now it resembled some vile warning against the evils of drink with shattered empty bottles and tattered party streamers calling out the irony of the Merry Christmas banner hanging above them all.

'I t-tried to wake him up.' Rowan stared at the blood on her hands.

There sprawled out amid the debris was the lifeless body of Harry wearing a jumper which proclaimed "HO-HO-HO!" Maxie looked down on the face that was slightly bruised but otherwise still the fresh-faced man she'd very briefly known. She pulled Rowan towards her and wrapped her in her arms while Andrew walked up to Harry and checked for a pulse. He looked back at the women and shook his head. Rowan collapsed onto the floor, screeching silently. Maxie held onto her until the forensics came in and then had to drag Rowan away from the scene so they could do their work. A uniformed officer held an arm out for Rowan to follow her and Maxie watched as the girl who had already suffered so much this week tried to take in the fact that she'd lost another friend. Harry hadn't been particularly helpful or amiable towards anyone in this investigation and he'd made his feelings about Kelly abundantly clear but he'd also made it clear that he loved Rowan and Maxie knew she felt the same about him.

Maxie walked up to Andrew who almost looked worse than the dead man they'd just encountered. She rubbed his arm supportively. 'How are you holding up?'

Andrew simply nodded and swallowed. 'I don't think I'll ever get used to seeing dead bodies but he just looked asleep didn't he? If I didn't know the circumstances I'd probably be trying to wake him up and give him a paracetamol. It must have happened recently.'

'How did he die? Is there an initial verdict yet?'

Andrew told her that there was bruising on the cheek but initial observations suggested that the area of fatal impact was the back of his skull where it had hit the wall and that was presumably the source of the blood on Rowan's hands from when she tried to wake him up. The disturbance throughout the rest of the warehouse looked like a robbery.

'They think he took a punch and then fell backwards?' asked Maxie. 'So this could have been an accident then? He disturbed the burglars and they shoved him out of the way?'

'Forensics said it's as plausible as any other theory at this stage.'

'It would be one hell of a coincidence,' Maxie said.

As they talked, more officers and photographers entered the building and Maxie knew that they'd be scouring the scene, dusting for fingerprints and bagging items that might later be the downfall of whoever did this. Maxie wondered whether the person who'd pushed him even knew what had happened. If it was a burglary, she wondered what they'd actually stolen and why they'd decided to risk doing it in the afternoon. Unless it was an inside job and whoever did this knew the company was now closed for Christmas. Even so, it didn't add up.

'What do you think?' asked Andrew, his voice breaking through the sadness she felt as she watched the scene.

'I don't buy it,' she said. 'Maybe the two cases aren't connected but it also seems too much of a coincidence for them not to be. He wasn't the friendliest towards us but you wouldn't wish this ending on anyone would you?'

'No, I really wouldn't.'

'Come on then, it looks as if they were having their end of year party before all this happened?' continued Maxie. 'Do we know if Harry was the last to leave?'

'You're right, we need to get on with this.' Andrew rubbed his face. 'I'll call in everyone who was there.'

He made some calls then led Maxie to a nearby coffee shop which had been speedily requisitioned for questioning. A woman Maxie recognised arrived and sat weeping into a paper tissue.

'Jasmine,' said Andrew. 'I understand you were Harry's right-hand person. I'm presuming there was some sort of party here this afternoon.'

Jasmine simply nodded and burst out crying again. Maxie moved to sit beside her and Andrew signalled for hot drinks to be brought over. Maxie knew that there wouldn't be a thimbleful swallowed by any of them but the warmth of a cup in your hands somehow eased things, no matter how bad they were.

'Where did all the summer scenery go?' Maxie started the conversation as gently as possible.

Jasmine took a deep breath and wiped her hands across her eyes. 'The shoot finished yesterday and it all went back to the props company.'

'Summer rolled up and shipped out eh?'

Jasmine smiled faintly. 'It was a really good shoot – great for the company to have those brands on the cred sheet. Harry was delighted. We were finishing for Christmas anyway so combined it with the wrap party.'

'You really say that? "It's a wrap"? I thought that was just in films,' said Maxie.

'No, we do say it and we do have parties at the end of each job. Usually they're just a drink in the pub but this time we persuaded Harry to do it properly,' said Jasmine. 'He wasn't going to, he didn't really want to be seen out having a good time after, you know, Luis's girlfriend disappearing.'

Maxie nodded her understanding. Jasmine continued, 'But we forced him and so he said we could have a big lunchtime session then take the rest of the day off. He even started enjoying himself. He doesn't normally, we all call him Ebeneezer. Or we used to,' she added quietly. 'That's kind of why we forced him to wear that jumper. It was supposed to be ironic.'

The tears returned so Maxie paused and took both Jasmine's hands in hers. 'I didn't think he'd have bought it for himself.' She smiled.

'Jasmine – do you think there was any link between Kelly's disappearance and … what's happened here?' asked Andrew. 'Did Harry ever mention her?'

Jasmine shook her head emphatically. 'No, I mean she worked at the PR company and they were a client so she sometimes came round but usually it would be the juniors who supervised shoots,' said Jasmine. 'We all know Luis though because he helps with some of the sets. He came round earlier this afternoon but he didn't stay long.'

Maxie looked at Andrew whose jaw had dropped to his chest. 'You're telling me Luis was here today?'

'Err, yes,' replied Jasmine, 'but only for a little while. I don't think he knew there was a party going on.'

Andrew turned his head towards Maxie. He looked furious. Maxie ignored him and focussed on Jasmine.

'Is there anyone who'd want to hurt Harry?' she asked. 'Was he popular? Was there a fracas at the party at all, maybe with Luis?'

Jasmine's smile widened and she threw her head back in a sad laugh.

'No never – Harry really liked Luis,' she said. 'But every single one of us has wanted to thump Harry at some time. He's an absolute perfectionist. He never misses a detail and he never compromises. That's why clients love him but it makes him bloody difficult to work with.'

She turned to Maxie. 'But he's like, taught every single person in this company how to do things better and we love him for it. It might seem like he's this complete tyrant but he'd do anything for you. He didn't deserve this.'

'Was he the last to leave the party?'

'Probably,' said Jasmine. 'He'd have wanted to make sure everything was locked up for Christmas.'

'Was there anything really valuable still left here during the party?'

Jasmine shook her head. 'We hire the big cameras and they'd been returned. All our Macs and laptops are gone but the files and rushes get backed up every night so we haven't lost the shoot and that's the really valuable thing. Harry would be furious if we had …'

She stopped herself and sniffed away another tear.

Andrew had stood up and was pacing around when an officer walked up to him and whispered something in his ear.

'I'll be right there.'

Asking an officer to continue the interview with Jasmine, he signalled Maxie to join him and they walked out to see a group of officers surrounding an opened rucksack.

'What's in it?' she asked.

Gloved up, Andrew then pulled a damp dress partially out of the bag so the sequinned neckline could be easily seen. Maxie's heart sank. It looked exactly like the clothing she'd seen in the numerous videos and photographs she'd been staring at over the past week. It was Kelly's.

'It certainly looks like her dress,' said Andrew. 'But let's get the lab to check it and the bag – see if it can give us anything to work on.'

'Where was it found?' asked Maxie, certain that she hadn't seen a rucksack like that when she had a snoop around. They were led to cupboards that Maxie hadn't been permitted to look through on her last visit, the cupboards she'd asked the police to search. She'd been reassured that the search had happened and nothing had been found at the time.

'To think we were the ones to let Luis go,' said Andrew clenching his fist. 'I've had it for this.'

Maxie followed him out of the warehouse and alongside her Harry's lifeless body was bagged and lifted onto a trolley. Maxie skipped a breath as it was wheeled past and could imagine his weight in her arms, could imagine how Karl would feel. The weight of a young man, helpless and alone; she wanted to take hold of him and make everything right. It took all her strength to hold it together. Suddenly there was a commotion at the warehouse door. Maxie turned to see Rowan fighting with an officer to be allowed near Harry. The girl's face was a portrait of agony as she broke free from the officers and threw herself over the trolley.

'You can't do this!' she screamed. 'You can't take him.'

Maxie pulled her into a tight hug while the police moved Harry out. 'I'm sorry, Rowan. You have to let him go. He's gone.'

Rowan fell to the floor screaming. Maxie watched the grief flow from Rowan and dreaded the moment they would have to prolong this agony for her, but there was no avoiding it. They had to ask Rowan to identify the dress.

Maxie held on to Rowan on the journey to the station. They walked through its corridors and into the interview room. Maxie kept a tight hold on Rowan's hand as they waited. Then the knock on the door came and Andrew walked in. Rowan instinctively tightened her grip on Maxie's hand as if she knew there was more bad news to come. Andrew put the envelope Maxie guessed would contain a photograph of the dress on the table in front of them. He told Rowan he had some pictures that she would find distressing and Maxie felt Rowan's body tensing even more. As Andrew lay the pictures on the table in front of them, she was initially puzzled.

'What is it?' she asked, looking at the picture from different angles, then it dawned on her and she gasped. 'It's Kelly's dress isn't it?'

'Can you confirm that?' asked Andrew and Rowan nodded. Then she scraped back her hair and pulled her hand away from Maxie.

'Are you telling me that you found Kelly too?' she demanded to know. 'Was she with Harry? Is she dead?'

Maxie tried to put a calming hand on her shoulder but Rowan shrugged it off and kept her eyes glaring at Andrew.

'No,' Andrew replied with exaggerated calmness. 'We haven't found Kelly but we did find her dress in a rucksack at the Looking Glass Productions office. They were locked up in a cupboard.'

'Why? And how?' Rowan asked.

'That's what we need to work out,' Andrew said. 'Is she likely to have gone to see Harry after being in that nightclub, maybe to get changed out of these things before going home?'

'Of course not,' Rowan snapped.

'What if he'd been the person she was waving to outside the bar?' asked Maxie. 'Could he have come to collect her, seen the state she was in and taken her back to sober her up before Luis could see her like that?'

'Harry wouldn't have left me there on my own,' replied Rowan.

'He may not have known you were still there,' said Maxie, knowing that what Rowan was saying was true – Harry would never have left Rowan. 'He might have looked around for you when you were in the toilets. Do you think he would have hurt Kelly – even accidentally?'

'No, no, no and no!' yelled Rowan.

'Rowan,' asked Maxie. 'Do you know where Luis is right now?'

Rowan shook her head.

'How do you think Luis would have reacted if he'd thought Harry had hurt or hidden Kelly?' Andrew persisted.

'For God's sake, Harry would never do that. Now can I leave this place before you start on me?'

'What do you mean?' asked Maxie.

'I mean first it's Luis who's beaten up his girlfriend, then it's Harry who's hurt her, there's only me left isn't there? I must have done something to her. I must be lying about the night out.'

Maxie put her hand over Rowan's. 'No one thinks that but the police have to do their job.'

'It's a bit late for that!' she shouted.

Rowan got up to leave and Andrew nodded to say she could go. When she'd left the room leaving just the two of them, Andrew sat silently and Maxie knew she'd have to be the one to speak.

'Jasmine said Luis left the party early and she saw him go. There's no reason to suspect he had any involvement in this. His profile …'

'For goodness' sake, Maxie, his friend is dead hours after we release him and he's nowhere to be seen. I don't want to hear any more about his profile. I think you're wrong!' Andrew got up and walked out.

Chapter Twenty-Seven

They drove back to Harry's warehouse in silence and by the time they got there, the media had heard the news and stood behind the cordon, battling for an update.

'Is there blood on the dress?' they called out.

'Do you blame yourself for this detective? For letting him go?'

'Do you still believe she's alive?' That was the question now on everyone's lips.

The DI was already on the scene and he strode up to Andrew. 'Just to be clear, I see no reason for us to change our theory about Kelly's disappearance,' he said. 'You have always thought Kelly had to have help and here's the evidence. She always planned to escape and left her overnight bag and a change of clothes here. Harry knew about it all along but lied during the investigation. Luis may or may not have found out and confronted Harry but until we know for certain, the party line is that he didn't. We're going to look pretty stupid for letting him go and for not finding the dress earlier but we'll just have to ride that out.'

Maxie knew the DI meant that Andrew would have to ride it out. There was no way he would take any blame. Maxie guessed that she was also in line to be the fall guy for Andrew if they couldn't solve this case and hoped the DI wasn't planning on meeting with DCI McAlister to question the role of ACU within their force. Maxie believed McAlister would continue to want ACU but would she be persuaded to have its Head of Unit changed?

The DI continued, 'This could be a straight forward burglary and the missing person's case isn't connected in any way although it is possible that in highlighting Kelly's life and job, the media have highlighted the amount of equipment that's kept down here – laptops at Christmas will sell in any dodgy pub.

'I'm going to authorise a dive team and some dogs just to be certain we haven't missed anything but be very clear as far as the media are concerned, we are looking for evidence in relation to the attack on Harry.' The DI turned to Maxie and emphasised, 'Professor, I would like to be clear that your input was authorised on the missing person's case and not this attack. We now have one narrative on that case and one only.'

Then he turned to Andrew. 'Get the Kelly report written up and have it on my desk before you leave on Christmas Eve.'

'But even if they're not actually connected, Harry's death and the burglary will still need looking into,' Andrew said. 'Luis is a link – we have to bring him in again.'

'Not by you.' The DI raised a palm in emphasis. 'I'll put another team on that. You're far too close.'

Maxie thought for a moment about protesting on Andrew's behalf but she guessed that wouldn't make the slightest bit of difference. The DI had made his decision but even if he was right and Kelly had left with the help of Harry, Maxie still needed to know where the young woman was, to know she was safe and well. Not just because that's what she should want as a concerned citizen and a mother but because Maxie had grown to like this woman she'd never met. Her audacious, ravenous lust for life and disdain for its polite conventions. Kelly went for what she wanted and Maxie had developed a respect for the girl who reminded her that she'd once been like that. The one who drank more than the medical bods advised, the one who danced till the music stopped, the one who turned down the offer of a man walking her safely home – unless of course she planned on getting him into her bed at the end. Although the town had come out in search for Kelly, the underlying current was still "watch yourself" and "women shouldn't go out alone". Maxie believed that Kelly's disappearance had absolutely nothing to do with her partying but that wouldn't matter if she wasn't found happy and healthy. She'd be the tattooed, pierced waster that got blind drunk and vanished forever more, a moral tale for society to debate. Maxie checked her watch. If she really wanted to find out what had happened she had less than thirty-six hours to do it in.

The dog team arrived and started to search the studio and after that they'd move onto the wasteland immediately surrounding it. The search area had been mapped out covering the rest of the warehouses on this small industrial estate, the underground car parks of the riverside apartments and the river itself. Every employee of Looking Glass Productions had provided fingerprints for elimination and they'd pretty consistently told the same story of the party.

Out in the car park, three coaches suddenly appeared and Maxie saw Orlando jump out of the first one, followed by people she'd seen manning the phone lines. Kelly's Army were here all wearing beanie hats with integrated head torches which bobbed around in the dark of the early evening. Andrew's shoulders drooped at the sight of them and Maxie knew that with the media still championing this group of young volunteers, the police had to find a use for them. She heard him introducing Orlando to the detective in charge of the search and he in turn asked them to focus on the distant car parks. She knew it was an area that had already been searched and cleared and at least giving them this to do would keep them away from the river. The dive teams were in place and the monitors ready to capture any images their cameras and sonar equipment picked up. The blackness of winter didn't bother either the dogs or the diving teams.

'It's blacker down there,' they'd once told her.

Maxie stood in the cold air as the officers descended into the river. A shiver ran through her body as she imagined being swallowed by its depths again. She'd almost drowned in a previous case and the sensation haunted her. Maxie couldn't bear to think of anyone down there at this time of year and silently prayed that they wouldn't find Kelly here even if it meant they never found out what had happened.

The team leading this investigation asked Maxie for a statement and they dropped back into the studio to take it. After they'd finished, Maxie was led out of the building and was about to leave when Orlando walked up to her.

'Are you okay?' he said. 'Do they know what happened in there?'

'They think it's a burglary gone wrong,' replied Maxie, sticking to the party line. 'A life gone for some computers.'

'They would have been state of the art knowing Harry. But he'd have handed them over if they'd just asked. What a waste – he was a good guy.'

Maxie could imagine that Harry wouldn't have handed anything over and maybe that's what really had happened. She and Orlando walked together in silence as the forensic team left the building and started to pack up, their task now to process the material they'd found and decide if it meant anything.

'Oh,' started Orlando. 'I'm sorry but I completely forgot to send over the contact details of those people in the photo. It's been a bit hectic. I'm really sorry. I'll call Andrew with them tomorrow. Do you want a copy too?'

'If you don't mind, although I very much doubt he'll be following them up now,' she said. 'The police think we've reached the end of the road on Kelly I'm afraid.'

'I heard and I can't quite believe we've reached this point,' reflected Orlando. 'I keep checking my phone to see if she's called me. The DI mentioned they think that Harry met her at the club and helped her get away. I wish Harry had said something, just to let us know she was safe.'

'Perhaps he would have done soon.' Maxie sighed. 'We'll never know.'

'Anyway I'll send over those names. If it's any consolation, I very much doubt any of them would be able to tell you anything. They probably haven't seen Kelly for months.'

There was a shout on the river bank following the sound of a commotion. Maxie put her hand above her eyes to block out the glare and see what was happening. The long dark shadows of two people stumbled towards the police cordon and the media parted to let them through but kept the camera lenses fixed on them. At the cordon an officer tried to stop them and managed to get hold of George but Patricia wriggled from his grasp.

'Where is she?' she cried.

A female officer grabbed her and Patricia collapsed into her, clinging to her uniform and sobbing. The sight of Karl's former headmistress, a dignified and caring woman with no strength left in her made Maxie gasp with sadness. They looked as if they'd lost the will to live. Mr Hendry put his arms around his wife and pulled her into his chest where she rested her head and wept quietly. The media started yelling their questions and moving in as close as they could.

'Is she dead?' they cried.

'Is it true they've found a body?'

Maxie tried to get through to them so they wouldn't have to bear these horrific questions. She battled the cordon and fought her way through to join the couple and put her arms around both of them. They looked into her eyes for a sign of hope but Maxie had nothing.

'They're saying you've found her dress.' Mr Hendry broke down and sobbed as he finished the sentence. Orlando appeared and placed a hand on George's arm.

'Mr and Mrs Hendry, there's no news and really nothing any of us can do here,' he said, his Scottish tones dialled up to soothe their angst. 'And it's freezing cold. I've sent for a car. Please let Maxie and I drive you home and we'll stay with you until the police have some news, whatever time that is.'

He nodded to Maxie and together they led them back towards the car, aware that the cameras were flashing, catching every moment of this encounter. Patricia walked holding her weeping husband in her arms, calmed by the need to ease his distress. She reached into her pocket, pulled out a paper handkerchief and reached up to wipe his eyes.

'It might not be her dress is what you're saying,' said Patricia, looking pleadingly at Maxie and trying to comfort her husband.

Maxie paused for a moment, choosing the fine line between wanting to ease their pain and needing to prepare them for possible worse news by the end of the night. She knew from studies of victims of crime, the worst thing she could do right now was to lie to them. She stopped walking and turned to face them both, her hand on Mrs Hendry's arm.

'The police will need to do a DNA analysis but until then, they can't be one hundred per cent sure. However, I need to be honest with you and say that from the photographs and videos I have seen from that night, I strongly believe it is Kelly's. But the police think she only came to the studio to change and that she's still out there somewhere.'

'At the bottom of the river?' George gulped. 'Is that where they're going to find her?'

They broke down and clung to each other, silent glottal tears overcoming their power to make any sound. Veins stood out on their necks as they clenched their jaws and tensed every muscle, trying to release the pain. Maxie knew nothing she could say would ease their suffering, that they just needed to know where their dear friend was. She took Patricia's skeletal hand and helped her into the back seat while Orlando took George round to the other door. As Orlando got into the driver's seat, George suddenly collapsed against the vehicle. He slid down the side of the car as Maxie and Patricia rushed to him and Orlando leapt back out.

George lifted his head and looked at Maxie. 'Help,' he said.

Patricia struggled out of the car to her husband. Maxie rushed up to him and tried to untangle the woollen scarf wrapped around his neck.

'Call an ambulance,' Maxie told Orlando. 'I think he's having a heart attack.'

She moved Patricia to one side and manoeuvred George into a recovery position. Putting her first aid training into action for the first time in her life, Maxie loosened the clothing around his neck and spoke calmly to him.

'Let's see if either of the two women you're saddled with right now actually have something useful with them.' She smiled.

Maxie looked up at Patricia and asked her to check both their handbags for aspirin. Like the practical woman she was, Patricia didn't stand on ceremony and quickly dumped the contents of each bag on the ground in front of the headlights, then started rummaging through as aggressively as she could. She found a strip of silver foil with two small tablets still intact. Patricia handed them to Maxie, who placed them on her husband's tongue and held his mouth closed before taking off her poncho to make a pillow for the sick man.

'The ambulance is on its way,' Orlando said, following Maxie's lead and giving his overcoat as a blanket. They could do nothing but wait and stay calm. The ten minutes it took for the ambulance to arrive felt like ten hours but the crew dealt with their patient promptly and soon had him wrapped up in a blanket on the stretcher with an oxygen mask.

'Good call on the aspirin,' said one of the paramedics to Maxie. 'You might have just saved his life.'

Maxie watched as the ambulance containing George and Patricia drove away and she picked her poncho up out of the mud and grit. She wanted to cry, scream and get blind drunk in that order but she knew it wouldn't help. She had to fight the oncoming sensation of defeat.

'I get the feeling you're not going to give up now,' said Orlando.

Maxie shook her head. 'I won't leave that couple not knowing what has happened.'

Orlando took her hand and she led him assertively back to the police team. They found Andrew and asked if there was any news, knowing full well if there had been, the whole world would have heard by now and the notifications on both their phones would be going crazy. Nevertheless, a shake of the head from Andrew confirmed it. The divers were coming up, the dogs had found nothing and Kelly's Army had retired to the nearest pub.

'It's over, Professor.'

Despondent, Maxie watched Orlando leave to join his team, then the police officers and finally the media who'd accepted there'd be no gruesome find tonight. As she stood in the cold of the night, a large flake landed on her shoulder, then another. Maxie looked skywards to see the dark sky speckled with large white flakes and she stood letting them land and watching them cover all the tracks of the search.

Chapter Twenty-Eight

Friday, 23 December

'You'd think they'd have learnt to shut their mouths by now,' said Karl, walking into the kitchen as Maxie stared out of the window watching the snow land and melt – it wasn't quite ready to stay but it would soon.

'With one breath they wish that old couple a speedy recovery,' continued Karl. 'And with the next they announce that they're thinking of suing the police force for incompetence.'

'It's hard on everyone,' replied Maxie, turning round to face him and stretching her arms above her head with a big yawn. 'We should cut them some slack. We still haven't found that woman's daughter and that's all that matters.'

Karl was fully dressed, prompting Maxie to say, 'Blimey what are you doing up before midday?'

'Going into town to find something for Olivia,' he said. 'And her folks – I can hardly turn up empty-handed on Christmas Day.'

Maxie's heart dropped in her chest but she said nothing and stood motionless in front of him, trying not to show how she felt. Karl read the silence and blushed awkwardly.

'I did tell you I'd be having lunch at her place on Christmas Day,' he continued. 'You said you were okay with it.'

'I know and I am – really I am'—Maxie wiped her hands—'but a mother can dream …'

Karl stood with his arms drooping by his sides. Maxie rubbed them and put on a big smile. 'I didn't mean it. I'm fine and can't wait to have a whole day on the sofa.'

She kissed him on the forehead, hoping she was managing to hide her true feelings. After Karl and Olivia had spent the nights here, Maxie quietly hoped their visits would slide seamlessly into a longer stay. It would have meant everything to have her son around on Christmas Day but she knew she still had to go slowly with him.

'So get yourself out there and do some shopping. I'm heading into work to write up this whole investigation for the department as well as my speech. Catch you later?'

Karl nodded so Maxie picked up the bag and coat she had primed and ready on the kitchen table and walked out. She closed the door looking up and down the corridor of the apartment block she'd chosen for this fresh start. The doormats were starting to look familiar but she knew no one behind the front doors bedecked with their festive wreaths. It seemed like a building where suppers and drinks invitations might happen and in fact a couple of neighbours had tried to make friends when she'd first arrived. Now having spent every waking hour either at the university or working alongside the police, Maxie guessed they'd given up on her. She certainly wouldn't be getting any invitations to join anyone on Christmas Day. She couldn't blame Karl for going elsewhere as it had barely registered in her house that any kind of celebration would be in full swing in only a couple of days. She certainly didn't have a tree up.

Maxie consoled herself by deciding that she'd just work most of Christmas Day and then relax with a movie. She still had to use the insight from this investigation in one of the ACU research studies. Finding Kelly wasn't the point of the research which focussed on the people left behind and how the current procedures made them feel. The case had certainly provided extensive insight into the emotional impact of a missing person on everyone, not just those close to them. The strands around public prejudice, unconscious bias and "unlikeable" victims would also warrant further research. Maxie still felt slightly ashamed of herself for thinking in this way – Kelly was a person not a research subject. However, it hadn't been the first time and it certainly wouldn't be the last that the public raged against the victim just because of their background or appearance. *"None perfect, all important"* – it had been the rallying call of the investigation and it could live on as the title of an academic study aiming to ensure that police procedures enabled everyone, no matter their walk of life or the circumstances of their disappearance, to get the justice they deserved.

Maxie was now even more determined to create something positive from this experience, whatever the outcome. She got into her car and switched on the local radio station to hear the news. Amongst the Christmas travel and traffic warnings, the reporter announced that the police were closing down the active investigation into the disappearance of Kelly Ingles after Christmas.

'A spokesperson told this station that many young adults choose to leave of their own accord and begin a new life at this time of year. They added that the death of a young man in a photographic studio was not thought to be related to the case.'

The new detective inspector was preparing the public for the narrative to come – that Kelly had chosen to leave and that Harry had died in a burglary gone wrong. But would Harry have helped her? Would he have watched the anguish of his friends over recent days, knowing where she was? Putting herself in Harry's shoes for just one moment, she could imagine him believing that without Kelly in the picture, Rowan and Luis might have a chance of lasting happiness – maybe with each other as he'd originally planned. When she thought back to the interview with him, she realised that he'd practically told them what he'd done. What was it he'd said? That she wasn't worth it and that everyone was better off without her? He could have told her to stay away from Rowan and Luis but Maxie still doubted Kelly would take any notice if she hadn't wanted to.

Despite her positive-thinking efforts, Maxie pulled up at the Criminology Building in a worse mood than when she'd got into the car. She paused by the vending machine on the way to her office and stocked up on chocolate. She had it piled in the crook of her arm as she nudged her office door open. Andrew was sitting there waiting with a box of doughnuts.

'I thought if I brought these you might help me with one final push,' he said. 'But I can see you've brought your own.'

'Great minds think alike.'

Although she'd come into the university to do her own work, Maxie was relieved to be able to have one final attempt to find Kelly. She and Andrew grabbed their case folders and took them into a meeting room with the diabetes-inducing picnic. Spreading out their notes, they chewed and sipped quietly, reviewing what they'd learned about Kelly since her disappearance. Andrew's phone rang breaking the silence.

'Hello?' He listened, raising his eyebrows occasionally and finally sighing with relief.

'What is it?' asked Maxie when he'd finished the call.

'DNA on the dress matches that from Kelly's other clothing in the wardrobe,' replied Andrew.

'Well it confirms what we already knew I guess,' said Maxie. 'Anything else?'

'We had to fast-track that,' replied Andrew. 'It's the day before Christmas Eve, the lab is swamped and we won't get anything else until after the holidays.'

'Bloody Christmas,' said Maxie. 'Well, we don't need it anyway. It won't tell us anything useful.'

'How do you work that out?' asked Andrew.

‘Hairs, fibres, residues – the girl was at a nightclub,’ said Maxie. ‘So let’s use our common sense here. If Harry did help Kelly then he has to have helped her hide somewhere until that flight. She’s a pretty distinctive-looking girl and isn’t in any hotel we know, Harry wouldn’t have let her stay at his flat – he doesn’t like her that much, so where is she hiding?’

Andrew shook his head.

‘I’m going to get hold of Rowan,’ said Maxie. ‘I’ll give your theory one more chance. I’ll try once more to drag Kelly out of hiding and then you have to start accepting this isn’t a voluntary disappearance. I’ll tell Rowan to meet us at the hospital.’

Maxie scrunched up the paper bag and slam-dunked it into a waste-paper bin on the other side of the room.

‘That has to be a sign that our luck is changing,’ said Andrew.

When they reached the hospital, Mrs Hendry was by her husband’s bed, where she’d been the whole night. He was surrounded by machines monitoring his every vital sign but the doctors assured them he was now in a stable condition and simply sleeping. Maxie opened the door to his room slightly and Mrs Hendry looked across at her, waving them in.

‘He’s going to be okay,’ she murmured. ‘The aspirin worked – thank you.’

‘I’m so glad,’ said Maxie.

She and Andrew led Patricia on a stroll down the corridor and told her about the lab results on the dress.

‘It doesn’t really mean anything though does it?’ she said, looking at them both through sad and weary eyes. ‘It doesn’t mean that we’re going to see her again.’

Maxie had to concede that it didn’t but Andrew said he still had a few hours and promised to personally keep them up to date. Patricia thanked him and walked back to her husband’s room. Before walking in, Maxie watched her take a deep breath and swallow back her emotions. If Mr Hendry had opened his eyes right then, he’d have seen a smiling wife walking assertively in rather than the frail, broken old lady they’d just spoken to.

A text arrived from Rowan saying she’d arrived and was waiting for them in the hospital foyer. They studiously followed the overhead signs to find their way back to the entrance. The place was an absolute labyrinth. Rowan stood up as they approached.

‘What can I do?’ she asked.

Maxie took the lead and told Rowan about her last conversation with Harry, how he'd said he hated Kelly's influence on her. The police thought he'd helped Kelly to run away and if he had done that, he'd probably told her to go once and for all.

'I think he'd have told her to stop screwing up your life. He might have told her that you were better off without her. If she's watching any of this, she'll know Harry is dead but she'll still think you hate her. Send messages, text her on every number she's ever had, send photos, WhatsApp – anything and everything. Over and over again. Tell her to get in touch with you, that you still care about her and that you won't give away her location to anyone else but that George and Patricia need to know she's safe. Tell her that you'll get her in to see them without anyone knowing. Play on every emotion you can and say *anything* you think will work to get her to respond but keep it going. Every message has to be completely private so she starts to trust you.'

'Is Mr Hendry dying?' asked Rowan.

'We all are. Will you do it?'

Rowan nodded and as she left for home they agreed to keep in touch regularly with any updates. Both Andrew and Maxie's phones vibrated with a text message from Orlando. He'd sent the contact details of the ex-employees and promised the final couple of numbers as soon as possible.

'I'd better get onto these people,' said Andrew. 'Do you think this Rowan thing will work? Why would Kelly contact her now?'

'Because it's Rowan who's asking her to,' replied Maxie.

Andrew's phone beeped with an email. 'The lab did me a favour but you were right – multiple DNA on the dress unfortunately and the underwear. They're guessing that came from people at the nightclub. There is one sample however that appears on both the clothing and the rucksack.'

'The rucksack isn't Kelly's so that has to belong to the person who stuffed her clothes in there,' said Maxie. 'Let me guess – it's not on your database?'

'Correct.'

'Does the report say anything else?'

'Nothing useful, residue from a damp stone floor but that could be anywhere.'

'Come on, think,' Maxie growled at herself, banging her fist on the side of her head. She looked up at Andrew and added, 'Maybe there's another building Harry has access to, somewhere he does shoots when they're not in the studio. I know you can offer your house as a location – you get paid quite a lot for it. Maybe one of them is empty at the moment.'

'It's a long shot but I'll get the team to speak to Jasmine again – while there still is a team and you speak to Rowan. We'll get to the bottom of this f—flipping case.'

He called in the instruction and found Maxie smiling at him as he put down the phone.

'Steady on DS, I didn't know you swore. I had you down as a polite young man.'

'That's two things you know about me now – I love Christmas and I swear. And I'll tell you this for free, I fart too.'

Maxie stifled a laugh. It felt so wrong to have any moments of levity but they were only human and were holding on to any tiny ray of hope they found.

Chapter Twenty-Nine

Andrew took the wheel and made his calls to the contacts provided by Orlando from the car. As each number he dialled simply rang and rang, he was having very little luck getting hold of anyone. Then finally there was a response and the ex-employee they now knew to be called Becky answered her phone chirpily. He explained what he needed and then Maxie sent her a copy of the photograph. She called back straight away.

'The guy judging the event is Stuart Rhomilly,' she explained. 'He owns Rhomilly-Ward but I'm sorry I can't remember the name of the client. He worked with Kelly and I wasn't on her team. I shouldn't have been in that picture actually but I was drunk and photobombing all of them that night. It was a great party as far as I can remember.'

'Do you have a number for this Stuart guy by any chance?'

'No but it'll be on Google. They're a pretty big company.'

Andrew thanked her and Maxie immediately searched for Rhomilly-Ward.

'So who are they then?' asked Andrew.

Maxie read from their website. *'We are experts in global communication providing a seamless international strategy for your brand.'*

'Fancy,' replied Andrew. 'I'll give them a call, see what they know.'

Andrew got straight onto them.

'He's taken his family away for Christmas,' said the voice over the Bluetooth connection.

'Lucky him,' replied Andrew. 'Somewhere with a different time zone by any chance?'

'Cancun … Mexico.'

Andrew thanked the voice and turned to Maxie. 'Nice of her to tell me where Cancun is, I'd never have guessed. What are they, six hours behind us?'

Maxie searched then looked up at him. 'Spot on. Well done clever clogs.'

'He's probably not up yet but I think I should still try to talk to him. I'll ring back and get the name of his hotel when we park up,' said Andrew.

Andrew had taken the turn-off to Rowan's house and was snaking through the traffic more easily than they'd anticipated. Maxie left Andrew in the car to make his calls, strode up to Rowan's front door and pressed the bell like someone who was going to finally get some answers today. Rowan stood aside as she bouldered into the hall.

'What on earth,' Rowan flustered. 'I haven't heard from her yet.'

'I'm not here for that.' Maxie noted but ignored her exhausted expression. 'Do you have any friends or know of any places that might be empty right now? Maybe somewhere that Harry used for shoots? Somewhere with a stone floor? It might even be somewhere quite derelict – somewhere no one would go.'

Rowan held her hands up in despair so Maxie explained the rationale behind her question.

'Kelly? Hide somewhere derelict? You've got to be kidding. She complains if there's no moisturiser in the loos.'

Rowan actually gave a little smile at her own joke but the deadly serious expression on Maxie's face didn't move an inch.

'You don't really think she's actually hiding, do you?' added Rowan. 'You think she might be hurt. I saw this film once where a kid fell down some steps in an old house, he broke his legs and couldn't get back up but no one knew where he was so he died down there. You think that might have happened? Oh my word, we have to find her.'

Rowan looked shocked by the thought of that as Maxie held her by the arms.

'That was just a film,' Maxie said. 'I remember seeing it too. Look, Kelly isn't in one of the city hotels – is there somewhere you can think of? Somewhere Harry would know?'

Rowan thought then nodded. 'Yes, actually, Harry bought this old cottage out in the sticks to do up. He said it was going to be his sanctuary, somewhere no one could bother him.'

'Do you know where it is?'

'Sorry, I don't,' said Rowan. 'I saw pictures of it on Rightmove but it looks a bit of a dump. He may have said where it was but I don't remember. I'd recognise it though.'

They quickly got the property website up on the phone and searched for cottages that had sold recently.

'That's it,' shouted Rowan as they opened the details of a renovation project in the foothills of the Pennines. Maxie noted the postcode and the two women ran out of the house, meeting Andrew coming towards them.

'That's an email sent to Rhomilly's address and the hotel,' he told them. 'The receptionist will print it off and give it to him at breakfast which will be around three o'clock our time.'

'We've got another lead too,' said Maxie as they bundled back into the car.

The height and oppressiveness of the town-centre buildings faded and the sky opened up as they left the busy suburb behind and the dark silent landscape opened up before them. Out here it was several degrees colder and sparkles of ice on black tarmac shone in the headlights.

'These roads look lethal,' said Andrew, slowing down slightly.

'Why would anyone want to live all the way out here?' asked Maxie as they reached a stone cottage, sitting alone and surrounded on all sides by fells. They all got out of the car and stared at the ramshackle building in front of them.

'He likes his privacy,' replied Rowan. 'Liked.'

Maxie placed a hand on Rowan's back and checked that she would be okay to enter the cottage. Rowan sniffed back a tear and nodded.

At one time this cottage would have housed a farmer, someone who worked this land and lived every day seeing the seasons change from the light of spring to the black of winter. It would need a lot of work to make it habitable but the setting was stunning – if you enjoyed solitude which Maxie generally didn't.

Andrew pushed his shoulder into the ancient wooden door and it caved in easily. Maxie walked in and adjusted her eyes as she entered the dark hallway. Andrew felt for a light switch on the wall and finding it, flicked it up and down – nothing. Rowan and Maxie turned on the torches on their phone, while Andrew went back to the car to get something stronger. Maxie walked through a doorway leading off the hall, the windows were boarded up and even by the torchlight she could barely see a thing but the empty chill filled the space. There was a rustling sound on the floor and both Maxie and Rowan screamed.

'Was that rats?' asked Rowan.

'Probably,' Maxie said as her heart rate started to get back to normal.

Andrew returned, turned on a big torch lantern and shone it around. Birds that had also made this place their own bristled from the disturbance. Maxie was relieved to see they weren't bats.

'Wow,' said Andrew as they all took in their surroundings. 'This place will be gorgeous when it's done up.'

A big stone hearth dominated the room and wooden beams ran the length of the ceiling. Maxie thought it looked exactly the kind of room where Christmas should be spent, just not in these circumstances.

They cautiously walked up the bare wooden staircase, with Andrew testing each step before putting his full weight on it. There were three doors leading off the landing and they each took one of them. In the corner of the bedroom that Maxie entered was a mattress and pile of blankets that looked as if they were being used by a rough sleeper. Maxie walked up to it grimacing and behind her something moved in a decrepit old cupboard. Maxie jumped and yelled out, 'Who's there?' Rowan and Andrew rushed into the room. The door of the cupboard creaked open and Andrew shone his torch directly onto the occupant.

'I'm sorry,' said Luis, holding his hands up against the glare of the light. 'This place is just so quiet, away from all the chaos. I needed some time so checked it with Harry then got a bus to the nearest village and hitched the rest of the way. Seems I'm not as infamous here.'

Rowan rushed over to him and hugged him. She told him that Harry was dead and the two friends clung to each other, sobbing until the tears ran dry.

'Why is this happening to us?' asked Luis.

Rowan held him tightly and he kissed her lightly on the top of the head.

'We thought Kelly might be hiding out here,' said Andrew. 'I don't suppose you've seen any sign of her in the cottage.'

'No – she's not here and she hasn't been,' replied Luis. 'I would know. I would be able to sense her.'

'Nevertheless, I'll get a dog and forensic team down here,' Andrew said to them.

Maxie looked around while Andrew explained that if they could find any traces of Kelly it might suggest this as a stopping off point but there was certainly no obvious trace of her here now. Someone keeping low for a few days would have bottles of water or food wrappers and as Maxie walked from room to room she could see there were no signs of either.

They waited for the police teams to arrive and Andrew asked one of the officers to take Maxie, Rowan and Luis back so the force could get on with their job. The three of them left the cottage silently, each deep in their own thoughts. It might have been a long shot but Maxie had certainly hoped it could lead somewhere and she suspected that Andrew had too.

'Can we stop for a coffee and warm up before we head back?' Maxie asked their driver, seeing a service station when they reached a main road. The officer stayed with the car while the others trudged wearily towards the neon lights of the café.

They gave their orders at the counter and then sat down in a quiet corner. Maxie picked up a long thin sachet of sugar from the bowl in the middle of the table and started scrunching and rolling it between her fingers like a stress toy. She liked the sound and the texture. The sharp granules started to cut through the paper sachet and before she knew it, she'd split open the packet and the grains were all over the table. The waiter arrived with their order and Maxie mouthed an apology. He put their coffees down in front of them then sighed and swept the grains into the palm of his hand. Maxie had actually wanted a sugar for her coffee but didn't dare take one now. All three quietly took first sips. Luis spoke first.

'This is all my fault.'

Maxie looked up to see what he'd say next.

'If I hadn't tried to pressurise her into moving in with me she wouldn't have gone and maybe none of this would have happened, maybe Harry would still be alive.'

He looked at Rowan who sat staring into her cup.

Maxie could see that Luis would always blame himself for this, as would Rowan. Luis said nothing more and just sat stirring his coffee while the silence at the table made the ambient jazz muzak even more irritating to all of them.

'I wish they'd switch that noise off,' said Luis eventually.

'At least it's not Slade,' said Rowan giving them all an excuse for the briefest of smiles.

Luis sighed. 'When all this started I read everything I could on missing persons. I looked at the database, all those faces, all those people – gone. And now Kelly's one of them.'

Rowan put her hand on top of Luis's and squeezed it.

'I even looked up what you said about the December disappearances,' continued Luis. 'I thought that was quite funny at the time – in a tragic sort of way. All these men drinking more than they're used to and forgetting where they live. I bet their wives took some persuading that's what happened.'

'I bet they did,' replied Maxie softly.

Luis paused as if trying to find the right words.

‘I don’t know how I’m supposed to feel right now.’ He looked at Maxie as if she might be able to explain it to him. ‘I walk round the house and she’s just not there and I don’t know why she’s not there. Sometimes I get angry that she hasn’t even bothered to text me and leave me properly. Then I feel ashamed for being angry – what if she’s been hurt? Then I think that if she’d been hurt, we’d have found her by now. In the hospital or in the morgue even but we’d have found her. I feel guilty if I’m hungry and have something to eat thinking I should be doing more than heating a pan of pasta while my girlfriend is still out there. If she comes home to a clean house or a dirty house, either way it’ll look like I didn’t care where she was or what was happening. It’s driving me mad.’

These were exactly the emotions Maxie was documenting through her research, the sheer helplessness that people felt. Luis put his hands through his hair and then dragged them hard down his face, pulling it into a demented mask.

‘If I knew she’d died, I could say goodbye,’ he continued. ‘If I knew she’d left me I could say fuck off. And then there’s Harry too – I just don’t know what to do.’

‘There is very little you can do,’ said Maxie as gently as she could. ‘Stay healthy and be ready to listen to Kelly’s story if she does make contact but be prepared that it may not happen quickly. There are people who go missing for years and some who never return as I’m sure you’ve read.’

‘They just sound like stories, like someone else’s life. You read them and think someone knows where they are or that there must have been something you missed but here I am and I have no clues, none at all.’

‘None of us do,’ said Rowan.

‘Harry may have done,’ said Luis. ‘But we’ll never know now.’

Rowan began crying and Luis pulled her in towards him and held her tightly.

‘We haven’t really spoken about Harry,’ said Maxie, handing Rowan a clean tissue. ‘And that’s the only concrete lead that we have right now – her dress turning up at the warehouse. What did you think when you heard that?’

‘Harry was always trying to look out for me, although as you’ve seen I can handle myself quite well,’ replied Luis. ‘Honestly? When I heard that, I could believe that he’d seen her in that state and got her out of those clothes. He wouldn’t want me to see her like that. He might have let her sleep things off but that’s it. He’d know I would be worried and he wouldn't hide Kelly. He was a good guy, maybe a bit serious but honest and now I've lost him too.'

The officer who'd driven them from the cottage appeared at the door of the café and told them he'd had orders to bring Luis straight into the station. Maxie guessed that they had to question him over Harry's death and now that the young man seemed emotionally broken, they'd go over his statements about Kelly's disappearance again. Maxie could see Luis was holding in a huge deal of hurt and anger.

'DS Dawson is on his way to escort you home,' the officer said to Maxie and Rowan. 'He's only five minutes away – are you okay to wait?'

Maxie nodded as she watched Luis reluctantly get into the back seat of the police car. Almost as soon as the police car left the service station, Andrew's car drove in and he screeched to a halt in front of them and wound down the window.

'That Rhomilly guy is up and wants to talk to us,' he called out. 'They're setting up a video conference at the station. I'll drop you off on the way, Rowan.'

'As one door closes …' said Maxie as she climbed in beside the DS.

Chapter Thirty

'Another wild goose turned up?' said the DI as Andrew charged towards his desk. Maxie tried to sneak in after him but still caught his exasperated glance.

'I know you want all your team to be as thorough as possible,' replied Andrew, shrugging off his coat and rifling through the papers on his desk in one move.

His boss made a show of checking his watch. 'I certainly want you to be as thorough as possible within the restraints of this force. I mean it, DS Dawson. This gets signed off and closed tomorrow.'

Andrew found the notes he needed and, nodding to the DI, strode back out of the office beckoning Maxie to follow him. They sat down in the video conference room and dialled the number they'd been given. On the other side of the world, a face appeared against the backdrop of a clear blue sky and a glorious ocean. Maxie recognised the blond-haired, blue-eyed man who was now slightly tanned and very much at ease. She thought the face looked even more handsome than it had done in the photograph and wondered yet again how Kelly had managed to surround herself with such gorgeous men. Academics never looked like this.

'Hi there, I'm Stuart,' said the face.

'It looks beautiful over there,' replied Maxie.

'It is. I'll give you both a tour.'

Stuart picked up his tablet and manoeuvred it round to give Maxie and Andrew a view of the brochure-perfect setting from his balcony.

'Thank you for getting in touch,' said Andrew before explaining the situation and asking how he knew Kelly.

'Most people in the industry would know her. She's a force of nature and if there's a party, Kelly will be there. How long has she been missing?'

'Nearly a week now,' said Maxie, knowing that she shouldn't be interrupting the interview process but still not wanting to waste time going over the history. 'Do you know who the other man is in the photograph that Andrew sent you? We're told he's a client.'

'He certainly is. He heads *Get Into Sport* and we'd just started handling his account when we won that award. It was a fabulous night.'

'How well would he know Kelly?'

'Not well. Look, there's something you should know and that's really why I got in touch. It's completely confidential although I'm not sure how much that matters now.'

Stuart leaned into the camera as if there weren't several thousand miles between them and somehow he could whisper. Andrew put down his pen and leant back in his chair. Maxie couldn't decide whether leaning in or out was the right response here so rocked back and forward for a couple of seconds before deciding to mirror Stuart and lean right into the screen.

'I offered Kelly a job just over a week ago,' continued Stuart. 'I've offered her the chance to go out to New York and handle some of our international clients. It's a big promotion for her but I think she'd do a good job out there.'

'New York?' blurted Maxie. 'So you bought that plane ticket?'

'Yes, it was a gesture – here's the job and the ticket. She was really excited about it but said she'd have to talk it over with her boyfriend before letting me know formally.'

Andrew put his elbows on the desk, interlinked his fingers and rested his chin on his hands and Maxie could sense the frustration he was feeling. She knew that when Andrew told his boss about this it would simply add weight to his theory that she'd run away. And maybe she actually had. Was it really feasible that Kelly hadn't mentioned this job to anyone? Surely if Rowan or Luis had known about it they would have said something by now. She listened as Andrew calmly confirmed the details of the job offer with Stuart: he'd interviewed her at the beginning of December and had called her on the Thursday before the office party to offer her the position. She'd seemed really pleased but had asked for a few days to talk it over with her boyfriend.

'It was a big move,' said Stuart, 'so I understood completely.'

'And you haven't heard from her since?' asked Maxie as Andrew sat looking lost in his thoughts. Stuart shook his head.

'So you don't know whether she spoke to her boyfriend?'

Stuart confirmed that he hadn't heard from her since making the offer but hadn't expected to. He'd come out for his family holiday and as ever, his wife insisted that he leave the world of work behind for one week of the year. He'd planned on calling Kelly the day after Boxing Day to see if they could make a New Year statement.

'It's always good to have something to announce first thing January. Now I guess I'll have to think of something else.'

Maxie shook her head in disbelief. These PR men and their statements. Kelly was just an acquisition to him. She knew her indignation was quite hypocritical given that this whole case should just be another research study to Maxie but, in fairness, it had always been more than that from the beginning. Stuart noticed her reaction.

'I'm sorry,' he said, 'that sounded heartless. I made the job offer because it needs filling at some stage soon so I have to decide whether to leave it open for Kelly or not. Have you absolutely no idea where she is? Can we help at all?'

The words sounded like criticism and if they did find Kelly before she accepted this role then Maxie would be warning her that this Stuart might be all smiles on the outside but there was a very definite hardness to his nature. She might be better off staying where she was.

'This isn't a stunt is it?' Andrew asked suddenly. 'Your agency locates her when OrlandoPR fail then celebrate her joining you? That would make a good January statement.'

Maxie silently applauded his suggestion; he'd learnt a lot this week. The PR world seemed to be able to twist any tragedy. Stuart laughed.

'Maybe I should employ you. If she were an international celebrity then that might work but if I turn up with Kelly in January, I'm going to get arrested for wasting police time aren't I? Honestly, I spoke to her once before I came out. I made the job offer and said I'd wait to hear from her. That's all I know.'

In the background a little girl started shouting "Daddy, Daddy" then ran up to the screen with a seashell. Stuart picked her up and sat her on his knee; it was his signal that the interview was over.

'Thank you for your time,' said Maxie.

'Call me back if you need anything else and definitely when you hear from her,' said Stuart, waving his goodbye and getting his daughter to do the same.

'Yes sir, no sir, three bags full sir,' murmured Andrew after the call closed.

Maxie made no move to leave the VC room. She couldn't decide whether this was good news or not. She was also aware that this piece of news had somehow changed her relationship with the girl she'd never met. She had looked at the pictures of Kelly, seeing the girl that she once was. If that were the case, what would Maxie have done with a red-hot job offer? What did she do when she was first offered the professorship? She upped and left.

'It's no use,' said Andrew suddenly. 'I can't read your take on all this.'

Maxie looked up and realised Andrew had been staring at her. She said nothing but instead started scribbling on her notepad. 'Did you check Kelly's work PC as well as her home one?'

Andrew nodded.

'How did she apply for a job without leaving a trace?'

'Internet café? Post?'

'Shall we add carrier pigeon to that list? No one applies for a job without an email so she must have one that we haven't found. We should get in touch with Stuart's secretary and find out the email address they used for all the correspondence and we should give Kelly's friends and family a call to see if any of them knew about this. They might be keeping it quiet if she's asked them to.'

'I'll go and tell the DI that there's some new information.'

'Really, I wouldn't,' said Maxie. 'He'll have your guts if he thinks you're not wrapping this up right now. Let's see if there's anything in it first.'

A nod sealed their pact. Andrew left Maxie to make her calls while he pursued Stuart Rhomilly's secretary.

Kelly's mother knew nothing about the offer nor did the Hendrys who were sad to hear that even when their friend came back, it wouldn't be for long.

'It's so far away isn't it? New York.'

Rowan sounded completely hacked-off at the news. 'Absolutely typical,' she said. 'She's putting us through all of this and when she turns up she's going to have some glamorous job offer ready and waiting. She'll just swan off without a care for any of us.' Rowan sniffed and choked back a tear before falling silent.

Maxie knew she was simply frustrated and worried. She promised to call with any further news and then went to see Luis who was still in the interview room.

'*Por el amor de Cristo*,' he exclaimed. 'How many more things do I have to find out about my girlfriend from a complete stranger?'

Maxie apologised and then questioned him about the Thursday she received the offer. Had she been excited or secretive about anything? Is there an internet café or another PC she might have used for the application? Had she even hinted at them living in New York?

‘No, no and no,’ replied Luis to every question. ‘Although she was always excited – about everything.’

‘Would you have gone with her?’

Luis sat shredding the paper cup in his hand. ‘It’s not my idea of a good time, being in a big city I don’t know, surrounded by Kelly’s work friends. But I love her so I’d have to give it a try or let her go. I would never hold her back from her dreams.’

Maxie heard the sadness in Luis’s voice; this job offer certainly didn’t seem in keeping with the engagement and the future he’d planned. Kelly’s disappearance had almost fast-forwarded their relationship to the point where he could see it wouldn’t work, that they were too different. Life had moved on and no matter what happened, they wouldn’t be returning to the same start point.

Maxie made the same promises to Luis as she had done to Rowan then scrolled through her numbers for the final call to Orlando.

‘I’ll kill him.’ Orlando reacted to the news. ‘Poaching someone else’s team is just not on. Was she taking any accounts with her? What did he say?’

Maxie could hear the cogs whirring as Orlando tried to work out the implications for his business. There was clearly no love lost between himself and Stuart.

‘Look Maxie,’ he continued in a state of panic. ‘I’ll do anything I can to help but I didn’t know about this and I really need to call round my client base to see if there’s any hint that they’re going to defect to that snake in the grass. Can I do that and call you back?’

Maxie agreed and left him to it. Behind her the door crashed open and she swung round on her chair to see Andrew with a triumphant look on his face.

‘No one knew a thing,’ she offered.

‘Au contraire,’ declared Andrew. ‘You were right. There was another email address and Harry knew everything.’

Rhomilly-Ward had provided Andrew with the email address Kelly had used for the application. It was a new web-based address which didn’t seem to have been used for anything other than this. They’d also told him that a Mr H Marlow from Looking Glass Productions had provided the reference as well as the client who’d been in that photograph with her. Andrew told her that although some laptops had been stolen from the warehouse, the company backed everything up into the cloud each night and amongst Harry’s private correspondence there was a disguised folder containing Kelly's CV, the interview dates and the offer letter. The letter said she had to bring an up-to-date passport into the Rhomilly-Ward office on Thursday for the final right-to-work checks.

'It looks as if she used his computers to do it all and keep it a secret. It also explains why her passport was missing – it's with Rhomilly-Ward.'

Andrew handed her copies of all the paperwork they'd found. It all looked in order; a perfectly normal job application that Kelly had kept quiet about.

'There was a lot Harry didn't tell us wasn't there?' said Andrew. 'This means it looks likely that it was him who met Kelly at the club, took her back and cleaned her up. That's why her clothes were in his locker. He was actively encouraging her to get a job as far away as possible. We know he thought Luis and Rowan deserved better than her.'

Maxie threw her hands up in exasperation. 'That still doesn't answer the fundamental question – where on earth is she? Her friend is dead, her boyfriend is being questioned – she can't be so heartless that she's ignoring both facts. Come on Andrew, what are we missing? I need to find her.'

'I'm supposed to remind you that in this job you can't get too emotionally involved … But I feel the same.'

'How can you not? This woman is driving me nuts. She has a gorgeous man who wants to marry her, a fabulous job, a boss who appreciates her and the offer of a promotion and a huge salary increase. The world is her oyster.'

'It's a lot of people wanting something from her though,' Andrew said, 'pulling her in every direction. To take the dream job she has to lose the dream boyfriend – whichever way she turns she'll hurt someone. But she never planned for it to get this bad and now she is scared to reappear. If I were her, I'd want to vanish. I'd speak to no one and take up that job offer. Go somewhere no one knows me and start again. There's nothing left for her here. It all fits, Professor and there's been nothing new from Luis we can use. Unless you can think of something we've missed, I think we both have to accept that it's time to move on.'

'I always thought that I'd get the chance to meet her.' Maxie exhaled. 'It looks like I'm going to have to go to New York for that. I'm going to need a drink – do you fancy a quick one? I'll buy.'

Andrew apologised and told her he was due at home. He planned to tell his DI the news and leave this all behind him.

'I still don't buy that she'd just vanish. I do hate cases with no resolution,' said Maxie.

'I've accepted that you have to get used to it but writing that end report helps. You get to close the book. It's not the exciting part of the job but it helps.'

Maxie could imagine that it did, just like the final draft of a dissertation or getting through all the exam papers.

'Could I help in any way with the report you write?' she asked.

'I'd love your input.' Andrew grinned. 'Let's get on with it.'

As Maxie followed Andrew to his desk, her phone rang. She picked it up and saw Orlando's name but also that she'd missed a call from Karl. He'd left a message which Maxie decided to listen to first and she sighed as she heard his voice.

'Hi Mum, was hoping you'd be home by now but I guess you're busy. Just to let you know that I'm heading out to Olivia's tonight so won't be in when you get home. Don't worry about me – I'm really going to Olivia's – you can call me there. It's been lovely to see you. Have a lovely Christmas and there's a little pressie from Santa under your bed but no opening it until the big day. Love you.'

He sounded happy and at least Maxie knew he was safe. Those two things should never be taken for granted and she doubted she ever would again. She rang Orlando's number and he picked up immediately.

'The good news is that no one was about to defect to that swine,' declared Orlando, sounding exceptionally relieved. 'The bad news is that none of them have heard from Kelly, so I can't be much more help.'

Maxie thanked him for calling her and as he spoke, knew she just couldn't let this case drop until she had the full picture. She'd come back to it in the new year even without the police force. She wished Orlando a merry Christmas and was about to end the call when she paused. 'If this isn't completely inappropriate,' she asked. 'Would you like to come for a drink later on?'

'I thought you'd never ask.'

Chapter Thirty-One

As Andrew collated his notes, he actually seemed quite agitated. Maxie guessed he was probably keen to get this stage over with, to get all the reports drafted, to keep his boss happy and then get on with his family celebration. She knew he would keep looking if he could but the case would become inactive tomorrow evening. Even Kelly's friends and family now assumed she'd bagged a new job and was going to jump on a plane to New York without telling them. Then one day, at a time of her choosing, she'd get in touch. It was at least a hopeful scenario and much better than the worst-case scenario Maxie had let herself imagine at the start of this case: finding Kelly floating in the river. That would have been unbearable.

Although the "moving abroad" theory was everyone's favourite, Andrew told Maxie he had to stick to the bare facts for this report. When she read the report which separated facts from the emotion of Kelly's life, it amounted to very little:

> "On Friday 16 December, Ms Kelly Ingles – 24 attended a work party with colleagues and her friend Rowan Peters. Kelly and Rowan continued on to a night club – The Printworks on Millgate Street and danced until approximately 2.15 a.m. Rowan went to the toilet and when she came out, Kelly had left the building. CCTV footage showed Kelly leaving willingly although under the influence of alcohol. Police were alerted as to the disappearance by Mrs Patricia Hendry who is a friend of Kelly. Neither Rowan nor Kelly's boyfriend, Mr Luis Caballero had heard from Kelly who had sent Mr Caballero a text at 3 a.m. saying she was staying the night with Rowan but never did. There has been no sign of or contact by Kelly since that date. Her dress from the nightclub was found in a rucksack at the premises of Looking Glass Productions on Friday 23 December. The owner of that company was found dead at the premises following an apparent burglary. An extensive search, incorporating dogs and diving teams, together with members of the public was undertaken and organised crime consulted but neither have resulted in any concrete evidence as to likely whereabouts of Kelly Ingles. Her mother is alive although she is not close to Ms Ingles. Instead, Kelly is close to an elderly couple Mrs and Mr

Hendry. Mr Hendry had a heart attack during the investigation. Attempts were made to contact Kelly with news of his condition but she has not come forward. Ms Ingles has a new job offer which would require her to move to New York. It is assumed that Kelly has disappeared voluntarily and will take up this offer in the new year. Ms Ingles' details are now with Missing Persons and the case will remain open pending her appearance in the new job. It will be subject to regular reviews in the event of further information becoming available but will no longer remain active."

It was what his boss wanted to read but not what Maxie wanted to do. She still wanted to search forever.

'Okay,' said Andrew pressing "save" on the report. 'The last bit is the worst. We have to go and explain what all of this means to Mrs Ingles.'

'I'll come with you,' said Maxie, dreading her reaction and wondering whether it would feel any easier than having to tell them they'd found Kelly's body. Not knowing was often worse than knowing.

Andrew called Mrs Ingles' number and she answered saying that she was in the hospital visiting George and Patricia. Andrew told her he'd be there within the hour but emphasised that he had no new news. Maxie noticed he was using a very dour voice to really set the expectation.

'It's best that she's prepared,' he told Maxie.

They walked through the hush of the hospital wing. Maxie knocked quietly on the door to the private room and opened it slowly to see Mrs Ingles sitting in a chair by the side of the bed, talking to Patricia. Maxie looked around the room for Dave and Mrs Ingles caught her looking.

'He's gone,' she whispered. 'He was only ever interested in the money wasn't he?'

Patricia put a hand on Mrs Ingles' shoulder as she dropped her head.

Maxie looked over at the bed and saw that, thankfully George was sleeping. It was one thing telling the perfectly healthy women by his side that they'd be stopping the investigation and quite another risking the heart of this poorly man. Mrs Ingles looked up and took a deep breath. With her drawn complexion and dark-circled eyes, her whole demeanour looked set for further bad news. She picked up a shoulder bag and asked Patricia if she would come too. Patricia nodded then kissed her husband on the forehead and linked arms with Mrs Ingles as they joined Andrew and Maxie in the corridor.

Wordlessly they walked to the canteen where Christmas music played over the speakers and snowflakes were stencilled on the windows. It looked odd to see any effort of cheer in this place of perpetual illness. Andrew suggested everyone sit down and asked Maxie to collect some hot drinks. She ordered all of them creamy hot chocolates, thinking they might be the best drink to serve with bad news. She joined Andrew on the opposite side of the table to the ladies and they all blew on their drinks then took small cautious sips. Andrew went to open his mouth but Mrs Ingles put a palm up to silence him. She shook her head and sobbed into her mug.

'How is George?' asked Maxie, breaking the silence after a few minutes.

Patricia nodded and murmured, 'He's okay.'

'When will he be allowed home?'

'They imagine it'll be just before New Year if his condition continues to improve.' She looked up at Andrew. 'So we'll spend Christmas Day here unless you're about to tell us there's some good news and we should all go home to celebrate.'

Andrew hugged the warm cup and shook his head. Patricia took hold of Mrs Ingles' hand and squeezed it tightly.

'I'm sorry,' said Andrew. 'I wish there was. There has simply been no trace of Kelly since last week and despite all our best efforts, we have no further leads to follow up. We would look for Kelly forever if we simply had any evidence to point us in a clear direction. The only lead we have is New York and we won't know if that's real until she tries to board the plane.'

Mrs Ingles smiled weakly. 'Her old school reports always said that she was good at anything she put her mind to. Back then they just wanted her to put her mind to her lessons rather than fooling around. Now it seems she's put her mind to disappearing.'

Maxie returned the smile.

'You think she might have just moved to New York for this job and not told anyone?' continued Mrs Ingles.

'We know the ticket we found isn't valid until January and she hasn't boarded any plane on another ticket yet,' Andrew said. 'It doesn't mean to say she's not going to at some time.'

'Maybe she will. Maybe when all this is over she'll turn up and have a big party to celebrate. She'll make us promise to visit,' murmured Mrs Ingles to Patricia. 'She's a real force of nature my daughter. She'd probably even manage to persuade that lovely boyfriend of hers to pay for the drinks.'

'I get that impression,' Maxie said and they smiled at each other.

'So what happens now?' Mrs Ingles asked Andrew.

He explained that the case would remain open and would be reviewed regularly but that post-Christmas, there would be no active investigation.

'At least she's not dead is she?' She gasped fighting back tears.

Maxie tried to reach out and hold her hands but Mrs Ingles pulled them back and folded them on her lap.

'There's no need for either of you to pander to me,' she added. 'I know that it's all about budgets and not about people.'

'It's about both Mrs Ingles,' Andrew said. 'I can't deny that there are other cases that need our attention but I have sisters Kelly's age and I would be fighting for more time if I could find anything at all I believed would help. Is there a route you feel we haven't pursued? Anything at all?'

'It's not like it is on the telly is it?' Mrs Ingles shook her head. 'Finding them tiny bits of plant and dirt under the microscope and discovering that they're only grown in one field in the whole county.'

'I'm afraid it's never been like that,' Maxie said.

'If she'd moved to a big city instead of here, there'd have been CCTV everywhere.'

'Maybe, it seems Helmsforth doesn't have it in the right places,' Andrew replied.

Mrs Ingles and Patricia sat quietly looking as defeated as Maxie felt. She so wanted to console these women who'd already been through so much but it wouldn't help. She knew that the only thing these ladies wanted to hear from her was that Kelly was safe and well. It was the only thing Maxie wanted to be able to say.

'So we won't hear from you again?' Patricia now spoke with words so soft and lost they barely broke the silence between them. Maxie felt them rather than heard them. She watched as Andrew looked straight into Mrs Hendry's eyes.

'It would be so very wrong of me to offer either of you any false hope,' he said. 'The statistics really do show that after this length of time we're unlikely to find Kelly unless she wants to be found. But I will make you this promise, if anything comes up, even if it's news that she doesn't want to come back, then I will come and tell you both personally.'

Mrs Ingles nodded and reached across the table to put her hand over his. 'Thank you.'

The conversation and the hot chocolate finished, Mrs Ingles told them that she was going to get herself home and Patricia said she'd better get back to her husband so the four weary souls got up and strolled back along the corridor. They walked Mrs Ingles to the exit and then turned to escort Patricia back to her husband.

'Will you have your family around you this Christmas, Professor?' asked Patricia as they walked.

Maxie shook her head. 'My son wants to spend this one with his new girlfriend. I'll miss him. We have this tradition, it's daft really but we always turn the volume down on the Queen's Speech and make up our own words. Knowing me, I'll have a couple of glasses of wine and I'll probably end up still doing it all by myself.'

'What a shame,' Patricia said as they reached the door of George's room. 'Even the silly things you do together are important aren't they? And the problem is you never know whether this one will be the last. If I've learned anything in the past few days, it's that.'

She said goodbye to Maxie and Andrew then stood for a few seconds to compose herself before heading back into her husband's room with fake cheer on her face. Sometimes it took a woman who'd lost almost everything to make you grateful for what you still had.

Maxie said goodbye to Andrew and then bounded to her car with renewed purpose. She practically skidded out of the car park and kept borderline legal with the speed limit until she'd reached the shopping mall. She could have Christmas with Karl – just not Christmas lunch. Swerving through the clichéd muddles of men traipsing zombie-like from store to store in the search of their last-minute presents, Maxie made straight for the food hall. She knew it had to close tomorrow so the shelves would be full of cut-price cakes and biscuits. Maxie was the absolute dream customer buying up the last of the hams, the cheeses, the liqueurs, the chocolates and what the heck, even the snow domes no one else wanted. The reindeer she'd seen made from fir cones and scraps of wood seemed to be pleading with her for a home of his own so she picked that up too. Her house would look like Santa's grotto this year.

'Build it and he will come,' she said to the assistant, handing her the reindeer.

She ploughed through the mall laden with bags, aware that she still didn't have an actual gift for her son. A jewellers seemed to sparkle in her direct line of sight and beckon her in. She walked up to the window and looked at the stunning array of designer watches and the ads featuring footballers and action heroes sporting these timepieces. Maybe you were supposed to pick the celebrity most like the person you were buying for she mused. None of them said "Karl". They were all far too sure of themselves. Her son still hadn't found his place in the world and she knew her lifestyle hadn't really helped. She looked around and then realised what she had to buy for him. Maxie marched into a travel agent's and asked for five hundred pounds worth of gift vouchers. Her son loved Olivia and this would delight them both. She'd encourage him to travel but to always come back. As the assistant was putting the vouchers into an envelope, Maxie stopped her for a second.

'Make it a thousand pounds,' she said, much to the assistant's delight.

On her way home and sure that she'd turned a disastrous Christmas into something they'd look back on with at least a giggle, Maxie called Karl. It went straight to voicemail.

'It's me, the worst mother in the world. Just calling to say I got your message and I promise not to peek at my pressie. I'd really like to see you and Olivia on Christmas Day. When you've finished all the proper turkey business with someone who can cook, come round. I'll put on a fabulous supper of things that don't need cooking and we'll make fun of the Queen's Speech. Hope you can make it.'

She waited hopefully for a witty text from her son but none came.

'Please Karl don't make it just me and Her Majesty this year.'

Chapter Thirty-Two

Maxie checked her phone every five seconds but still nothing from Karl. She fretted over her message, wondering whether it was witty enough or whether it'd be seen as downright embarrassing. She hoped he wouldn't start the Queen's Speech tradition at Olivia's house if that was her only bargaining chip. She still had to get ready for the drinks date tonight so stood the phone on the toilet cistern while she took a shower. Murphy's law, it beeped with a text when she had a headful of shampoo. She struggled out and dripped over the floor, shaking the water from her hands so she could pick it up without destroying it. Her hands were too wet to swipe the screen, the shampoo had started dripping into her eyes and as she reached blindly for the towel, it tangled around her legs making her stumble forwards, cracking her forearm and wrist against the tile floor as it took the brunt of the fall.

Maxie propped herself upright to catch her breath and picked up the phone. If this was one of those sales texts, she was going to find their head office and wring the neck of the person in charge. It was Orlando, confirming the arrangements for tonight.

Thought we'd try The Mermaid – good reviews x

Maxie looked down at her legs tied up in the huge bath sheet and snorted to herself. 'Maxie darling, that doesn't mean to say you have to go dressed as one.'

The trauma of the shower over, Maxie waded through her wardrobe looking for something suitable. Her arm and wrist were throbbing so she was sure she'd be sporting black and blue bruises by the end of the night. She needed something with long sleeves. She picked up a dress and thought about Kelly and her need to cover up the bruises from her kick-boxing. The guilt of not being out there, still looking, welled up in her but maybe Andrew and the DI had been right. They really had no idea where to look next and Maxie had to start focussing on her own life for a while which wasn't exactly looking like a winter wonderland right now. Building a proper relationship with Karl and having some fun of her own would be her New Year resolutions. She didn't know how she'd do the former but at least she was about to have some fun. She had a date and they were meeting at The Mermaid, somewhere she'd always wanted to go. It was a gorgeous place, known for its wine list and gin range; the evening would be a positive smorgasbord of pleasure for her.

'I've got a *date*,' she kept saying to herself.

An actual date with someone who'd come to know her quite well over an extremely short period of time and hadn't run away. Not someone who'd swiped her photograph and decided to give her a go and certainly not someone who'd be sending her obscene images after a bottle of wine. Maxie laughed out loud at her reflection, just thinking back to that encounter. She wondered who he'd end up with next. He'd seemed so nice and normal at the beginning of the date. That's why she'd let her guard down and relaxed a little. Maxie's mind wandered to imagining whether he expected a photo of her in return – something hot and steamy?

'I'd send him a picture of me doing the ironing.' She giggled to herself. It felt strange but good to laugh and she deserved a night out but all this contemplation wasn't getting her ready for her evening out with that handsome Scotsman. The occasion called for her black leather skirt and ankle boots, topped with a dark aubergine coloured cowl neck top. Her lipstick matched the top so with her colouring and a dash of eyeliner she looked slightly exotic – just as she remembered her mother managing to do every day effortlessly. A notification on her app told her the taxi had arrived so with one last check, she took a deep breath, picked up her bag and set off with the aim of thoroughly enjoying herself.

Orlando was waiting at a table in the bar when she arrived. She knew he would be. Men don't get to his position without knowing the rules and arriving before your female companion to secure her a table is one of those rules. He stood up to kiss her on the cheek and as she took off her coat he whistled.

'Professor Reddick,' he said. 'You certainly scrub up well. Go to the top of the class.'

'Why you smooth-talker you.' She laughed. 'I have to warn you that flattery will get you everywhere.'

Orlando checked that it would be okay to have a drink at the bar before going to the table and asked her whether she'd prefer wine or something else to start. Maxie was mentally giving him marks out of ten and so far couldn't fault him. She hated men who simply went ahead and selected a Chardonnay for her, uttering something inane like "you can't go wrong with a Chardonnay". You absolutely could especially if like Maxie what you really liked to start the night off with was a large gin. She accepted the balloon-shaped glass full of ice and herbs then sighed with delight as the crisp clear liquid sparkled through her body, rejuvenating her. She hadn't realised just how tired this case had made her feel.

'I wanted to ask you out when we first met but I didn't think it would be very appropriate,' said Orlando.

'It wouldn't have been,' acknowledged Maxie. 'And besides which I wouldn't have accepted. You came over as a bit full of yourself.'

Orlando dropped his head and groaned. 'I said all that stuff about honouring our heritage didn't I?'

Maxie nodded then they both grimaced. Orlando mouthed a "sorry" and Maxie sat up tall in her seat.

'I like to tell my under-r-r-lings,' she mocked doing a very bad impression of his accent. 'That we me-e-e-e-re mor-r-r-tals must raispect their-r-r-r memor-ree.'

'I do not sound like that.' He laughed. 'Okay maybe I did.'

A waiter approached to say that their table was ready. Orlando held out his hand to escort Maxie and she paused before accepting it. As they sat down she reflected that it had been quite some time since a man had offered her anything to lean on. Maxie wondered whether it was all too good to be true and couldn't help but notice how he handled himself throughout the whole meal. It was pretty damn perfect. He didn't order for them but made suggestions of things she might like to try, promising that he'd eat anything she didn't like. Maxie tested him by ordering the strangest selection of side dishes to accompany her sea bass and then telling him she'd only done it to see how he reacted.

'If you want beetroot with your bass then who am I to comment on your weirdness?' He held his palms up in defeat.

Maxie let herself flow into the fabulous food, witty conversation and effortless company until just as the plates were being taken away, a young woman with cropped blue hair entered the bar with a group of friends. Both Orlando and Maxie stopped mid-mouthful to look at her smiling and lighting up the room.

'I don't think I'll ever stop thinking about her,' said Orlando.

Maxie swallowed and patted her mouth with her napkin. 'Me neither.'

'I tried not to feel guilty about coming out tonight,' Orlando continued. 'Because there's nothing we can actually do, but that doesn't really help does it?'

'We could be out ransacking the streets until she's found.'

'But you've done that and she's not there.'

They looked at each other and knew the carefree conversation was over. They both had a need to talk about Kelly in the same way that you need to try and understand any tragic death when you're at a funeral.

'What do you really think has happened?' he asked.

'I honestly don't know. She seemed to be an open book when I first started following the investigation. Everyone knew what she was like and she didn't try to hide it. I really admired her. Then the more everyone looked, the more we found that no one knew her.'

Orlando nodded. 'That job offer knocked me for six. I taught Kelly all about PR and she was just going to up and leave. And to think Harry knew about it from the very beginning. I can't believe he gave her a reference. Do you think if he'd told us, before the attack, we'd have found her by now?'

'I can't see what difference it would have made. It's as if she's vanished into thin air.'

'When I was wondering whether coming out tonight was the right thing to do, I couldn't help but think that sometimes things turn up when you stop looking for them,' said Orlando. 'If you weren't out searching but relaxing instead then something would catch the corner of your eye and it would all make sense.'

'I know exactly what you mean. I guess I was hoping for that too.'

'So I was just a decoy.'

Maxie put her hand on his. 'Of course not,' she said, perking up the tone of the conversation. 'You're here to keep my son off my back. He says I have to get out more and stop thinking about the job. Not that this worked completely.'

'I hope the next time we go out,' Orlando said, 'there is no case or study we're both connected with and we talk about films and music like normal people do.'

'To being normal.' Maxie raised her glass and they clinked, holding their glasses together for a moment longer than they needed to.

Out of the corner of her eye, Maxie spotted someone she recognised entering the restaurant. It took her a moment but then …

'Oh no, it's him,' she said, ducking her head down.

'Who?' asked Orlando.

Giggling, Maxie pulled his head down towards the table and told him about her blind date and the photo she got afterwards.

'A dick-pic?' Orlando snorted. 'It's a classy dating site then.'

Maxie sneaked a look across the restaurant. The blind date fortunately had his back to her and was standing up now, kissing a woman on both cheeks and inviting her to sit down. From their body language, she could tell this was a first date.

‘His next victim arrives,’ said Orlando.

‘It’s not really funny,’ said Maxie. ‘I hope she’s okay.’

Neither Orlando nor Maxie could keep their eyes off the blind-date couple. Then, when the man got up and headed towards the bathroom, Orlando grabbed Maxie’s hand and pulled her up.

‘Come on,’ he said. ‘Let’s go.’

Orlando took her hand and hurried her towards the blind-date table. Once there he picked up the guy’s phone which had been left by his glass and dropped it into the water jug in the middle of the table. The woman sitting there looked shocked.

‘Escape while you can,’ Orlando whispered to her as he and Maxie ran towards the exit.

Outside they hailed a cab and snuggled into the back seat. ‘That was naughty,’ said Maxie with a big smile on her face.

‘Well I can’t have him shocking any more innocent women.’

‘Thank you for avenging my honour,’ she said, turning towards him and kissing him softly.

‘My pleasure,’ Orlando replied, responding to her lips. ‘My place?’

Maxie nodded. The taxi drove into a cul-de-sac of smart modern homes, not at all what Maxie had expected. Orlando watched her appraising the location.

‘I had you down for the warehouse conversion type,’ she said to him. ‘Living in a dank building while you do it up.’

‘Not when I work in one all day. Nope this place is maintenance-free and filled with gadgets.’ He touched an app on his phone so every room in the house lit up.

Maxie laughed and took his arm as they walked towards the front door. It opened as he approached and inside there was already music playing.

‘Can it mix a gin and tonic?’ she asked.

‘I’m working on that bit.’

Orlando showed her to the living room while he went into the kitchen. Maxie took a stroll around the room, checking out his books and his photographs. She picked up a very old picture of a rugby team where a young Orlando stood proudly holding a trophy as Captain of the team.

‘I didn’t know you were sporty,’ she said as he came back into the room, holding a glass out to her.

‘Oh I would have loved to play professionally,’ he replied. ‘But it’s that age-old story.’

'Injury?'

'No, just crap at sport.'

Maxie laughed and looked at the picture again. 'Why does it say Roland not Orlando?'

Orlando tried to take it from her as she held it behind her back, teasing him. He held his hands up in a "you got me" gesture. She handed the picture to him.

'I was born Roland but there was this cartoon puppet on TV back then – Roland Rat.'

Maxie nodded that she remembered it.

'So I got called Ratty all my teenage years. You can't really run a PR company being called Ratty. I swapped round the "o" and the "r" and voila – I have a name fit for the industry I've chosen to work in.'

'It's a very PR type name but it suits you far better than Roland.'

'Thank you,' said Orlando. 'Kelly used to make fun of me something rotten. The team came round for a barbecue and I thought I'd hidden it but she found it. She'd sing out "roly-poly pudding and pie" if she wanted to tease me, which as you can imagine was quite a lot.'

'Well roly-poly is one thing you certainly aren't.' Maxie rested her palm on his perfectly flat stomach.

'Shall we take these drinks to the bedroom?' asked Orlando.

'I thought you'd never ask.'

Chapter Thirty-Three

Saturday, 24 December

Maxie woke up with Orlando spooning her. She carefully unravelled herself from his embrace and reached out for her phone. It was only 5.30 a.m. but she was wide awake. Orlando groaned and tried to pull her back but she redirected his arm to snuggle a pillow. It had been so long since she'd enjoyed a man's company and Maxie knew she should feel guilty for having enjoyed herself at a time like this but she'd needed it and felt so much better for having let herself go. She leant over and kissed Orlando gently on the forehead.

'I'm going to head home then have to go into the studio to record a podcast,' she said. 'Speak later?'

Orlando half-opened his eyes. 'I'll drive you,' he moaned sleepily.

'It's far too early, you sleep.' She pulled the duvet up over his shoulder. Without protest his eyes closed again and Maxie got out of bed and dressed. The cab she called arrived quickly and within an hour she was singing happily to herself in the warmth of her own shower. She felt totally revitalised and as thoughts started pinging through her head, she wondered whether having good old-fashioned sex had helped her synapses fire-up again.

'That would be an interesting strand for Alzheimer's researchers,' she murmured as she wrapped herself in a towel.

Every Saturday, Maxie recorded the *Criminal Thoughts* podcast with her co-presenter Craig Johnston. This would be a Christmas Eve special and Maxie knew the only thing any of their audience would want to hear about was Kelly and the missing person's case. She'd asked for permission from Mrs Ingles to discuss it and hoped it might help anyone else going through something similar. The emotions Maxie had felt and noted in Kelly's friends were still raw so today was a perfect day to talk about them and to tell the whole messy truth of real-life investigations. Her challenge was going to be getting through the broadcast without breaking down. Just remembering the despair, the sadness and loss on the faces of everyone she'd met during this investigation created a lump in her throat that made talking difficult.

Maxie threw on some black trousers, a black polo neck and a simple locket. She looked at the locket in the mirror; it contained a picture of Karl and when she touched it she thought about him not being there and that led to thoughts of Kelly. Now that the thought association was there, the locket would be a constant distraction whenever she touched it and that was no use if she wanted to be objective all day. She changed it for a pendant set she'd bought at a craft fayre, something that had absolutely no emotional significance at all. Even though she wouldn't be seen today, Maxie needed warpaint to face the world. She brushed on mascara and then a layer of a dark plum lipstick and she was ready. She was Professor Reddick – Head of the Applied Criminology Unit and co-host of *Criminal Thoughts*.

The studio was practically empty and Maxie knew that many podcasters had recorded their shows earlier in the week. Not only had she not had time, but also both she and Craig wanted the details they presented to be as up to date as possible. The sound technicians nodded at her as she walked past into the recording booth. Shortly after she'd arranged all the information she wanted at hand, Craig arrived.

'Are you ready for this?' he asked and Maxie nodded. They put on their headphones and adjusted the microphone as they did a soundcheck before kicking off.

'Welcome,' announced Craig. 'And a Merry Christmas to all our listeners. This is Craig Johnston and I'm here with my co-host Professor Reddick for a special edition of *Criminal Thoughts*. Today we're going to hear about the case of Kelly Ingles and discuss how it feels when a person goes missing at Christmas. Over to you Professor Reddick.'

Maxie began by asking everyone to think about a person they knew who had been to an office party without them. 'Think of someone very close like your partner, your child or your sibling,' she said. 'They work somewhere different to you and therefore obviously they're at the party without you. They may have bought a new outfit, have had a glass or two before they went out but they told you they were going and you thought nothing of it. You had your own party to go to.'

'Okay,' said Craig. 'I'm imagining my wife – she went to an office party last week.'

'Now imagine she just doesn't come home,' said Maxie. 'What would you do?'

'I'd call her friends and then I'd call the police,' replied Craig.

'No one has seen her and the police have no leads – she's vanished and she doesn't come back.'

They let the airwaves go silent to make the point then Maxie asked Craig how he'd feel.

‘My body has turned cold just thinking about it,’ he said. ‘How much do you think the way Kelly looked hampered the search?’

The presenters discussed the bias that had emerged towards both Kelly and her parents then Maxie presented some other research where prejudice had impacted the justice system.

‘If anyone out there is thinking of making a New Year’s resolution,’ she said. ‘I would ask you to be aware of when you’re judging the book by its cover. We all do it but if we’re aware, we can stop.’

The show had to end on a hopeful note so Maxie and Craig said they hoped that Kelly was safe and well and that all those who loved her would hear from her soon. As she said those words, Maxie felt a gloom settling over her. She hated not knowing whether Kelly was safe.

Maxie drove home unable to shake that mood. She had to get in a better frame of mind if she was to host her son and his girlfriend tomorrow – not that she’d heard from him yet. Once in her flat, she plonked herself down at a table and took out a box of Christmas cards. It was a box of twelve and she knew she would probably only use half of them at a push. She wrote the first and put it in the envelope just as the doorbell rang.

‘I hoped you’d be back home,’ said Andrew through the intercom – he was holding up a Christmas card. ‘I just wanted to say thanks for your help.’

Maxie buzzed him in and when he reached the door, they exchanged cards – his was the first and only one she’d written.

‘Thank you,’ said Maxie opening the card. ‘Is everything signed off now?’

Andrew nodded. ‘I’m going back to the office now. I’ve got a meeting with the DI later and then I guess it’ll go in the inactive pile.’

‘I’m sorry I couldn’t be of more help,’ said Maxie. ‘I feel as if I’ve let everyone down.

‘Me too,’ Andrew said. ‘But we’ve done all we can.’

He shrugged and Maxie guessed he didn’t really want to let this one go yet. She offered him a coffee but he said he needed to get back to the station and after giving him a peck on the cheek and wishing him a merry Christmas Maxie waved him off at the door.

She went back to her Christmas cards and wrote out a couple more – to people she’d only just met then headed out to her car. She reached the street where Rowan and the Hendrys lived. Rowan wasn’t at home so she popped the card through the letter box and then walked down to the home of the elderly couple who'd first reported this case. To Maxie's surprise, Patricia opened the door and squeezed Maxie's hand sympathetically before leading her into the toasty-warm living room.

'I thought you'd be at the hospital,' said Maxie. 'I just brought a Christmas card round.'

'I'm heading back there shortly. George needs clean pyjamas,' replied Patricia.

'I'm so sorry I didn't find Kelly,' added Maxie.

'It's not your fault,' said Patricia. 'We're sure we're going to get a postcard from her in the new year.'

Maxie wished her well and left, driving on to the street where Luis lived. When she got there, it looked strange and she realised it was because for the first time in days, there were no journalists here waiting to record or pester Luis – even they'd given up. Luis opened the door as she walked up the drive. He looked weary – ten years older than he had when they first met. He invited her in.

'I don't know what to do with the rest of her things,' he said although he wasn't really talking to Maxie just letting his own dark thoughts stream out, trying to make them real. 'I mean if I knew she was gone for good I could give them to a charity shop but if she might come back or send for them from New York then maybe I should keep them. Why didn't she say goodbye? I guess I just wasn't good enough in the end.'

'Do nothing at all for now,' said Maxie softly. 'And know that when people walk away without saying goodbye, it's usually because they can't face themselves rather than anyone else.'

'Maybe when she's been away long enough, she'll send me a message,' Luis said. 'I just need to know she's okay. That job did sound fabulous didn't it?'

Maxie nodded. 'What are you doing for tomorrow?' she asked. 'Will you go to your brother's?'

Luis shook his head. 'No I'm not good company at the moment. It wouldn't be fair on his kids to have a mopey uncle around.'

'Are you sure you don't want to be with someone? You could spend the day with Rowan maybe?'

'She's going to be with her folks and no matter how miserable any of them feel, they'll still be sitting there pulling crackers, wearing stupid hats and trying to make the best of things. I can't do that.'

There was really nothing Maxie could say to make this situation better. This was the void she'd written about in her research, the emptiness that accompanied not knowing. It was no time to be alone.

'Luis, I know you don't really know me but could I call in on you tomorrow? Check that you're okay? I promise there'll be no stupid hats. I'm probably going to be on my own too.'

Luis nodded his appreciation. 'Thank you but I'll be fine I promise. Harry's parents have also asked me to their house in the morning and I think that's where I should be. They need me there. They want to go to church to say a prayer. It's not my kind of thing but I think this year I might try to believe. It can't hurt can it?'

'It can't,' Maxie said gently, touching his arm and leaving him to it.

Back at home, Maxie walked into her kitchen and flicked on the radio. Among the "non-stop feel-good classics", an early-afternoon news reporter told of last-minute bargain hunters creating pre-Christmas chaos at the shopping mall. Maxie imagined the same people would be creating the post-Christmas chaos with gift returns and Boxing Day sales in just forty-eight hours. She felt that this Christmas had somehow forgotten she even existed, no gifts, no parties, and no family. She checked her phone but there was still no message from Karl.

She slammed down her phone in a burst of self-pity. She had no right to be angry with her son's choice but he could at least call her back. She went upstairs and to avoid the temptation of peering under her own bed at the present he said he'd left, Maxie walked into Karl's room and started tidying up. She found a lone sock as she'd guessed she might. She took a photo of it and sent it to him, writing: *You forgot something.*

There was still no reply.

The radio announcer cued up the next song and "Goldfinger" from the James Bond movie filled the room. Maxie smiled. She used to sing this to Karl when he was a toddler and now he cringed whenever he heard it. She sent another text.

Think HRM might channel a bit of Bond tomorrow – hope Olivia doesn't mind ☺

A royal message voice-over and a Sean Connery impression? If that didn't get her son home, she'd pretty much played every card she had. Her phone beeped and her heart jumped almost simultaneously. It was a laughing emoji from her son.

Okay so he hadn't confirmed anything but at least she knew he wasn't ignoring her. She hugged her phone, the little piece of plastic and glass that linked her with Karl. It beeped again and with joyous expectation she quickly opened the message. Her heart dipped a little. It wasn't her son but it was Orlando telling her he'd enjoyed the evening. Perhaps she should accept that one man was moving on in her life just as another was moving in. After all, he'd been kind and funny and he seemed to really like her – even if he did have a silly name.

Suddenly a wave of nausea ran through Maxie. She slouched in her chair feeling faint. She had to make a call and she really didn't want to. She called Andrew, asked the question and got the answer she knew she would.

'I've got my meeting in less than an hour. You know you have to let this go now,' he told her.

Maxie was already running down to the hall, picking up her coat and car keys.

'But I know what's happened to her Andrew. And if I'm right, I know where she is.'

Chapter Thirty-Four

Kelly heard footsteps and tried to drag her body from the heavy stupor holding her down and keeping her fixed to this cold stony ground. God knows how long she'd been here now. Everything ached and muscles that had once taken her effortlessly anywhere she wanted to go, now cried out at any attempt of movement. Her brain alone seemed willing to try and piece things together. It knew this was not a normal hangover, even for Kelly. And her brain had worked out that she must have been drugged. It had to have been in the water and bread left for her each day. Her brain had persuaded her not to eat or drink anything at all yesterday and she guessed that's why she was thinking a little more clearly today. Her body wasn't happy with this arrangement, it was starving and so, so thirsty. But Kelly had to prioritise, to think, to work this out.

At the beginning, she was so shot through with the pain of the hangover that she couldn't work out whether she was dreaming or awake. Only as the drink started to loosen its hold on her brain so that she could believe what she remembered and what she felt, did she realise that she was very much awake but imprisoned. Her body was bound, trapped by cords. She remembered the confused panic of that first morning. Waking up and trying to pull her hands and legs free, to rip those cords but every time she moved they just got tighter and tighter. Now as she lay here, every part of her body cried out in pain.

Through the hood encasing her head she could see a shard of sunlight and shuffled her aching limbs towards it, feeling warmth. It didn't last long and soon this dungeon was pitch black. Did that mean it was night? Kelly remembered it was still December so reasoned that it might not even be so late. She was pleased to have remembered this as it meant she'd really started thinking again. She had to pull herself together and try to figure out what the hell was going on.

In the beginning she'd thought it might be some kind of joke. She vaguely remembered a film where a debutante's friends hired a kidnapper for her birthday. She'd been bundled into a van and blindfolded. Then they took her to a surprise party venue and took the blindfold off. The girl thought it was hilarious. Kelly would have been absolutely furious. And anyway, if any of her friends had that kind of money to waste, surely the blindfold would be off by now.

She was filthy and wrapped in a sleeping bag under some old blankets. The dirt which seemed to seep from her own pores clung to her body alongside the dust and grime of the floor. She'd woken up one morning to find that her own clothes had been taken off her while she was unconscious and now she was lying in this dank space naked. Kelly hadn't known why and for the brief moments she'd been conscious had been terrified that she was being held by some pervert. She had to stay awake, she had to work this out.

The footsteps were getting closer, echoing along a corridor and then a barrier of some kind sounded as if it were being pushed aside – a makeshift door maybe. Then she knew someone was in this room. Kelly instinctively curled up in a ball, burying her head down in the blankets and tried to steady her heartbeat. She couldn't do it and started hyperventilating not knowing what was coming or what to do next. A hand reached towards her and her whole body tightened expecting pain. The hand pushed aside the blankets and lifted the hood halfway up her face so that her mouth could seek out air. Kelly yelped in fear, aware of how utterly pathetic that sounded.

In a movie, she thought, the captive would have said something meaningful, would have tried to reason with her captor. She was shaking too much for that. The hand forced some water into Kelly's mouth. Oh God, her body cried, how good that feels. How much we needed it. Kelly didn't care whether the water was drugged or not, she swallowed again and again trying to take in as much as her parched mouth would allow. She needed to breathe and take a big gulp of air through her mouth but she needed the water more. She kept swallowing until she choked and spluttered, taking in the damp air as she did. Then the hood was pulled back down and too late she tried to reason, 'Please don't …'

The hand checked the ties which bound her and as the person leant over her, Kelly inhaled their scent. They walked away but Kelly knew that smell. It was so familiar, her brain cells fired and screamed as they tried to remember how they knew it.

'Come on brain, come on,' she screamed internally. Then it came.

'Oh my God, it's you.'

The footsteps stopped and turned back towards her. For a fleeting moment Kelly thought they were going to untie her. She heard them bend down and pick something up. Then all she felt was the cold air swoosh as something solid was whipped through with anger and hitting her hard across the head. A surge of pain. Then complete and utter blackness.

Chapter Thirty-Five

'I called this meeting to close the investigation so you'd better have a really good explanation as to why you've pulled in this team on Christmas Eve against my express instructions,' Andrew's boss said, throwing his pen to the desk.

The officers who'd worked the case and had expected to have headed home, now sat waiting, arms folded, for Maxie to tell them her latest theory.

She looked devastated. 'I've long thought that Kelly was the sort of girl who wouldn't just disappear. She's too gutsy for that. She winds people up the wrong way but then she turns on the charm and they forgive her. And it was this lack of personal awareness that turned out to be a problem for her. She hacked people off, she threatened their masculinity and their dignity. She draped herself around another man while the one who wanted to marry her sat at home and she was leaving the company that had trained her and given Kelly her first break.'

'We know all of this, Professor.' The DI sighed.

'We focussed on Luis, not the other man she'd hacked off,' continued Maxie.

'Luis obviously has a violent streak and as even you say, he's been well and truly shafted by her,' countered the DI.

'But that's not enough to take it further,' Maxie said. 'He loves her and described her as a shining light, a beacon, the type of person who lights up a room. Most people would probably count themselves lucky to be in her presence. Luis thought he wasn't good enough for her and that's why she'd left. We're looking for the person who felt he was too good for Kelly, a real narcissist.

'The text Kelly sent on the night she disappeared said she was staying with "Ro" – her boyfriend Luis took this to mean she was staying with her friend Rowan and we never questioned that. There wasn't anyone on the radar called anything like "Ro" but there is now.'

She explained the photograph she'd seen revealing Orlando's real name and the nickname Kelly had for her boss.

'He acted shocked when we told him about Kelly's job but he knew about it beforehand. In a private discussion, Orlando told me it was a shame Harry hadn't come forward earlier with information about Kelly's new job. I hadn't told him that Harry had helped with the application or that he was giving Kelly a reference and I now know no one else involved in the investigation did either.'

This was the fact she'd checked with Andrew. She had been slightly surprised that Orlando knew about Harry's role but had assumed it had been discussed by someone else. Andrew confirmed that it hadn't been mentioned by him or the DI and added that neither of them made a habit of discussing cases with interested parties. Maxie had been about to say that she didn't make a habit of sleeping with them but thought better of it. She continued.

'So Orlando did know that Kelly was leaving and he had to have assumed that when the move was complete he'd lose clients. He said it himself – she was extremely important to his business. I think that when Orlando found out that Harry had provided the reference, he went to Harry's studio to confront him and things got out of hand. They may have struggled and Harry may have slipped and banged his head. That part could very well have been an accident. However, leaving Kelly's clothing there wasn't and I think at that point, he was trying to frame Harry or throw us off the trail.'

'This is a good friend of mine we're talking about,' said the DI. 'I can't see him doing any of this.'

'We still have unidentified DNA from that scene,' said Andrew. 'So we'll know if he touched that rucksack.'

Maxie nodded. 'I believe he found out about Kelly's new job on the Friday and that he went back to the club to try to talk her out of it. She waved at him across the street and agreed to go back to the office to discuss it, maybe even negotiate a deal for herself. We've heard time and time again that this girl was good at her job but Orlando believed that he'd taught her everything. The PR world will have its jungle drums like any other workplace and Orlando knew that some of Kelly's clients would definitely follow her to the new company when she left. The motivation is money, pure and simple. He'd have been hoping to persuade her to stay but when he saw her laughing and drinking, absolutely delighted to be leaving his company – well that was the real trigger.'

'You think he killed her when she said no?' asked Andrew.

'No, I really don't,' Maxie said, wondering about the man who'd had them completely fooled all this time. 'I actually think he's a passive aggressive. He doesn't have the guts to go through with anything like that. Like with Harry, I believe they had an argument when Harry was drunk, he slipped and Orlando left him there to die. I think he's far more likely to lock someone up and let them wither away rather than actually do the dirty work himself. I know it's been over a week but there's still a chance that Kelly is alive.'

'But where?'

'Somewhere damp with a stone floor.'

The team were given their instructions. The DI would head to Orlando's house to bring him in; one of Andrew's constables would be waiting at the hospital to tell Mrs Ingles if and when they found their daughter while Andrew and Maxie would lead the team searching the OrlandoPR offices.

As they sped towards the office building they'd visited so many times in this past week, Maxie watched the angst on Andrew's face.

'The most important thing is to find Kelly alive,' he kept saying.

Maxie knew he meant it but she also knew that after that, this case would come under some serious scrutiny and not just for him. Kelly's Army had been set up in the very place the girl was imprisoned. Andrew had followed up every lead meticulously but that's not how it would appear. Questions would be asked about his boss's connection with Orlando and someone would have to take the flak. Maxie hoped it wouldn't be Andrew. She felt so loyal to the DS who'd welcomed her into his case and it had to end as well for him as it did for Kelly.

They pulled up at the office. Maxie and Andrew ran towards the door with the squad following. Andrew's phone rang and he stopped briefly to take the call from the DI. He pulled his shoulders back and stood tall as he turned to the team.

'Watch it everyone, he's not at home. He might be here.'

The front door of the office was unlocked and Andrew entered first with Maxie close behind. The corridor was empty but Maxie took the lead and signalled Andrew to follow her as she traced the route they'd taken that first day. In the room decorated with old photographs, Maxie studied the pictures and when she'd worked out where she needed to be strode back into the corridor, past the former war room and through the door she guessed led down to the basement cellars perfected by those Victorian industrialists.

The air grew cold and damp as they descended the steps. He hadn't oversold the achievement down here. Although she'd looked at those old photographs on that initial tour of Orlando's office, they hadn't given any indication that the cellars would be anything like this. She had imagined a series of smaller spaces – like a wine cellar in a chateau – somewhere that could be easily searched. Instead huge disused storage rooms led from dark corridors and were filled with ancient machinery hinting at the building's former use.

'This is nothing like I thought it would be,' she whispered to Andrew who was now leading the way. 'It's enormous.'

The torchlight picked out the sturdy brickwork of each room, built with more care and consideration than some of the modern-day buildings found above ground.

'My dad told me they have chutes down here,' whispered an officer behind her, sounding as overawed as she was. 'For loading and offloading direct from the canal.'

At that word, Maxie shuddered. There was still time for Kelly to become one of December's water-babies and she couldn't let that happen.

'Where would they be, these chutes?' she asked and a torch was shone on the most likely direction. 'We need to get there fast.'

Getting anywhere fast was not an option. The depth of the darkness and their unfamiliarity with this environment forced them to check every step they took. It would be easy to choose the least foreboding turn each time, simply to avoid having to enter the suffocating blackness. They stuck closely together so that each officer was able to hear and see the heavy breaths of his or her colleague. Maxie was sure they could all hear her heartbeat too. She wasn't afraid for herself but for the woman they were here to find. A person could survive seven days without food in normal circumstances but down here? Had that bastard fed her or brought her water? The police had her party clothes so what was she wearing? She could have frozen to death down here whether she'd been fed or not. Maxie could feel fear spreading through her body; fear and guilt. How the hell could she have slept with him while Kelly lay down here? She'd never forgive herself if they didn't find this young woman alive. She must have sniffed back a sob because the officer in front of her turned round. 'Don't worry ma'am, we'll find her.'

When Maxie reached up to wipe her cheek, she found her face sodden with tears.

They reached a crossroad of tunnels and Andrew suggested that they take one each to speed things up. Maxie was scared but couldn't doubt the logic so agreed and turned right with one of the officers while Andrew turned left. The air changed and she now felt the unmistakeable chill that signalled an outlet and water close by. Maxie looked down and saw the ground shine like wet tar. They had to be close.

Maxie thought she heard a noise and stopped dead. She stood completely still and listened intently. The lack of movement allowed the cold to permeate Maxie's clothing and take a grip on her body. The clouds of breath grew thicker and more frequent as her heart rate increased. She was sure she'd heard something. She shone her torch to either side but there were just miles and miles of cold stone walls. Then that sound again. There was definitely someone else down here. Or heaven help her, more rats. Please let it be the king rat and not his minions. She shone her torch towards the direction they'd just come from and the instant the light hit the blackness, a shape lurched towards her and knocked her full force to the ground. She flattened the officer behind her and cracked her head against the cobbled ground. She watched Orlando take off as she lay there.

'It's him,' she cried out in agony. 'Get him.'

Andrew and his team ran in pursuit of him while one officer tried to help her up. She'd been winded pretty badly and her body didn't want to move. She needed a moment to steady herself but she wouldn't stop anyone searching.

She told the officer to stop fussing and told him to check the opening in the side of this tunnel where Orlando had emerged. The officer swallowed hard before switching his torch onto full beam and vanishing. Maxie sat in the dark, listening for any sign that Orlando might be close. The longer she waited, the more certain she was that he was hiding out there, waiting for her to be alone. She couldn't take it any longer and had to get up. She struggled to prop herself on her elbows.

'Hello – are you still there?' she called out.

There was nothing but the echo of her voice. She tried to get up but the pain was excruciating. She reached up to the back of her head. It was wet and when she put her fingertips to her nose, the metallic scent of blood was unmistakeable. What on earth would she do if the officer got lost and didn't come back? This was where Kelly had been living, this was the darkness she'd suffered and the freezing cold she'd endured and now she was caught in it too.

Maxie gasped with relief when she finally saw the officer's torch beam again.

'I think I've found something ma'am,' he whispered.

'Then let's go.'

She held out her arm for help and he pulled her to her feet. She winced as she put weight on her ankle but this was no time to let any injury hold her back. If she'd got up to find her leg broken she'd have forced herself to walk on it right now. The officer led her to a heavy door, thankfully left unlocked as Orlando made his escape. The officer dragged it open and they looked into the overwhelming gloom of a space that stretched out before them. There was no sound and no movement. A cry of help or a shuffle in the corner would have told them there was a living being in this room but there was nothing. They stepped inside and shone the light: it was cavernous. Maxie and the officer walked through the room with the meagre torchlight, shining it into corners where old piles of rotting rope and rusting metal lay as remnants of the past. In the farthest corner from the door lay a bundle of duvets and blankets. They were definitely more twenty-first century than twentieth. Maxie held the officer as she hobbled up to them and shone the light more closely.

'Kelly,' Maxie called out, hoping to get a response.

Nothing.

She signalled the officer to move the blanket. Tentatively, as if expecting vermin to scurry out, he lifted a corner with the edge of his foot.

Again, nothing.

He handed Maxie his torch and she shone it on the bundle while he crouched down and lifted all the filthy layers of fabric carefully. Then the officer jumped back and Maxie saw it too: a foot with the unmistakeable shooting-star tattoo they'd come to know too well. Maxie dropped to her knees to help pull the rest of the blankets off Kelly. Still she didn't move. Underneath the layers, the naked, lifeless girl was swathed in random remnants of cloth and curled up against the cold. Maxie tore off her own coat and got the officer to do the same, then she lifted the girl's bloody body and wrapped her in them. She felt for Kelly's pulse. It was barely perceptible but it was there.

'Can you carry her?' asked Maxie of the officer, knowing that the delicate bundle of skin and bones in her arms right now would take no effort. He simply had to hold her gently.

Maxie stroked Kelly's head as the officer tenderly picked her up. Maxie could barely walk unsupported but she had to. She sent the officer off, telling him to get out of that place as quickly but as safely as he could. Maxie struggled through the tunnel, knowing that every step she made was making her ankle much worse. Eventually she emerged into the daylight and saw Kelly being safely handed over to the medics. She turned away from the rescue scene and looked up to the sky, screaming silently. She struggled to fight back the tears but along with the pain, they were working their way to the surface. It wasn't her injury causing the grief, rather the sheer emotional relief.

Kelly was safe but she very nearly wasn't. Mrs Ingles would have her daughter back.

'Your colleague says you were knocked down,' called a paramedic behind her. 'We should take you in to have a look.'

Maxie allowed herself to be led to an ambulance. She really wanted to speak to Karl now and hear his voice, then to call Luis and Rowan and the Hendrys but she felt faint. Andrew rushed up to the ambulance as she was about to be driven off.

'Well done,' he said. 'If you hadn't found her, she wouldn't have survived tomorrow.'

Maxie nodded but felt no better. She'd taken too long to think this one through. Next time she wouldn't make that mistake.

'Did you find Orlando? What's he said?' she asked groggily, noting the grimace on Andrew's face.

'He knew the labyrinth in that basement better than anyone. We didn't catch him.'

Chapter Thirty-Six

Christmas Day

Maxie thought the media had been kind to the investigation team. They rightly focussed on Kelly being found and not on the fact that it took a university professor to sleep with a criminal before they worked out what on earth was happening. The police statement simply confirmed that Kelly was recovering in hospital and looking forward to spending Christmas with her mother. A full account would follow after the holidays. By then of course, no one would be interested. The old saying "news today, chip paper tomorrow" bizarrely had even more pertinence when your news came from a digital device. By the afternoon there'd be a natural disaster or a celebrity death somewhere in the world and the abduction of a local girl wouldn't be worthy of a swipe.

Orlando's car had been found abandoned in a multi-storey car park just outside London. Maxie could see him being so deluded he actually thought he could blend in and start again in a big city. He'd done it once before when he changed his name but this time the Met would be on his case. He didn't have it in him to live anonymously for too long. Maxie imagined he'd be more comfortable as a famous and notorious criminal than an unknown council clerk or whatever he'd have to become. He'd find a certain prestige in being the Jeffrey Archer or O J Simpson of the PR world.

'Watch this space, it'll happen,' she said to Andrew when he arrived at the hospital to drive her home.

Right now, all Maxie wanted was to get Orlando out of her head. She'd been ordered to rest for a week and although her head injury was superficial, her ankle was very badly sprained and she'd been ordered to rest it as much as possible. She shuffled to the side of the hospital bed and picked up one of the crutches she'd been given.

'You look like that little boy from Dickens – Tiny Tim.' Andrew laughed.

Maxie shook her crutch at him. 'Watch it you ragamuffin,' she croaked, channelling Scrooge. 'Or I'll put you over my knee.'

She began shuffling along the corridor clumsily getting used to the crutches then paused. 'I need to say goodbye first.'

Andrew nodded, pressing the button for the lift. Up on the second floor they hobbled towards Kelly's room where she lay with drips rehydrating and nourishing her slender body. Her mother, together with Luis and Rowan sat around her bed as she slept and they looked up but didn't move as Maxie and Andrew entered the room.

Maxie felt lost for something appropriate to say then Mrs Ingles walked towards her with arms outstretched. She hugged Maxie – a long and hard and thankful hug that squeezed the tears from both of them. They both knew that they'd been a whisker from not finding Kelly alive.

The police now believed that Orlando had intended to "discover" Kelly after Christmas and after the new job had been taken by someone else. There'd been a press release drafted on his PC where he announced that she'd wandered into the office confused with no memory of where she'd been but was glad to be back.

Kelly had been drugged and blindfolded throughout her ordeal to try and make sure she couldn't identify Orlando or the place she'd been held but when Kelly recovered she was able to verify that she'd recognised his scent and let slip that she knew who he was.

'It was then that Orlando had to take action. If the subsequent blow to the head hadn't killed her, a few more days down there would have done.

'I'm sorry it took us so long,' Maxie whispered through the sniffs.

Mrs Ingles stood back, still holding Maxie's arms. 'You never gave up. I saw it in your eyes. You got her back for Christmas and somehow I knew you would.'

In the bed, Kelly stirred slightly causing everyone to turn their attention to her. Maxie watched as Luis gently kissed her hand. The professor left quietly with Andrew.

They said very little as they drove to Maxie's house. Andrew made sure she was sitting comfortably and checked that everything she needed was within hobbling distance.

'You go, have your Christmas. I'll be fine,' Maxie told him as he stood there, reluctant to leave.

'Don't you want me to call your son and tell him to come round and look after you?'

'No,' she replied firmly. 'He just knows we've found Kelly. He doesn't know I'm hurt and I *don't* want him to. I've said I want to relax today and that he is to stay exactly where he is. I want him to enjoy himself with his lovely girlfriend and not feel that he has to come and look after his stupid mother.'

'If you're sure,' said Andrew.

‘Go. What more could I want than being told I absolutely *have* to sit around with a box of chocolates and watch TV. It’s every girl’s dream.’

Andrew smiled and raised his finger to tell her to wait there. He left the house and then reappeared with a cool box; he opened the lid to reveal several tinfoil containers.

‘I know how you love curry so got one of the guys at the station to rustle up these for your Christmas lunch. His mum’s a brilliant cook – they just heat up in the oven.’

Maxie took a closer peek and inhaled the heavenly spicy aromas.

‘Oh my word – how utterly fabulous. Put these in the kitchen then go look in the cupboard above the kettle,’ she instructed Andrew. He walked over and opened the door to the selection of Christmas food she’d bought, thinking Karl would be here.

‘Take a Christmas pudding and as many cakes as you like,’ she said. ‘Tell your family to enjoy them and thank you so much for the curries. I am going to have the best day ever now.’

Andrew took a couple of cakes, pecked her on the cheek and waved goodbye. Maxie leaned back into the sofa and closed her eyes.

Two hours later, Maxie woke up in the exact same position that she’d fallen asleep, flat on her back with her hands nestled around her phone resting on her belly. Her eyes opened to complete silence and it took her a moment to realise where she was. She went to push herself upright and realised that the painkillers had worn off. Everything ached, even the parts that hadn’t been injured in the fall – she guessed they’d simply come out in sympathy.

She swung her legs round and put her feet on the floor, pressing down to test out her ankle. It cried out with pain in retaliation so she quickly brought it back to rest on the sofa. She looked around for her crutches and saw that Andrew had left them standing tidily in the hallway. Somehow she had to get over to the freezer without them as she desperately needed an ice pack and a refill of painkillers. Her phone beeped to tell her she’d missed a call and had a message.

She played it out loud and heard her son say first of all that he’d had a lovely Christmas lunch and that if she was sure she could cope with it then he and Olivia would be round for tea. Maxie then heard what she assumed was Olivia’s family yelling “Merry Christmas” down the phone. She could picture them all gathered together, cheery with their Christmas jumpers and rosy cheeks.

A couple of seconds and a bit of rustling later, the background voices vanished and Karl whispered into the phone, 'Right they're gone – look, it's all been a bit too dull. Let me know you're in. We so need some entertainment Maxi-mum-style.'

Maxie kept her voice calm as she called her son and confirmed that she'd love to see him and Olivia today. As soon as the call ended she hollered out loud across the room, 'Hurray! He's had a hideous time!'

And he'd called her Maxi-mum again! No matter what had gone on in the past twenty-four hours, this was shaping up to be the best Christmas in a very long time. Determined to ignore each screech of pain, Maxie forced herself up and hobbled over to the kitchen, clutching each piece of furniture to propel her on as she went. She could imagine she looked like some earthbound primate trying to get to the other side of the jungle. It was bloody exhausting, and the next time she shouldn't let Andrew tidy things away. Maxie propped herself up against the kitchen bench standing on her one good leg and started unpacking the cartons Andrew had brought.

There was so much food it was just as well Karl was coming over. Maxie hoped his Christmas lunch hadn't been up to much and he'd arrive ravenous. Even if he was stuffed to the gills, she'd defy any mere mortal to turn down this banquet. It would only take twenty minutes to heat up when he arrived, just enough time to have a drink and make up a reason why she was doing her best impression of Long John Silver.

She could at least set the dining-room table. No, on second thoughts, they'd snuggle together on the sofa and eat from bowls. She'd lay a banquet out on the coffee table and they wouldn't have to move all afternoon. Wine and beer – where could she put them so they were in easy reach? His present – what about his present? How could she give him that? Despite the negative press giving gift vouchers always got, Maxie had really thought about what her son would like most of all. He'd always said that what he wanted was to get as far away from his dysfunctional family as he could. The travel vouchers weren't an afterthought but a genuine act of redemption and he would recognise that. Nevertheless, however meaningful she knew they were, right now the bits of paper in a plain envelope looked fairly pitiful. How could she wrap them up and make them look exciting? She suddenly had a thought and hobbled her way to the corridor – it was exhausting.

She eventually got to her bedroom and pulled out a pair of cowboy boots from the bottom of the wardrobe. According to Karl and his father, these had been one of her biggest fashion mistakes (and again, according to them, she'd made very many of them), but they undoubtedly said America and that was one of the places Karl really wanted to see. She could put the vouchers in one of the boots and wrap it in one of the sparkly gift bags she kept in the kitchen, the ones that other people had given her over the years and that she recycled religiously.

A glance in the mirror as she was preparing to negotiate her way back gave her such a fright. Apart from the bruises down one side of her face, she was a ghostly white and anything but festive. There was only one thing for it – the Christmas onesie. Maxie pulled her clothes off, wincing as her battered body was forced to move. She couldn't get in the shower like this so pulled out several face wipes and cleansed herself as best she could. Then she sprayed her perfume liberally above her head and let it settle on her body. She brushed some bronzer over her cheeks, flicked on the mascara and topped it off with a lipstick so red, Rudolph would have been proud of it. She looked and felt a lot better.

'It's going to be okay,' she told her reflection.

The doorbell rang and she whooped. She grabbed the cowboy boots and hobbled back along the corridor.

'I'm coming,' she hollered. 'Did you forget your keys?'

She put the boots in the shoe rack where she'd be able to reach them later for wrapping and, pulling herself upright with the help of her crutch, composed herself before throwing open the door.

'Merry …'

Orlando reached out and grabbed her throat, pushing her backwards and kicking the door shut behind him. Maxie just didn't have the strength to do anything about it. She tried to pull his hands off but couldn't. She collapsed to the hallway floor, gasping for breath as this angry man pressed his body weight into her, tightening his grip and seeming to enjoy the picture of hopelessness beneath him.

'I might not get away with this but you won't be around to know, you bitch.'

Maxie reached out her hands, trying to get hold of the crutch which had fallen to the ground in the struggle. It was millimetres from her fingers but it may as well have been miles because she just couldn't reach it. She was helpless and she was blacking out …

Whack. The sound was so loud she couldn't tell where it had come from and in her daze she cowered, waiting for it to hit her next. It didn't. The weight lying over her fell flat, crushing her body but losing its grip on her neck. She pulled the hands away but couldn't move him.

'Mum, are you okay? Mum?' It was Karl's voice and then his face. He was here. Maxie reached up and touched him. It was real.

He started hauling Orlando off her with the help of someone else, then two people lifted her up. It was Luis and over in the living room, Rowan and Olivia were calling the police.

Karl helped his mum to the sofa while Luis knelt on Orlando a little harder than was necessary just to stop him getting up but the blow to the head had been a good one and he wasn't going anywhere.

The squad car arrived with the ambulance and they removed that man from all of their lives once and for all or at least until the trial after Christmas. Maxie refused the offer of more help from the paramedics. She had everything she needed right here.

Karl sat her down on the sofa and propped cushions around her. 'Painkillers or wine?' he asked but knowing her answer, already had the glass ready. He poured everyone a drink and they sat around the coffee table.

'We met Luis at the Kelly's Army offices and I gave him my number. He called me and asked if he could come round to thank you while Kelly was sleeping,' explained Karl.

'But I could never thank you enough,' added Luis, taking her hand.

'I don't know, knocking out my attacker with a cowboy boot comes close.' Maxie was trying not to laugh for the pain along her neck.

'What on earth were they doing out anyway?' asked Karl. 'You're surely not going to start wearing them are you? Especially not with an ankle the size of Texas.'

Maxie tapped the side of her nose to tell him it was a secret.

'I hope you're all staying for food,' said Maxie. 'Andrew brought round a whole banquet and it looks fantastic. It just needs heating up.'

The youngsters looked at each other as if wondering what the polite thing would be.

'Really, it would make my day to have you all here,' Maxie added.

That settled it. Coats came off, the girls settled down beside Maxie while Karl and Luis brought everyone drinks then worked out the order food needed to go into the oven. Bhajis and samosas soon appeared and then disappeared.

'You've no idea how good this is,' declared Olivia, savouring them. 'My dad always cooks on Christmas Day and no one has the courage to tell him how bland it is.'

Maxie smiled, happy to hear that. The boys brought in several dishes and laid them on the table, giving everyone a bowl to help themselves. Food and wine served, they raised their glasses in a toast.

'All's well that ends well?' suggested Maxie, so that's what they called out.

'Are you ready?' asked Karl, his finger poised on the remote. Maxie nodded and he pressed "play".

Her Majesty the Queen appeared before them looking elegant and regal, the tasteful palace Christmas tree twinkled discreetly in the background. She faced the camera, the commensurate professional that she was and opened her mouth to speak. Simultaneously, Karl hit mute and doing the worst Sean Connery impression anyone had ever heard, Karl and Maxie began their own private Christmas tradition:

'Mshter Bond … we've been exshpecting you.'

Thank You

Dear Reader,

Thank you for choosing *Wrong Sort of Girl* – I really hope you enjoyed it. I developed Professor Maxie Reddick to be the kind of woman I'd want fighting my corner if I were ever in trouble and I hope you feel the same way about her. She's not perfect herself but really does care about the underdog and does all she can to help secure justice for those who ask for help. If you haven't had the chance to read the first book in the series, *One by One*, please do take a look and read about the first crime Maxie solved and about her personal journey to this point in time.

If you've enjoyed reading *Wrong Sort of Girl* please leave a review for the book on Goodreads or the website where you bought the book. You can also follow me on Twitter for news on my other books (see my 'About the Author' page next).

Looking forward to hearing from you.

Helen x

About the Author

Helen Bridgett lives in the North East of England. Outside of writing feel good fiction, Helen loves the great outdoors and having a good laugh with friends over a glass of wine. Helen lives with her husband and their chocolate Labrador, Angus; all three can often be found walking the Northumberland coastline that inspired her first novel, *Summer at Serenity Bay*.

To find out more about Helen, follow her on social media:

Twitter: www.twitter.com/Helen_Bridgett
Facebook: www.facebook.com/HelenBridgettAuthor

More Ruby Fiction

from

Helen Bridgett

One by One
Book 1 in the Maxie Reddick Files

When practising what you preach is easier said than done …
Professor Maxie Reddick has her reasons for being sceptical of traditional policing methods, but, in between her criminology lecturing job and her Criminal Thoughts podcast, she stays firmly on the side lines of the crime solving world.

Then a young woman is brutally attacked, and suddenly it's essential that Maxie turns her words into actions; this is no longer an academic exercise – this is somebody's life.

But as she delves deeper, the case takes a sickening turn, which leads Maxie to the horrifying realisation that the attack might not have been a one-off. It seems there's a depraved individual out there seeking revenge, and they'll stop at nothing to get it … little by little … one by one.

Visit www.rubyfiction.com for more details.

Summer at Serenity Bay

What happens when you send a group of celebrities to a tiny seaside village?

Advertising executive Chloe Walsh thought she was visiting her friend Roisin to get away from it all, but little does she know her kooky friend has a master plan to breathe some life into her sleepy seaside village through a new wellness retreat – and she needs Chloe's skills.

So starts a community effort to put the retreat, Serenity Bay, on the map. Everyone from Andy at the Surf Shack to Tony at the chocolate shop is involved – even Roisin's Gran has a few ideas!

But Chloe strikes gold almost too soon, attracting the attention of a major production company. Now a colourful group of celebrities are preparing to descend on Serenity Bay to film a reality TV show. Is the village ready for the fun and scandal that are bound to follow?

Christmas at Serenity Bay
Sequel to Summer at Serenity Bay

A peaceful Christmas in Serenity Bay? Think again!
Chloe Walsh's skills as location manager for the beautiful seaside village she calls home have come up trumps again, and Serenity Bay is now the setting for cosy crime drama *The Montgomery Mysteries*, starring amateur sleuth Dominic Montgomery and his crime-solving dog, Agatha.

But Chloe is in a race against time. Filming has to finish before the village Midwinter Festival but schedules are tight – and a mystery saboteur is intent on slowing things down even further. Not only is Chloe facing problems with the shoot, she also has some personal conundrums to solve – a diva actor has commandeered her flat, her mum is having a late mid-life crisis, plus she has no idea what to buy for her Christmas-obsessed boyfriend!

Can Chloe sort out her life and save Christmas for an entire village?

Visit www.rubyfiction.com for more details.

Introducing Ruby Fiction

Ruby Fiction is in imprint of Choc Lit Publishing.
We're an award-winning independent publisher, creating a delicious selection of fiction.

See our selection here:
www.rubyfiction.com
Ruby Fiction brings you stories that inspire emotions.

We'd love to hear how you enjoyed *Wrong Sort of Girl*. Please leave a review on the store where you purchased this novel or visit www.rubyfiction.com and give your feedback.

Ruby novels are selected by genuine readers like yourself. We only publish stories our Tasting Panel want to see in print. Our reviews and awards speak for themselves.

Could you be a Star Selector and join our Tasting Panel?
Would you like to play a role in choosing which novels we decide to publish? Do you enjoy reading women's fiction? Then you could be perfect for our Tasting Panel.

Visit here: **www.choc-lit.com/join-the-choc-lit-tasting-panel**

Keep in touch:

Sign up for our monthly newsletter Spread for all the latest news and offers: **www.spread.choc-lit.com**

Follow us on Twitter: **@RubyFiction** and
Facebook: **RubyFiction**

Ruby FICTION

Stories that inspire emotions!

Printed in Great Britain
by Amazon

83225085R00137